Union

Spirian Saga Book 2

Rowena Portch

ᘁ n i o n

Originally published in America by Rowena Portch, in
2010 as *The Union*

FIRST AEON ENTERPRISES EDITION,
DECEMBER 2012

www.Aeon-Enterprises.us
Cover illustration and book design by
Aeon Enterprises

ISBN-978-0-9886275-1-2
V2.0_r2
Printed in the U.S.A.

ACKNOWLEDGMENTS

Gregg, you are a wonderful mate. Thank you for sticking with me through all my adventures in life. I know it's hard to be married to a female with a gypsy soul. God bless you, my angel. You are and always will be my best friend.

Daughter, Erika. Your skill of storytelling inspires me to continue writing. I know your own novels will be a huge success. Thanks for your undying support and cheerful spirit. Most of all, thank you for my wonderful grandchildren who make me smile.

Nick, Andrew, and Zach, you are the most gifted sons a mother could ask for. Not only do you encourage me to continue pursuing my dreams, you call when I need to hear the words, "I love you, Mim." Thank you.

To the females in my life, Mum, Evelyn, and Georgian, bless you for the girl time, the laughs, your support, and most of all, your unconditional love. I couldn't make it without you.

To my fans, thank God for you all. You inspire me to continue pursuing my passion.

Chapter 1

The dark side is like quicksand. You know you're sinking, but you have limited time and resources to free yourself before it swallows you whole.

THE PAST SIX MONTHS PROVIDED blissful and much needed normality after last fall when I discovered I was a Spirian. My existence as a mere human had ceased and I quickly found myself rushing headlong into a world where good versus evil leaned more toward the evil side. I was destined to wed Khalen—a man who could easily end my life if anger had a hold on him—and to fulfill my role as a legend I didn't believe in.

Spirians, I learned, often lived in self-supporting communities called clans. Each member of the clan filled one or more roles that kept the clan fed, clothed and sheltered. Those who did not contribute were asked to leave. The elders often watched and taught the young ones, while the younger members performed more physical duties.

Khalen and I returned to work at The Wellness Center, his professional health practice that was managed by our good friends, Gregg and Ro. This is where Khalen offered natural and traditional healthcare, while three others and myself offered massage therapy and acupuncture.

At home, I was becoming more involved with the daily activities. I rather enjoyed tending the gardens with Jade and Ember, and caring for the animals with Ian and Aidan. My primary role, however, was tending the physical injuries of the clan members; they came to me with everything from scraped knees to broken bones. My healing capabilities had grown stronger, as well as the intuitive gifts that I had developed even before Khalen's grandfather, Shanuk, awakened my ability to heal.

Since his death last fall, Shanuk often made his presence known to me in subtle breezes that kicked up out of nowhere, and a welcoming peace when I needed it the most. I missed his magnificent smile.

Today was a good day, with sunny weather, a pleasant spring breeze, and healthy plants to roam barefoot among—until Khalen's rogue twin, Traeger, entered the camp.

As I freed the asparagus patch of medicinal dandelions and plantain, the hair on the back of my neck stood alert. A familiar cold swept over me and Maiyun, my guide dog, released a low growl. Her mixed genes of Malamute and Husky made her appear more wolf than a domestic pet.

"What is it?" asked Ember, her hands filled with limp stalks of chickweed and speedwell.

I glanced toward the direction that held Maiyun's attention. A black Lincoln Continental was coming up the driveway. The pancakes I ate earlier suddenly felt like lead in my gut. I remembered all too well the time I had endured with Traeger last fall. I had made a grave error that forced me into his grasp and nearly cost me my soul.

His ability to draw me in was frightening, even though I wanted nothing to do with him. The calmness that I had enjoyed recently was about to end, I was certain.

Before the car came to a stop, Khalen and his father, Case stood at the end of the drive.

Stay there, Khalen warned me telepathically.

What's he doing here? I responded in kind. There was no answer. I was sure Khalen wondered the same thing.

Maiyun started to trot toward Khalen. I called her back to my side.

Although I could not see much detail due to my blindness, I recognized the body language of Traeger and, Seth, his quiet and ominous son. The other man who stepped out of the car was a stranger.

Case's inquiring stare made Traeger's companions uncomfortable; they kept their eyes lowered and shifted their feet. Traeger, however, sauntered toward the old man with sickening confidence.

"I request council with you," he said. His hair had grown longer since I saw him last. He had it tied in the back.

Case raised his head a bit, as if to remind the young man of his stature in the presence of a clan elder.

Traeger responded by lowering his head as a sign of respect. That subtle body language gained the attention of everyone around. Conversations ceased and a crowd began to form around the three outsiders.

"Come," said Case, leading the way toward his yurt.

Khalen waited for the three men to follow his father, and then proceeded behind, shutting the door of the yurt as he entered.

Eve exited the yurt shortly afterward. She had been baking bread for the evening meal. Her flour-dusted apron fluttered. A faint white cloud trailed in her wake as she hurried toward me. Her silver brows were creased and her long gray braid swung wildly as she picked up her pace. Under her apron, she wore blue jeans and a vibrant pink blouse. I still couldn't get over the fact that she was over fifty years old. She certainly didn't move like it, even though she was human.

When I had first entered the clan, Shanuk, Khalen's adoptive grandfather, explained to me that Spirians aged slowly because their pineal glands were so developed. He was over 300 years old when he passed away. My heart felt heavy with the loss, and now Traeger, the very cause of Shanuk's death, was here in this camp. Shanuk was more than just the eldest Spirian. He was my mentor, and something that mere words could not describe. When he passed into the Spirit realm, he took all that was dead in me and offered a stronger life in return.

I bit back the tears stinging my eyes. "What's going on?" I whispered to Eve.

She held up her hand, as if to silence me. After concentrating for a moment, she finally spoke. "Traeger is asking Case for help."

I knew better than to interrupt her while she was tapped into Case's mind. As his mate, she could communicate with him over any distance, which is probably why he sent her out to me. If he didn't want her tapping into his mind, he had the power to block her. I patiently waited for more information. It seemed an eternity before she spoke again.

The sisters, Jade and Ember, moved closer. Apparently, their curiosity was stoked as well. I noticed Jade staring out toward Ian, who was mending the goat pen. She was smitten with him and obviously disappointed with his perceived disinterest.

Eve brought her hand to her mouth. Her expression changed to concern. She started shaking her head.

Jade gasped and so did Ember. They were reading Eve's mind.

"What?" I finally said, feeling the odd woman out. Until I formally united with Khalen, I was not really part of the clan and was denied the gift of communal telepathy, or so I believed. The clan could read each other's thoughts, providing the distance was not too great between them. With mates this was different; once Khalen and I united, we would be able to communicate with each other over any distance, just as Eve and Case did.

I was ready for the union, but Khalen was not. He asked for time to sort things out and I vowed to give him as much as he needed. His last union ended very badly with the death of his mate, Valerie. When she fell into the trap of Traeger's allurement, Khalen was forced to kill her, ending their union. If she were allowed to live, she would have placed the entire clan at risk. That unfortunate demise nearly claimed all that was good in his heart, a fear he was not eager to revive.

"Traeger wants Case to train him. He wants peace between the clans," Ember whispered.

I waited for more.

"Khalen is arguing. He seems mad."

Yeah, I thought. That seems right. He should be angry. I wanted to ask him what his brother was up to, but I knew he wouldn't answer. He was purposely keeping me out of this. Providing we were close enough, I was able to read his thoughts when he kept them open to me. My thoughts, on the other hand, were inexplicably open to the entire clan. I had much to learn about the gift of telepathy.

"He and Case are discussing the issue," Ember continued. "Case believes that a bond between the clans would be good, but Khalen doesn't trust his twin."

"And Case does?" I asked.

"Shh," all three of them hissed.

I rolled my eyes, wondering if any of them knew how frustrating this was.

Again, Eve shook her head slowly. "No," she whispered.

Ember and Jade looked confused. "Case agreed," said Jade. "I didn't think he would."

She and Ember went back to pulling weeds as if the drama was over. It was far from over and I was not as accepting of Case's decision as the sisters obviously were.

I watched Khalen leave the yurt and head straight toward his thinking log.

Eve saw me start after him and gripped my shoulder. "You might want to give him some time, dear."

"What is Case thinking?" I asked.

Eve channeled herself back into his thoughts. "He begins Traeger's training tomorrow morning." Her shoulders sank and her jaw clenched. "I have a bad feeling about that one."

"Yeah," I said, knowing she spoke of Traeger. "Me too." I removed my gloves and stuffed them into the front pouch of my sweatshirt. "I'm going to talk to Khalen."

She squeezed my arm as if to say good luck with that.

I knew what she meant. Khalen was not the most pleasant person to talk to when he was angry and amped up.

Maiyun stayed close to my side as we walked toward the log. Khalen was nowhere in sight. I called for him in my mind. *Khalen?*

There was no answer. I reached out with my feelings and closed my eyes. I saw him by the water's edge. The trail leading down there was precarious for those who could see. It was stupid for someone, like myself, who was blind.

Maiyun stood between me and the trail. "I need to go to him," I said.

No! Khalen replied in thought.

Then come up here, I thought back. *Please.*

I heard him coming up the trail.

For a long moment, he said nothing. I knew better than to break that silence. In truth, I was happy just to be near him. We sat on the log overlooking the lake. His hazel eyes looked golden against the early noon sun. He was deep in thought, though he kept that thought hidden from me.

He wore blue jeans today, with a white short-sleeved shirt that could easily pass for dressy-casual. This was his day-off look, and it was about as casual as I would ever find him. He wore the moccasins that his mother made for him. I guessed it was his best attempt to connect with his Native American bloodroots.

His thick black hair shone with blue hues against the sun, and his eyes were golden green. His naturally-bronzed skin glowed hairless and smooth.

From his square jaw line and high cheekbones, I knew he was tribal, but little was known about his mom. His biological father, Damon, looked Native American as well, perhaps Cherokee or some neighboring tribe. Khalen wasn't too interested in sorting it out.

He took my hand in his and squeezed it hard. "My brother will be staying for some time," he finally said. "I want you to stay away from him." His voice carried the same British tone that his father and mother spoke, laced with elegant culture and refinement.

I huffed in reply. "No worries about that."

His grip felt crushing and desperate. "He will lure you to him," he said. "It's his gift. Understand?"

I nodded. "I'll be all right," I said quietly, not really convinced of my own words. I remembered all too well how easily Traeger had trapped me in his arms and kissed me last fall. My mind had gone blank and shockingly unresponsive. If it had been any other man, he would be clutching his groin in pain the moment he grabbed me. When he had held me, though, I was powerless.

"When I'm not around," said Khalen. "Stay with Ian and Aidan. They will keep you safe." His gruff tone did not catch me by surprise. His emotions were on edge and he was incapable of tender words now.

I raised my brow with playful apprehension. Ian and Aidan, the Irish brothers who had a reputation as the clan playboys, were going to keep me safe? Despite their reputation, I did trust them, as did Khalen. They had the gift of illusion and could easily make you believe just about anything, including flying. The flying squirrel suit adventure they took me on months ago still shone bright in my memory. It was a thrill I would not soon forget.

"I promise," I reluctantly said. Agreeing to his unreasonable request was out of form for me, but deep inside, I was relieved to have the protection. Having Traeger so close made me feel vulnerable; an emotion I was not used to entertaining.

We were silent for a moment before I spoke again. "Why is he here, Khalen?"

His golden eyes flashed down to meet my inquiring stare. They were distractingly hypnotic. "He wants Case to train him."

"Train him?"

"Traeger wants peace between our clans. He believes that if he learns our ways he will better understand how to calm the ill tendencies of the Shadows."

"And Case agrees?"

He looked at me. There was a faint hint of pain etched in his eyes. "Case is the clan leader. He cannot refuse to train anyone who approaches him, even if the person is a Shadow." His muscles tightened when he said it.

Like his twin, Khalen had been born into a Shadow family. At an early age, he developed his most powerful gift—reaping; the ability to take life. Not wanting to be a Shadow, he had also asked for Case's help. I doubted Traeger's intentions were similar.

Khalen was ostracized from his blood family and eagerly adopted by Case and Eve. The war between the clans had begun. To maintain some semblance of peace, a treaty was drawn to prevent the clans from entering each other's territory without prior permission. Along with that agreement, Spirians were not permitted to use their gifts against one another. This treaty was honored until last fall when I inadvertently used my gift to protect Maiyun against Talon's ill intent. Talon worked for Traeger's father, Damon. Talon was sent to discover the extent of my gifts, and to lure me away from the Protected clan. My ignorance delivered me straight into Traeger's clutches.

"How long will he stay here?" I asked. My palms were slightly damp.

Khalen stood. "As long as it takes." He offered his hand and led me back to our yurt.

As we approached the camp, Traeger was walking toward his car to remove his bags. Judging by the number of them, he was prepared to stay for quite some time.

Khalen wrapped his arm around my shoulder, protectively and possessively.

Traeger responded with a broad smile that made him look like the Cheshire Cat in *Alice in Wonderland*. His dark eyes followed us up the stairs and into the yurt. The hair on the back of my neck stood in eerie response.

Chapter 2

A silhouette looms like a shadow, void of detail and dimension,
distorting and darkening our feeble will.

IT WAS A CLEAR EVENING with a few clouds looming overhead. The fire crackled and provided a welcoming warmth. Khalen and I sat on a log opposite from Eve and Case. Ian and Aidan played with Maiyun and the other dogs near the lake, while various clan members gathered around neighboring fires.

In the distance, Jade watched Ian with admiring eyes. I could almost feel her heart heavy with longing and disappointment. I wanted badly to help her, but it was the Spirian man who chose his mate, not the woman.

"He knows," said Khalen, obviously reading my thoughts. "The match is not a good one for him."

I was still very unclear about the etiquette of proper matching. The rules were not defined. "She's a good woman," I said.

"Yes, but not a good woman for Ian."

My brows furrowed. "Why?"

He smiled down at me. "Jade is human and young in

spirit. She would never understand Ian's ways and it would cause strife between them."

"Hmm," I said, trying to mull over that weak explanation in my mind. There was so much to learn about the Spirian ways. I felt young in spirit myself, and precariously ignorant. "Perhaps he should tell her so that she can stop pining for something that will never be."

"That he has," Khalen assured me. "She is deaf to his words."

"Son," Case called from across the fire. "Walk with me." He stood, looming above us. When Khalen stood, he nearly matched his father's height of six-foot-four.

Eve came over to sit next to me.

"Is Traeger staying with you?" I asked.

She glanced over her shoulder. "He is staying in the guest tent behind our yurt."

I had to laugh. The great Traeger, staying in a tent? I wondered how long that would last. He was used to his large mansion with all the convenient amenities of a five-star hotel. "I'm sure he's very comfortable."

Eve chuckled, knowing exactly what I referred to. "I certainly hope not," she added.

We both laughed.

I studied the flames for a moment as they rose and fell, dancing on the gentle evening breeze. Case could extinguish them with a thought, but I still struggled with that one. Projecting my energy was unpredictable and often disastrous. I continued with my Qi Gong exercises as Case instructed. He assured me that it would take years for me to develop any kind of consistency with my new gifts. I would have to learn to be patient.

"He's trying to talk Khalen into claiming me soon," I said, almost as a spoken thought.

Eve nodded. "It is dangerous to wait any longer."

"He's not ready."

She reached out and patted the back of my hand. "His fear consumes his good sense," she said. "It will be his undoing."

I thought about Ian and Aidan and the number of women they had taken to their beds.

"Eve," I hesitantly said.

She raised her brow as if already knowing what I was going to ask. "Yes, my dear."

"Ian and Aidan have shared affections with many women. Why are they not claimed?"

"If a man chooses not to claim a woman, the woman will not be claimed."

I frowned. "Um," I hesitated. "How does a man claim a woman?" At first, I thought that he had to join with her and that was that. But now, I was confused and even more curious. Eve was human and had never really joined with Case as do Spirians, but I knew she was savvy to the their ways.

Eve lowered her head, collecting her thoughts for a moment. "Well," she said. "First, the man has to bring the woman to a state in which he can bond with her. Typically this involves a very intense orgasm."

My face instantly reddened and I felt uncomfortable.

"Once she is in that state, he connects with her and draws her into his spirit. The bond is painful at first, and then the woman feels a sense of completeness that is impossible to describe, or so I'm told." She smiled sadly. "Of course, some men are better at this than others."

"So, you can share affections with one another without actually uniting?"

"Yes," she confirmed.

I frowned. Khalen had not made love to me, nor had he even tried. I had thought that it was because he was not ready for the union. Now my speculation was heading in another direction. Perhaps he was not really attracted to me in that way.

"Khalen will not be intimate with you until the time is right," she offered. "To him, the entire act is sacred, not just the union."

I smiled and lowered my head. "I wish I could read your thoughts as easily as you can read mine."

"What stops you?" She turned to look at me with curiosity etched in her face.

"I am not bound to the clan until Khalen is ready."

"Jade and Ember do not have mates, yet they can hear your thoughts."

I had not thought of that fact, but yet it was true. There were many people in the clan that were not bound to a mate and they could all communicate without words.

"I can hear Khalen, but no one else."

"That is because you are entrained to him. When you open yourself to others, you will be able to communicate with them as well."

The thought of opening myself to others was fraught with feelings of vulnerability. "How can others hear me when I am not open to them?"

"They are open to you, and therefore, your thoughts enter their own."

"So, how does Khalen block me from hearing his thoughts?"

She closed her hands together. "He closes the energetic door that connects all things."

"How?"

"When you heal someone," she explained. "You empty

yourself of yourself, correct?"

I nodded.

"In a sense, you open yourself to the universal flow, God's energy. Now, what happens when you try to force something to happen?"

"I'm cut off. I can't make anything happen," I answered.

"Yes," said Eve. "Exactly. You cut off the universal flow so that nothing can get through."

It all made sense to me now, and I felt ridiculous for not being able to figure it out on my own. It was so simple. "That is why his energy closes in around him when he tunes me out," I said, again speaking my thought out loud.

She nodded, enthusiastically. "Yes, you have it, my dear."

Another confusing thought entered my mind. "So, how does Case break through, even when I cut myself off?"

She laughed. "He draws you in and invites your thoughts."

"Draws me in?"

"He taps into your vibrational pattern, entrains to it, and then changes your vibration to match his intention."

I frowned. "Why can't others do that to him?"

"Shanuk could do it."

"How?"

She placed her hand over my arm and gave it a gentle squeeze. "You are like an infant asking how to run a marathon, Skye. You and I have neither the strength nor the knowledge to comprehend the level at which Shanuk existed."

I nodded and thought about what she had said. In many ways, I did feel like an infant, especially in the presence of Case.

Union

~ K h a l e n ~

I FOLLOWED MY FATHER TO THE thinking log. We sat, maintaining the silence between us. He knew what had been on my mind, and knew my feelings about it full heartedly.

"You don't agree with my decision to allow your brother to stay," he finally voiced.

"I do not."

"Suggest a better plan, Son." His voice had a tenderness to it.

"Send him away, Father. He is poison here and will infect the clan."

Case pursed his lips in thought. "If you have a child, and protect him from the elements, the germs of the world, and the social drama, will he be stronger or weaker for it?"

I knew where he was going with this analogy. "Weaker," I sighed.

"If I send Traeger away, will he be grateful for my wisdom, or vengeful because of my rejection of him?"

I felt the blood heat my face. "He will be vengeful no matter what you decide," I growled.

"Is it his respect for me that angers you so, or is it my willingness to help him?"

"Neither. It is the danger he poses to our camp."

"Is your faith in me so shallow, my son?"

His words struck a chord deep within my soul. My faith in him was as strong as any I had ever felt. In my heart, there was nothing he could do to fail me. "My faith in you is strong, Father."

"Yet you doubt my ability to control your brother during his stay?"

"I do not."

Case sighed, something he did when his point was not finding its intended target. "Traeger believes there can be peace between our clans. It is a noble wish, but a feeble one. He is very much like you were when you first came to me, Khalen. He inherently wants to be good, and do the right thing, but his ego and desire for power will overtake him. His own clan members will turn against him. To rise above the pressure, he will have to allow his ego to die and accept a position beneath his current stature."

"That won't happen," I said.

"Yes, I know that as well."

My knuckles turned white. "Then why continue with this dangerous charade?"

"Events must run their course, my son. The journey provides the lessons, not the destination. By training the man, I will form a bond with him—a strong bond. With each passing day, he will find it harder to thwart me."

I knew that lesson all too well. Respect was a powerful thing. I nodded, acknowledging his wisdom and foresight.

"Have you considered the matter of Skye?" he asked.

"I have." My stomach wrenched with the thought of taking her for a mate. It felt more like I offered her a death sentence than the eternal love she deserved.

"She is not Valerie," said Case, referring to the mate I had ignorantly taken several years back. "She is strong, and she completes you."

"That she does," I said. "To the point where losing her will be the death of me."

"Then do the right thing and keep her safe, Son. Claim her now. Do not wait."

"She is not ready," I growled.

Case gripped my arm. "Then make her ready."

Chapter 3

*When misery's company parts ways, misery bands with anger
and hate, raising a formidable foe.*

-Traeger-

Traeger, **I HEARD IN THOUGHT.** It was the dulcet
voice of my alpha mate, Sunjia. She was a beautiful
Brazilian woman with obsidian eyes that shone like black
diamonds. She was the perfect, obedient mate with gifts
that complemented my own. Where I could manipulate
and lure people to do my bidding, she could make one
forget the difference between right and wrong, like a drug
that numbs the senses.

Yes, I answered. *What is it, Mate?* There was no need to
use names when it came to women. It was easier to simply
address them as their stature in life.

*The clan is turning against you. They doubt your strength to
lead them.*

Of course they do, I thought to myself. The benefits
of forming a bond with the Protected ones elude them.

The mere thought is so far out of the box they live in, how can they possibly conceive it?

Today's training with Case had been grueling and cruel, but well worth the effort. The man was a much stronger teacher than my father had been, and much more generous with praise. My father was one of the few clan elders who had seen more than two hundred years. Unlike the Protected ones, the Shadows seemed to have a shorter life span.

I intended to change that. Somehow, I would have to convince the Shadows that the elders contained the wisdom and power we needed to survive. We had to do a much better job at preserving our kind. There were too few teachers left to carry on the training of our young spirits.

Woman, I called to Sunjia. *Convince them that my gifts grow stronger every day. Tell them that I will not abandon them.*

Yes, Traeger, I understand, she responded.

Being confined to this blasted tent was almost more than I could bear. To gain Case's cooperation, I had to agree to stay in this hellhole until my training was complete. I was not allowed to correspond with the other clan members, especially the females. The agreement was unreasonable, and I was going to bring that to my teacher's attention this evening.

His mate, Eve, had graciously brought me my dinner: a scant portion of bread, cold ham and canned beans. I had unfortunately exhausted my bottle of wine last evening, and was in sore need of something refreshing. My best charm did nothing to melt the icy exterior Eve exhibited. She simply looked at me with those coal-black eyes, and softened my intentions with grace and kindness. Honestly, I wanted to choke her.

If I knew Case would never find out, it would have sufficed to have my way with her first. Like Skye, she was sure to offer some intriguing challenges.

Case entered the tent, a glass of brandy in his hand. "I trust you enjoyed your dinner?" he asked. His voice was as silky as the delicate threads of a Monarch butterfly's cocoon.

I glanced down at my half-eaten portion. "It was better than expected," I retorted.

His response was immediate and direct.

I found myself on the floor gasping for breath and fighting the pain that threatened to implode my organs.

"Am I to assume that you disapprove of my mate's cooking?"

I could not gather the breath to speak, let alone think of a suitable answer. His grip on me eased a bit. I breathed deep and stifled my instinct to be sarcastic.

He took a long, slow sip of his brandy as if purposely trying to taunt me.

My mouth watered in response.

He smiled. "I would offer you a drink," he said snidely, "but it seems you've indulged yourself already."

I assumed he referred to the two meager bottles of wine that I had managed to ration through the course of seven long days. It was ridiculous, really, having to go without for so long.

"Perhaps you did not hear me say that you were to have absolutely no alcohol or any other recreational substances during the entire course of your training?"

"I heard," I gasped. The pain ripped through me like rampant flames. I could not break his blasted hold.

"So then you willingly disobeyed me?"

The intensity of his grip thwarted my ability to stay

conscious. I was on the verge of fainting, a fact I was sure he knew. "I am weak, my teacher. Please have mercy." My plea disgusted me. I sounded like many of the females I had taken to my bed.

"You will learn to be strong, Student, or you will leave this camp and never return." His voice was calm and even.

I knew there would be no reasoning with him tonight.

Our training continued throughout the evening. I was exhausted and mentally spent. The morning sun filtered in through the door flap. "If it is your will," I said, with as much respect as my worn-out body could muster. "I would like to take a shower."

He eyed me suspiciously. "Yes, perhaps a bit of fresh air will clear your cluttered thoughts. You have two hours to see to your hygiene. Do not mingle with the clan."

I stumbled to my feet. Every inch of my body ached as if it had endured a thousand strikes from a formidable length of stiff hosing. Even my bones ached as I forced them to move. Crossing Case was clearly not an option. I was beginning to rethink my decision to stay here.

He watched me as I gathered my toiletries and headed for the door. As I crossed the camp toward the showers, I saw Skye, Khalen's female.

She glanced up at me, and then headed in the opposite direction. I willed her to turn around, but like most of my efforts to lure her, it failed. No woman had been able to resist my invites, but this one did, and she repeatedly ignored my efforts to sway her from my traitorous twin.

I continued my trek to the rural outbuilding that housed the showers, willing her to follow. I could feel her as if she were standing before me. Her scent tempted my hunger and my body responded in kind. I smiled, thinking how sweet she would taste. If Khalen would not take her,

I would, and soon.

I had about seven more days here before I could return to the comforts of my own home. Seth was charged with keeping things running smoothly in my absence. It was clear, based on what Sunjia reported, that he was not suited for the job just yet. He was seventeen already and had not shown any signs of having gifts of his own. Sunjia, his mother, explained that her own gifts did not manifest until she was nearly thirty. If our nine-year-old daughter does not show promising signs of gifts soon, Sunjia will lose much of her value to me.

Unlike the Protected ones, Shadows are able to take more than one mate without disapproval. I already had five. Sunjia was the only one I impregnated. I now wondered if that had been a mistake.

The shower's water trickled over my head like a poor excuse for a leak. Apparently, water pressure was nonexistent in this godforsaken dirt mound. I wouldn't doubt it if plastic bags had been placed on the roof of this shack and left for the sun to warm. That there was even a trickle at all was no doubt due to the sheer force of gravity. How quaint.

I made quick work of showering, and donned my clean clothes. They were pathetically wrinkled. Honestly, I had no idea how Khalen could stand living like this. It was just short of barbaric.

A lovely redhead met me on the path. She was obviously heading for the women's showers. I smiled and caught her attention.

"You're Traeger, right?"

I nodded. "I am. And you, lovely lady, are?"

She giggled like a young teen, yet this human was clearly in her forties. "I'm Jade." She glanced back at another redheaded woman trailing behind her. "And that is my sister, Ember."

The older one finally caught up and gave me a questioning stare.

"Good day to you, Miss," I said, offering an alluring smile.

She grabbed the young woman's arm. "Come on."

Jade smiled back at me. "See you later."

"No doubt," I said. It was reassuring to see that I hadn't lost my gift. Staying in this pit nearly had me convinced that I could not lure anything other than bad food and cruel lessons.

Skye tended the animals with Ian and Aidan as I made my way back. I tried to draw her attention, but she ignored me as usual. Aidan stood with his arm hanging over the end of a shovel handle, watching me pass. I had an odd sensation of walking through a long tunnel made of stone. It was cold and dark save the end, where the light shone through. "Damn illusionist," I cursed.

Case waited for me outside of my tent. He had the most disturbing stare, as if he could see right through my soul.

"I asked you to stay clear of our women," he said.

"I sought out no one," I said. It was the truth. Just because the humans happened to be on the same path as me, and caught my attention did not count as lying, so far as I was concerned.

"You spoke to Jade and Ember, and you tried to lure Skye."

The old man's talents knew no bounds. Even my late father could not perceive so much. "I was being kind to the humans," I explained, "and Skye just happened to gain my attention. Perhaps it was her trying to lure me?"

As expected, the remainder of the day was filled with pleasantries such as unbearable pain and impossible feats to perform. I felt like a polar bear expected to ride a bicycle three sizes too small. Case was ensuring that I had absolutely no energy left to cause more problems within the camp, I was sure.

At midnight, he left my tent. I was more than spent and was looking forward to a good long rest. He then informed me that training would begin at five in the morning. I was to meet him at the lake. Bloody hell.

I had to admit, the old man was making an impression on me. He had more gifts than I could imagine, and his style of training was unsurpassed. He had me believing that I could become one of the Protected. I even started feeling a bit guilty for trying to gain the attention of that young woman, Jade.

I turned out the light, hopeful that my newfound contentment would somehow rub off on my clan brothers.

I was wrong.

Are you becoming one of 'em then? A familiar voice chimed in my head. It was Sean, the leader of the Seattle clan. He was as powerful and ruthless as a hit mob. His clan was half the number of my own, but his pull with the surrounding clans was strong.

No, I assured him. *I am merely learning their ways to understand them better. They can be formidable allies.*

We don't need allies, Traeger. We need the woman that the legend speaks of. Tell me you are doing all this to steal her away and claim her as our own.

That was an added benefit, yes, but my pure intention was to gain the trust and respect of the Protected ones.

Myself and the others are questioning your loyalty, Traeger.

Understood, was my only reply. It was clear that an

alliance with the Protected ones was not an option at this time. If I sided against the Shadows, they would kill me. If I pledged loyalty to the Protected, I would be expected to follow Khalen's lead. Never would I claim loyalty to a brother who gave up his own family for another who was clearly not of his kind.

Taking Skye from him was a more attractive choice. As my mate, she would strengthen my clan and gain me the respect I deserved. With any luck, Khalen's anger would bring him back to us, his blood clan, and he would follow my lead.

Chapter 4

Integrity defines the heart of the soul.

~ S k y e ~

EVERY TIME TRAEGER'S COLD GAZE met mine, I wanted to claw his eyes out. His pitiful attempts to lure me toward him were like similar poles of two magnets. He repelled me. His intentions for wanting to be here were all wrong. He wanted to have an alliance with our clan, but there was something else underlying that desire.

It did no good to talk to Khalen about his brother. His father's mind was set and there was nothing he could do about it. Khalen rarely left me alone these days, and when he did, he delivered me directly to Ian and Aidan with strict orders to keep an eye on me. And that they did with grueling diligence.

I missed my alone time and craved it more with each passing moment, so much that I made every excuse just to use the privy. Aidan was beginning to think I was sick or something.

"Honestly, Skye, you just used the privy twenty minutes ago," said Aidan. "Are you not feeling well?"

My shoulders slumped. "To be honest," I explained, "I'm getting a bit stir crazy. I haven't been alone for the past ten days and it's getting on my nerves."

"Yes, well, you won't be alone anytime soon until that Shadow is gone."

"Please," I pleaded. "I just need some time to think, down by the lake. Traeger is in his tent with Case, they won't break for at least another two hours."

Aidan looked over at his brother, who vehemently shook his head. "I'm sorry, lass. Khalen—"

"Does not own me," I finished for him. "I am a grown woman, and not a possession to be held under lock and key." I tossed down the shovel in my hands and stormed off toward the lake. Maiyun trotted beside me.

I heard Ian grumble under his breath then follow me. He carefully kept his distance, trying his best to give me as much space as he felt comfortable.

If I weren't blind, I would try to outrun him. The thought almost made me laugh. His legs nearly doubled mine in height. It would not be a fair match. He was trying to read my thoughts, but I carefully kept him out.

My talk with Eve two weeks ago by the fire had proven very useful. Since then I was more conscious of when others entered my thoughts. I could feel their energies merging with mine. I learned to gently nudge them away, without appearing rude. I was simply drawing a curtain between my thoughts and theirs.

This new gift had also proven useful against Traeger's constant attempts to lure me toward him. I wanted nothing to do with that man.

I sat down on Khalen's thinking log, and then swung

my legs up and lay down on my back. Maiyun laid her head on my chest. I grazed my hand over her soft muzzle and she closed her eyes. "I wish I could read your thoughts," I said. She licked her lips, and then lay down beside me.

Clouds dappled the afternoon sky, offering little in the way of light. I closed my eyes and tried to tap into Case's mind. It was no use; he detected my effort the moment I thought about it. I wanted to talk to him, but he spent most of his time with Khalen's twin. Even Eve was getting a bit bothered by her mate's preoccupation.

I briefly wondered if Traeger was luring Case away from the clan, but quickly thought better of it. Case was much stronger than Traeger, and far more clever. I tried to envision what an alliance with the Shadows would look like. It was hard to imagine, really. We wanted such different things.

Theoretically, the two clans should be able to get along, just as the sun and the moon do. But we were not really like the sun and moon. We were more like fire and water. Both were valuable, yet together, we made a hazy cloud of steam that all too quickly dissipated.

I sighed and listened intently to the soothing sounds of the sparrows and finches, which beautifully orchestrated their musical songs to the breeze that combed through the trees. Spring had always been my favorite season here in Washington. Everything smelled so fragrant and fresh, even the earth, rich with rotting leaves and fat little worms.

I figured if I appeared to have fallen asleep, Ian would get bored and return to his cleaning duties. No such luck. I opened my eyes to find him sitting beside Maiyun, stroking her fur.

"I don't like him here," I said.

"None of us do, lass," he replied, staring out at the reflective waters in distant thought.

"My friends are heading back from Oregon," I mentioned. "I would like to spend some time with them."

He looked at me with a questioning glance as if he already knew what I was about to say but wanted to hear the words.

"I want to spend some time away from camp," I finally blurted out, probably sounding a bit more desperate than I wanted. In truth, I needed some time away from this situation—and from Khalen.

For the first time in many years, my heart ached for something it couldn't have. Khalen kept me close, safe, and made me feel very loved, but there was that one piece that was missing—intimacy. I wasn't sure how much longer I could hang on without losing myself completely. I knew it was difficult for Khalen as well. He left frequently during the middle of the evening. He needed a walk, he always said, as if that was typical for most people.

The draw we had toward one another was indescribable and was beginning to tear away at my soul with each passing day. Soon there would be nothing but shards left. My breath grew heavy with the thought.

Ian placed his large hand on my shoulder. "I'm not convinced he'll ever be ready, lass."

"I know," I sighed. The realization of it all felt heavy as dull lead in my chest. I forced a deep breath and held it for a moment. "I need some time away from here."

"Oh, lass," he said, his voice burdened with apprehension. "It's not safe, you know. The Shadows will find you easy enough and without the protection of the clan, you—"

"I know," I interrupted him. "Right now, I would

rather be dead than live with this pain." I stared into his languid green eyes as if trying to drive my point into his very soul.

"Aye, I'm not missing the point, lass. No need to throw daggers."

I moved back, my eyes wide. "You felt that?"

He rubbed his eyelids. "Like red-hot pokers."

"Oh, God. I'm sorry," I said, rubbing my palms together. "Here." I placed my hands over his eyes. "This will help."

"What were you thinking?" he asked.

"I don't know," I said. "I wanted to make my point clear and was drawn to your soul through your eyes. I—"

He reached for my hands and held them. I broke down and released the torrent of emotions I had been holding inside since my husband Derrick passed away ten years ago.

Maiyun looked concerned as Ian rocked me in his arms and whispered something in Gaelic against the top of my head. I felt a presence and glanced up.

I'm not sure how long Khalen had been standing there, but he made no move to separate Ian and I. When I managed to gain some composure, I pulled away from Ian's arms, and wiped my stinging eyes, red and swollen from the recent outpour.

Ian looked up at Khalen as if listening to a private thought. Ian nodded, squeezed my hand, and then quietly took his leave. Khalen sat down in his place.

"I'm sorry," he finally said. His hand shook as he fought the urge to touch me. When I reached out to touch him, he pulled away and shook his head.

Aidan came to us with grave concern in his eyes. "My brother said you wanted to see me." There was an edge to his voice that seemed unmerited. I gathered it must have been something that Khalen had said to Ian just a short time ago.

Maiyun nudged Khalen's hand to gain his attention, but her efforts were ignored. Khalen was acting very peculiar and my gut was not prepared for what he was about to say.

"Aidan," he began, his voice gruff and pitched with grief. "I want you to take Skye as your mate."

I stood, my despair suddenly replaced with anger. "I am not your property, Khalen Dunning. You cannot just offer me to another because you have no need for me." The last part came out broken and weak. I wanted to walk away, but held Khalen's stare instead.

"No need for you?" he questioned. The pain we both felt was amplified by the space between us like a giant capacitor of emotions, threatening to explode with deadly results. "God, woman. I—"

Aidan stood there, not quite sure what to do. To touch either one of us would prove fatal right now. He was in a precarious position and he knew it.

"Khalen," Aidan said. "You're not thinking straight, lad. Step away from Skye and we'll talk."

The hum in the air was deafening as thunder. I could feel the jolt of a thousand shocks coursing through my body, yet I held my position.

Case came running with Ian close behind. The next thing I knew, I was sitting on the ground with the wind knocked out of me. Khalen had been thrown fifteen feet away, also struggling to breathe.

Aidan was visibly shaking. He sat on the log and placed his face in his trembling hands.

Eve ran toward us. "What happened?" She rushed to

my side and helped me stand. "Are you all right?"

I nodded, not really sure what to think. I felt disjointed from life and confused, as if someone had taken a piece of my soul. Khalen looked pale.

The hair on the back of my neck stood upright. I turned to find Traeger watching us all with hungry eyes.

"Leave," Case warned him. "Now."

Traeger smiled down at Khalen and walked away.

Khalen tried to stand, but Case held him down forcefully. "Stay down," he commanded.

"I'm all right," said Khalen. "Let me stand." His voice had an angry edge to it, which seemed odd, seeing it was aimed at a man he obviously respected.

Case stared down at Khalen, his eyes glowing with opalescent hues. "You will stay down until I release you."

Khalen's intention was alarming. He was testing his father's strength and openly challenging it.

"Aidan," Case said, still keeping his eyes on Khalen. "Take Skye, Ian, and Eve to my yurt."

"Aye," said Aidan. He then ushered us all away. I looked back at the two men, still staring each other down. Khalen's intentions were clear and they frightened me. I had never seen this side of him.

"Come," said Aidan, encouraging me to follow the others. "They'll be all right."

At some point during my riff with Khalen, Maiyun left my side. I looked around the camp, but she was nowhere in sight.

"Where's Maiyun?" I asked.

"Ian had to take her away."

"Why? Where?"

"Don't worry, Skye, she's fine. She waits for you in your yurt."

"Khalen's yurt," I corrected.

I saw him swallow hard. "It should not have come to this," he mumbled.

By the time we reached Case's yurt, Eve had started serving a tray of cookies and hot tea. She gestured for me to sit but said nothing. Everyone was uncomfortably quiet.

Case joined us much later—too much later for my comfort. Khalen wasn't with him.

"Where is he?" I finally asked.

"Gone," said Case, nodding with appreciation as Eve poured him a cup of tea.

"Where—"

"Tell me what happened," he said, interrupting my inquiry. I could tell by the sharp tone in his commanding voice that his patience was short and his temper dangerously fanned to a red-hot warning.

"Khalen tried to offer me to Aidan as a mate," I explained, my hands twisting together. "I simply reminded him that he did not have the right to pass me off to another."

Case's cold stare made me feel like Jell-o inside, with no structure to hold me up. I struggled to swallow. He took a bite of shortbread, and chewed slowly as he pondered his thoughts.

Ian and Aidan looked noticeably alarmed, as did Eve.

"And then what?" asked Case.

"Khalen got angry." I looked down at the rug beneath my feet, temporarily mesmerized by the geometrical patterns and contrasting colors. "It was like we were caught in some electrifying field," I explained, almost as if I was questioning whether it was real. "I felt his anger and matched it with my own."

Case took a deep breath and closed his eyes. "You are his equal," he sighed.

"I read his intentions," I said, "and matched them with my own."

Case ran his formidable hands through his hair. "It all makes sense now," he mumbled, as if his words were not meant for any of us to hear. "The shield you cast toward Talon last fall, and your ability to thwart Traeger's lure."

"My eyes," Ian added. "The way you pierced right through them with your thoughts."

Everyone looked at him, and then at me.

"It appears," said Case, "that you are not only able to sense intention, you can also direct it with deadly accuracy."

I wrapped my arm around my stomach, feeling as if someone had just sucker-punched me. "I should leave."

"And go where, Skye?" Case asked.

"Back to my apartment."

"You are a Spirian. It is too dangerous to live without a clan, especially when you are not yet claimed."

"I'll manage," I said, feeling the anger well up in me like acrid vinegar. I knew Case would not allow me to go unprotected. He would no doubt instruct Ian and Aidan to watch me from a distance.

I stood, feeling that now was the best time to leave. Tears welled in Eve's eyes as she stood and offered me a lingering hug.

"Stay safe," she whispered.

"I'll take you into town," Aidan offered.

I nodded. "Thank you." I looked over at Case and met his steely stare. "Thank you for your guidance, Case." There was so much more I wanted to say, but my words were choked behind unbearable sadness.

Case nodded and watched me leave.

A part of me expected some fight, or even more of an argument from him, but I was disappointed. Even Eve looked surprised as he watched me walk out the door.

Aidan escorted me back to Khalen's yurt. I glanced up at the solid-looking door with a heavy heart. I went inside and immediately felt the emptiness. Maiyun greeted me enthusiastically, but her breath was tainted with the rancid odor of anxiety. Khalen had not returned here, nor was he anywhere near camp. His Escalade was gone.

I gathered a few of my things, stuffed them into a bag, and then called Maiyun to follow me. I'm not sure why I left some of my things; perhaps I felt a need to return at some point, or was just in a hurry to leave. I wasn't sure. I still felt the numbing affects of Khalen's anger and my opposition toward it. Right now, I cared very little about anything.

I took one more look around before closing the door behind me.

Chapter 5

In the wake of a storm, wisdom dictates a need to wait with quiet reserve and not rush in with fight in our hearts toward the lure of destructive winds.

-Khalen-

As CASE SUGGESTED, I DROVE straight for Grays Harbor and planned to stay there at my beach cottage until my anger cooled. Never had anyone matched my fury, let alone a female. Her strength both surprised me and infuriated me all at the same time. Did she not understand my position?

I knew that my indecision was causing her pain. I saw it in those silver-gray eyes of hers as she looked up at me, still quaking in Ian's embrace. Through his thoughts, I felt her pain and the emptiness in her heart.

Aidan could offer her safety, love and stability. Couldn't she see how hard it was for me to give her up? She said I had no use for her. I pounded the steering wheel with such force, the vessels in my hand burst open, causing a bright purple bruise to swell under my skin. The pain was a welcoming distraction. I released a primal roar, causing the passenger in the car next to me to take notice.

I wanted to rip my heart out and toss it out the window. I cursed the moment I saw that gray-eyed vixen. Of all the clans in Washington, what brought her to mine? Damn her heart. She was impetuous, independent, stubborn, and gifted beyond any young Spirian I had ever met—and I was in love with her.

I pulled into the driveway and parked the car. Unpacking could wait. Right now, I needed a swim. With any luck, some renegade orca would try to make a meal of me.

In the water, I could unleash my anger and vent without fear of destroying everything around me. At worst, the waters would become inexplicably turbulent and white peaks would form around me, but no one would notice this evening. There was hardly a soul on the beach, and the setting sun would soon offer useful darkness.

In the morning, of course, there would be unfortunate casualties as a result of my venting. That could not be helped. The coastal birds would make quick work of the carnage and nobody would think twice about the incident.

- S k y e -

MAIYUN RODE IN THE BACK of the Jeep with her tongue hanging out and her mind oblivious to the tension in the cab. A dog's life was so simple and uncomplicated. She felt the basic emotions, but she was blissfully spared the complex nuances that drove most people insane.

Aidan was silent at first, keeping his eyes trained on the road ahead, and his thoughts to himself. I did the same, appreciating the quiet time and a reprieve from what was sure to be awkward conversation. Unfortunately, that reprieve was short-lived.

"Would it be so bad to have me as a mate?" he asked.

Before my outrage back at the camp, I never considered how Aidan might have taken my response. My already burdened heart felt the weight of yet another quandary.

"No," I said. "I was just surprised at how quickly he tossed me aside without even a warning. He caught me off guard, that's all." I smiled, trying to assure him.

He must have seen right through it. His jaw tightened and his eyes darkened. "Would you consider it?"

I looked down at my hands, wringing together as if trying to rid my skin of some invisible parasite. "Yes and no," I said quite honestly. "Yes, because I find you attractive, kind, and persuasive. No, because I am hopelessly in love with Khalen, despite his uncontrollable anger, his stubbornness, indecisiveness, cruel nature, and arrogance." The last part probably came out a bit louder than necessary.

Aidan laughed. "You find me attractive?"

I rolled my eyes. Men could be so simple sometimes. "Yes, I do," I said. "Is that all you heard?"

"Aye," he said, "all I wanted to hear." His smile was genuine and welcoming.

I shook my head, but smiled at the same time. "Men," I said. "They are all impossible."

"I noticed," he said, "that you never once mentioned that Khalen was attractive."

I looked at him, my mouth hung open, and my eyes

wide in disbelief. "Right now, that is the last thing on my mind."

Still, his smile did not fade. Unbelievable.

Another period of time passed with unspoken words. The ride from Harstine Island to Belfair was only 45 minutes, but today it seemed longer.

"What was it like?" he finally asked.

I shook my head. "What?"

"Being caught in Khalen's wrath."

"Scary."

"And?" he prompted.

"Painful, imprisoning, frustrating, exhilarating— magical." That last word surprised me and apparently surprised Aidan as well.

He looked at me and nearly hit a car in oncoming traffic. The blare of the horn still sounded in the distance.

"Describe magical," he said.

He was genuinely interested. I detected no sarcasm, just pure curiosity in its truest form.

"It was as if we were one being, fighting the same demon, but not each other. We were connected."

His smile deepened.

"Now what are you smiling at?" I asked, irritated with his display of humor.

"Khalen thought you didn't care for him. He thought you wanted someone else."

I shook my head with the irony of it all. I knew that men could be dense at times, but God almighty, did it have to be at the most obvious of times?

"Let me guess," I drawled. "He thought I wanted you?"

"Aye, he did."

A moment of silence passed. "As did I," he added in a much more subtle tone.

"Aidan," I said, lacking something else to say. "I—"

"No need, lass. I understand." His brilliant smile dimmed to a halfhearted grin.

"No," I insisted, "I'm certain you don't."

"It doesn't much matter, now does it?" he said. "I am your faithful guardian for as long as you'll have me."

Lord, those words stung like a thousand bee stings. I had told Khalen almost the same thing. I would stay with him for as long as he'd have me. Only I didn't expect him to give me away so quickly.

"He didn't," said Aidan.

"Didn't what?"

"Give you away."

I would have to learn to guard my thoughts more carefully. "So, asking you to take me as your mate was not giving me away?"

"No, it was more like offering you a choice. One he thought you wanted to make."

I spat out my response. "Apparently, his thinker is broken. The only thing he managed to do was push me away."

"So you're not in love with him anymore?"

I shook my hands, imagining the heads of both men in my grip as I shook them senseless. Obviously, it didn't take much effort. "No," I said with as much venom as I could muster, "I'm not."

"Then I still have a chance?"

I looked at him squarely now, with no humor at all on my face. "No, I'm no longer available."

Confusion reigned over his emotions now, and perhaps a bit of hurt. At the moment, I didn't care. My heart was bleeding and was tapped out of compassion. Just like a country song I once heard, my give-a-damn was busted.

Chapter 6

Time offers us a moment to reset our expectations and perhaps our beliefs. It is a good place to start when the direction we take leads to an undesirable destination.

IT DIDN'T TAKE LONG FOR ME to settle back into my apartment. Maiyun seemed happy as well. Khalen's presence still lingered there, though. I tried smudging the place with white sage, and attuning it with numerous tuning forks in the chromium scale, but still his energy lingered.

During the night, I could feel his touch on my skin, his voice in my ear like the deep tones of a distant angel, and could smell his blasted scent in every room. I hadn't had a decent night's sleep since my return. I was hoping that Sam and Karin's arrival tomorrow would change all that.

Maiyun either sensed my unhappiness, or she missed Khalen as well. I wasn't sure. He hadn't shown up for work for two weeks, and even Gregg and Ro seemed concerned. On many occasions I had to offer remedies to his clients to address new symptoms as they arose. I almost looked forward to the earful I would certainly get for interfering with his clients' treatments.

I planned to take some time off to spend with Sam and Karin. I welcomed the reprieve I would get from passing Khalen's empty office every day. For the first time in months, I considered moving to another town altogether. At this point, another country sounded intriguing. Either way, I would have to seek employment elsewhere and make a new start. My soul grew dark and heavy with the thought. It was hard enough not seeing Khalen. The thought of never seeing him again hardly seemed plausible.

Back in my apartment, I sat in the dark, trying to imagine where he might be. All that came to mind was cold, salty water surrounding my body and the roar of angry waves. As far as I knew, he boarded the first ship to leave Seattle. I couldn't blame him, really. I wanted to leave as well and get as far from this place as possible.

I had not blocked him from my thoughts and often wondered if he even cared to read them anymore. I certainly couldn't read his. It was as if he had removed himself from my radar completely. Like a sick mantra, I called his name over and over in my mind, praying he would answer. He never did.

The next morning Sam and Karin arrived bright and chipper, knocking on my door at seven in the morning. I had fallen asleep in the chair, with my empty wine glass dangling precariously in my hand. I only had one glass last night, but it hit me hard on an empty stomach.

Maiyun paced between me and the door, eager to greet her bear-like friend, Sam on the other side. I acknowledged their arrival with a low and groggy, "I'm coming."

I opened the door to find Sam wearing a hunter-orange tee-shirt tucked neatly into his green and brown kilt, accented colorfully with a bright new pair of rainbow stockings. Karin, of course, looked much more practical in a pair of blue jeans and a lacy white blouse.

"You look like hell, Skye," Sam said with far too much confidence. It was quickly rebutted with a sharp poke from Karin.

"Did we wake you?" she asked.

I stepped away from the door to let them inside. "No," I lied, "I was just sitting for a bit."

"You're a horrible liar, Skye," said Sam.

"So I've been told," I replied, faintly remembering Traeger's words several months ago. In Sam and Karin's presence, that memory seemed like a completely separate life.

"Okay," said Sam, "where is your coffee machine? We need to get some life into you."

I pointed at the French press on the counter.

Sam pulled it apart and inspected it questioningly. "How do you turn it on?"

Karin snatched the parts from his hand and told him to sit down. He did so, looking clueless as a frog in boiling water. She found the container of coffee on the counter and expertly portioned some into the press. She then filled the water kettle and placed it on the burner.

I buried my face in my hands and groaned.

"Tough night?" asked Sam.

I peered at him through narrow slits between my fingers. Tough was an understatement. Hellacious was much more accurate.

"Never mind," he said. "I don't think I want to know."

"No," I confirmed, "you really don't."

"Sam and I wondered if you wanted to grab something for breakfast," said Karin, checking on the kettle as if doubting the heat of the flame.

"Sounds great," I moaned, standing from my chair. "I'll just take a quick shower."

"I'll have coffee for you when you come out," she said.

I offered a thumbs up and padded my way into the bathroom. I heard Sam's mock attack on Maiyun as they wrestled on the floor. He was used to my moods and never read too much into them, thank God.

I wasn't much of a morning person, especially when I hadn't gotten enough sleep for days on end. My bout with Khalen didn't help matters either, seeing I couldn't even talk to him to apologize—although what I had to apologize for eluded me. After all, he was the one who gave me away like an old dog who had outworn its use.

With a heavy groan, I pushed back the anger darkening my already black mood. Today was turning out to be a real hoot. I needed to get an attitude adjustment if I wanted to keep what few friends I had left. I missed everyone back at the camp, and wanted badly to return to see them again, especially Case and Eve.

As I stepped into the shower, I thought of Ian and Aidan, who took turns visiting me every day. Aidan's obvious courting ritual was beginning to get on my nerves, but I did enjoy his company. There were times he had me convinced that he really thought he had a chance at winning my heart. I did my best to assure him that my heart was still set on the one I couldn't have.

I wished Shanuk were here to consult. He would know what to do. In the depths of my mind, I could hear him say, "Pain is just an illusion." I wondered if that statement held true for matters of the heart as well. My heart felt cruelly trampled and bruised to the point where even Shanuk's blue mist couldn't remove the pain.

I stood under the steaming hot water, praying it would melt away my nagging anger toward Khalen Dunning and his blasted stubborn nature. I cursed my betraying feelings toward him, wanting him as if he were mine to have. God, I was truly blind and miserably stupid. I knew all along about his feelings toward me. Even Traeger tried to set me straight, but I was too ignorant to see the truth of it all. "Ugh," I cried, slamming the heel of my fist against the wall.

I purged the thought of him from my mind and turned off the water. Tears blurred my pitiful vision as I reached for my towel. I missed him. My heart felt empty and lost without him. It was pathetic, really. Our platonic relationship should not have merited this strong of a bond, but it did. With all the force of a tsunami, it did— and it left just as much destruction in its wake.

When I stepped out of my room, both Karin and Sam looked at me as if I were the Bride of Frankenstein.

"Hey," said Sam, "you okay?"

Karin handed me my coffee. I took it from her and forced a smile.

"No," I said. "I'm really not." I put the cup down and sat in the chair that Sam held out for me.

"Wanna talk about it?" he asked. His thick bushy brows were scrunched together with genuine concern.

Karin pulled up a chair and sat on the opposite side of me. She placed her hand over mine and patted the back of it. "This involves a man, doesn't it?"

This comment caused Sam's concern to morph into an irritable scowl.

"Yes," I confirmed before Sam could place his

Birkenstock-clad foot in his mouth. "It does involve a man."

Karin beamed with pride of knowing she was right, while Sam shook his head. Maiyun, of course, offered her bear-like play companion comfort by placing her head on his broad lap.

I told them the condensed version of what had transpired during the long six months of their extended stay in Oregon. I ended the story with an embarrassing display of anger while downing the last of the coffee, of which neither of them had a single cup.

Their blank stares and open mouths indicated a state of mild shock, but strangely enough, I didn't care. My coffee press was empty and my stomach was growling in protest. "Anyone hungry for breakfast?" I was suddenly feeling very light and slightly better about the day.

"Dang, Skye," Sam finally said as I got up from my chair. "I knew you were different, but never thought you were some famous legend."

The glimmer of light that had briefly revealed itself to me extinguished with the air that pushed those vile words from his mouth. I moved very close to his face and took a deep, calming breath before I emphasized the following exclamation: "I—AM NOT—A LEGEND!"

The confused look in his pale brown eyes made me want to slap him.

"But, you just—"

"Stop!" I commanded. I raised my hands as if to swat some annoying flies buzzing around my head. "Please, can we just get something to eat?"

"So," Karin inquired, as if to clear up the confusion clouding her mind, while leading us all out to their car. "Khalen is supposed to marry you, but he wants another man to take his place?"

"Sort of," I said, regretting having told them the story in the first place. "It's a little more complicated than that." I never told them about Khalen's past, or about his fear of taking another mate. I left out a lot, which was probably what caused most of their confusion.

"Maybe he, too, believes you're not the legend and that is why he doesn't want you," said Sam, opening the back door for Maiyun to jump in.

I decided to let this whole thing go and simply agree with him for now. "Perhaps," I shrugged.

That seemed to satiate both of them and it was a perfect time to change the subject. "Tell me about your trip to Oregon. You stayed there much longer than you intended."

Karin started telling me about the friends they met there and about the short writing contract Sam agreed to complete.

"I made a boatload of money in those short five months, he said. "I agreed to do some more writing for them offsite, so it looks like I'll have some steady work coming in, at least."

"That must be a relief." I pointed to an orange and black sign. "JR's is just on the left there. They serve a fairly good breakfast."

Sam pulled into the driveway and parked in front of the building.

I snapped Maiyun's service vest on, and then asked her to hop out. It had been a while since the last time I took her into a restaurant and I hoped she would remember how to behave. She had picked up some bad habits living with Khalen. Again, my heart sank with unbearable heaviness.

We walked into the restaurant and took a seat at the far corner, away from foot traffic. Since there was no room for Maiyun under the table, she curled up beside me, making sure to keep her tail tightly tucked. "Good girl," I said, scratching the soft fur behind her ears.

While waiting for our food to arrive, Sam told me about the adventures that he and Karin had at the dunes.

Outside JR.'s, four Harley-Davidson bikers pulled up. The hair on my neck immediately stood erect.

Karin laughed at something that Sam had said.

"Hmm," he added, "I guess you had to be there."

"Skye, are you all right?" asked Karin.

I took a sip of my coffee then pushed the mug to the edge of the table to offer the waitress a hint that it was empty. "Yeah, why?"

Sam rolled his eyes then sipped his tomato juice. "I think I liked you better when you weren't in love," he said.

The four bikers said something to the waitress, and then walked toward us. Maiyun lifted her head as if mildly curious, but not alarmed. I felt cold as the foursome sat at the table across from us. I looked over casually and found them all staring in my direction. I could not make out their faces in the dim light of the room.

Our meals arrived, but I had suddenly lost my appetite. One of the bikers was trying to read my thoughts. I shielded him out. The buzz in the room was audible to me, but Karin and Sam seemed oblivious to it.

"How's your breakfast?" asked Sam, watching me push my potatoes around the plate.

"It's great, how's yours?"

He frowned at me and shook his head with frustration. "So, besides getting engaged to Khalen and breaking it off, what have you been into?"

That bit of verbiage gained unwanted attention. The bikers apparently recognized Khalen's name.

"I've been spending quite a bit of time in Olympia," I lied. "Since Khalen and I didn't work out, I thought about buying a house there."

Sam looked doubtful. "You're thinking about buying a house?"

"Yeah, a cozy two-bedroom right on the water."

Sam finished the last of his juice. "Uh huh." It was clear he didn't believe me.

"And then," I added, "I got a great job offer to work in New Zealand for six months, so I accepted." This story sounded about as believable as me being pregnant. I just hoped it sounded more likely to the rude pack of men sitting across from us, hanging on my every word.

"New Zealand," Karin shrieked with excitement. "That sounds great. What will you be doing there?"

Sam looked amused, knowing full well I was lying through my teeth. He followed my gaze to the four men across from us.

"I'll be doing some ghostwriting," I said. "I leave in three days."

Karin's eyes grew wide. "Three days? But I—"

Sam nudged her under the table, earning him an angry glare.

"What was that for?" she said.

"We should be happy for her," said Sam. "This is a great opportunity."

"I know we had plans," I said, trying to look apologetic. This lying business was tougher than I thought. "I just found out, last night."

Something soft brushed against the side of my face. It was a wadded up napkin.

Sam looked over at the man who had obviously tossed it. I followed his gaze.

One of the bikers smiled. "Hello, Skye."

"You know those guys?" Sam asked.

I shook my head.

"She probably doesn't recognize me," the man said, "being blind and all." He started to stand.

He reached his hand toward me, and then suddenly pulled it back with a yelp of pain. Maiyun jumped up, apparently startled from a deep sleep.

"I don't know you," I said, almost as a warning.

He weighed my strength against his own for a moment, and then bowed his head with consent. "My apologies. I must be mistaken." He returned to his seat, clutching his hand.

"But he knew your name," said Karin, which earned her another painful kick from Sam.

"Are we ready to go?" I asked.

Sam looked at his and Karin's half-eaten meal, and then at my untouched plate. "Um, yeah, I guess."

I flagged the waitress down. "Excuse me, we are in a hurry. Can we have our check and a few to-go boxes?"

She looked at me with a hint of apprehension, and then said, "Sure, hon."

We paid our bill, packed our meals, and then left. My heart pounded so hard in my chest, I could barely hear what Sam and Karin were discussing.

"Skye!" Sam yelled. He grabbed my arm and spun me around. "What the hey?"

Karin clutched the bag of leftovers and looked at me with large doe-like eyes. She was genuinely worried.

I saw the foursome exit the building and walk toward us.

"Get in the car," I told him, "please."

"Not until you—"

Maiyun released a low, warning growl. My stomach felt hollow and it was not from lack of food. The four men stood right behind Sam. He turned around.

"Best do what the lady told ya," the skinny one said with a gold-toothed smile. His Irish accent was sharp as if he had just stepped off the boat from Ireland.

"Look," said Sam, "she said she doesn't know you, so move on." He placed his hands on his broad hips and had the look of an angry bear that had just woken up from its long winter slumber. He may have been more threatening, though, without the bright colored shirt and rainbow socks.

"Sam," I said, keeping my voice low and calm. "Get Maiyun and Karin in the car and start the engine."

The skinny man smiled. They intended to grab me once Sam was preoccupied. I had my own intentions. I used my shield to push their bikes down one by one.

"Shit," said the man with darker hair. "Our bikes."

It didn't take long for the other three to take notice. The first man, who had spoken my name, quickly turned his attention back to me.

"Very clever, missy." He stepped toward me. Maiyun howled in the back of the car and scratched at the window. My shield held the man at a short distance from me, allowing me to open the back door of Sam's Outback.

"We will find you," the man growled, his voice sinister and dark. I ducked into the car and instructed Sam to drive.

"Turn left out of the driveway."

"We should take you home," he said, his voice shaky and uncertain.

"No, I can't go back there, now."

Sam did as I asked and turned left onto Highway 3. "Skye, what's going on? Who were those guys?" He peered at me through the rear view mirror with steely eyes. Clearly he was not pleased.

"Shadows," I said. "I need to get somewhere safe."

Of course, he was not willing to let it go that easily. I had to tell him about Spirians, about my gifts, and a bit about the camp he was driving me to. I wasn't sure if my friends were permitted at the camp, but I was sure to find out.

Chapter 7

When embers are extinguished, a red-hot glow does not always betray the heat that lingers.

-Khalen-

I RETURNED FROM THE OCEAN WITH a new perspective and an emptiness in my soul that could only be filled with Skye. The thought of her being another's mate felt like death, dark, shallow, and heavy. I wanted to apologize to her and Aidan for ever suggesting their union.

I headed straight to our yurt, eager to see her face. She would just be getting up about now, her silver eyes glazed with peace. I opened the door quietly, not wanting to disturb her.

"Khalen," a familiar voice said in the darkness—a voice I hadn't heard for some time. I looked over at the bed; it was empty. Maiyun's bed was empty as well.

The fire burned bright in the circular pit, illuminating the face of an old acquaintance. Kiara sat on the couch, looking just as stunning as I had remembered her. Her auburn hair hung down in gentle curls over her shoulders and shone like copper embers. Her reddish-brown eyes glowed against the reflecting firelight, a stunning contrast to her brilliant smile.

I noticed the bottle of wine sitting on the end table beside her, next to two empty glasses.

"Nice to see you again, Kiara," I said. I looked around the yurt for any signs of Skye. "Have you been here long?"

She stood and walked toward me. Her long legs wrapped in silky sheers reflected the firelight. Her short, close-fitting skirt did little to hide the shape of her hips, and her white silk blouse played well with her ample breasts. The woman hadn't aged a bit.

"Since last night," she purred. Her long, delicate fingers stroked my chest.

My body remembered her skillful touch and reacted in kind. I stepped back. "Where's Skye?"

Kiara's smile broadened. "Khalen, my dear, you're frowning. Are you not happy to see me?"

"I'm sorry, Kiara, it is always nice to see you, but I was expecting someone else to be here."

It was her turn to frown. She stopped advancing toward me and studied my face. "Skye?" she asked.

"Yes, was she here?" My words sounded too desperate, even to my ears.

Kiara shook her head. "No, just me and the fire." Her eyes lit up with the word. Her gift was to will the flame. She could ignite an entire building with a mere thought, especially when she was angry, as I discovered way back in college. She had a talent in stoking fires in other places as well, I remembered. It was challenging to keep my head straight when she was so close.

"Can you excuse me for a moment, Kiara, I must find

her."

She reached for my hand. "Can't it wait, Khalen? You just got here and we have so much catching up to do."

"No," I said, it can't." I removed my hand from hers and headed for the door. I was relieved to know that age had dampened the lust in me that was once uncontrollable. Twenty years ago, I would not have been able to walk away from that woman.

Case was walking toward a cluster of boys engaged in a fight. Dust flew around them as arms and legs flung in all directions. Muted sounds of thumps and groans mixed with the scuffle.

"Enough," he roared. The thundering sound of his command made the boys stop and tremble, despite their fury. Case glanced around the camp. "Gauging by the look of this place, I would bet that most of you have chores to do."

Twelve boys scampered off in various directions, leaving two still on the ground, heaving from breathlessness and bleeding from their faces and hands. They were Pete, Ember's boy, and Thomas, a sharp-witted kid that came to visit from the Squaxin tribe now and then. He was Caleb's son.

"Now," said Case. "What is this about?"

Pete spat blood and stood. "He shoved my little brother."

Thomas stood and brushed the dust from his bloodied arm, making it a thick, sticky mess. "We were playing a game, Pete, I tried to tell you."

Case shook his head with disgust. "Both of you go to Eve and get cleaned up. We will discuss this later."

Pete touched his swollen nose. "I need Skye," he mumbled under his hand.

"Yes, well, she's not here, so you must see Eve."

The two boys hurried off toward Eve and Case's yurt.

"Where is she?" I asked.

Case stared at me with steely eyes. He looked tired and worn these days. I knew that he would have to return to England soon; it was clear he missed his homeland. Now that his father had passed, there was not much keeping him here, save me.

"She left the same day you did."

"Left?" My chest constricted with fear, as well as regret. "Where did she go?"

"Back home." He started to walk toward his yurt. I touched his arm to encourage him to stop. He did, momentarily, and then continued.

"Father, please," I pleaded. His distance felt worse than his rage.

He turned and placed his hands on my arms. "Aidan watches over her now, Son. She is safe."

Those words stung worse than his most forceful reprimands. My knees threatened to fold beneath me. "I am a fool," I growled.

A white Outback rolled into the camp, raising a cloud of dust. Case and I walked toward it.

I recognized the odd, rounded man as the one who helped Skye back to her table at the restaurant several months ago, when Skye had just started working at the center. His bright apparel was still an eyesore. The woman he was with was familiar as well. Skye, too, stepped out of the car. She looked pale and drawn. Maiyun howled in the back until the short man let her out.

Maiyun ran toward me. I removed her service vest and gave her a good rub. "Hey girl, I missed you." Her warm, wet tongue licked my arm. I kept my gaze on Skye, who stared back at me with empty apprehension.

She looked away from me and walked toward Case. "Case, these are my friends, Sam and Karin."

Case nodded to each of them, and then waited for Skye to explain her sudden reappearance without Aidan.

The door to Khalen's yurt opened, drawing everyone's attention. Kiara stood, dressed in Skye's robe, holding a steaming cup of coffee. She looked pleased to have drawn so many eyes to her presence.

Skye's face paled even more now, and her eyes dulled to a flat shade of gray. She was purposely keeping her thoughts from me. She drew in a deep breath and turned to Case. "Can we talk?" Her eyes turned back to me. "Alone?"

Case took her arm. "Yes, of course."

I looked at Sam and Karin, who also looked as if they had witnessed something terrible. Both of them seemed to have recognized me, but not entirely.

"What happened?" I asked.

Sam threw up his hands. "We should have stayed in Oregon, that's what happened." His voice had an angry edge to it.

Karin told me the story about what happened at the restaurant. "It was weird," she added, "the way that Skye could keep them from touching us. It was like there was an invisible sheet of glass between us and them. One guy even hit it with his hand and pulled it back in pain." Her eyes were wide now, with childlike wonder.

"What about what happened with the bikes," Sam added.

"The bikes?" I inquired.

"Yeah," he explained, "four heavy Harleys. She knocked them down one at a time. They were clear across the parking lot."

"And then what?"

Sam raised his arms as if offering a hug. "We came here."

"What did Skye tell you?" I asked.

Sam leaned against the dusty hood of his car. "Fragments of things that don't make much sense, really. She said you offered her to another man. Why would you do that?"

I could feel my frustration building. Humans were difficult to read, and even more difficult to be around. They had no attention span, and you had to explain everything to them in detail for them to understand. Spirians needed only a few words and the rest came naturally. Skye probably thought she had explained it all to them, but yet they still seemed perplexed.

"My reasons are unimportant right now. Were you followed?"

Karin shook her head. "No, I watched. There was no one behind us." The enthusiasm in her voice conjured images of an amateur spy vying for the approval of a seasoned veteran.

"What's going on?" asked Sam. "Skye is—different."

I did my best to fill them in on the details, but it was trying my patience and my mind was on other things. Skye continued to block me from her thoughts, just as I had done to her many times over.

I took Sam and Karin over to Eve's, and then planned to give Kiara a piece of my mind for her lascivious antics. She was too smart not to know what she was doing.

~ S k y e ~

CASE AND I WALKED IN silence toward the lake. I knew he was planning to take me to Khalen's thinking log, but that is not where I wanted to go. Right now, I wanted nothing to do with Khalen.

"Don't you, now?" Case questioned. His obsidian eyes looked right through me.

"No, I don't."

He led me there, anyway, despite my unspoken objection.

"Sit, Skye. We are at a crossroads and these petty feelings between you and Khalen are nothing but a nuisance." He sounded tired and disgusted with the whole ordeal.

The pain of his dismissal hurt me more than I wanted to admit. I sat next to him and wrung my hands together. "They don't feel petty to me," I said quietly. "I feel dead inside."

He sighed. "Because you and Khalen belong together, yet you both insist on pushing the other away."

"He pushed me away," I said.

"Did he?"

I thought about it for a moment, and then felt a sudden pang of shame. How easy it is to allow negative emotions to block the truth of what is real. I was so focused on Khalen's actions that I had become blind to his true feelings. Deep in my soul, I knew that he was mine and I was his. There was no denying it and Case was absolutely correct in seeing the pettiness we had allowed to govern our actions.

Case nodded and smiled. "Now you see the truth of it, don't you?"

I nodded. "Yes, I do. I feel young and foolish."

"Skye, you just realized something that often takes hundreds of years for most of us to see. Do not discredit yourself so easily. Shanuk saw power in you that put his own to shame; that's saying quite a bit, wouldn't you say?"

I nodded. "The life I once knew is gone forever, isn't it?"

"Yes, it is. You can never go back now."

"Even my friends, Sam and Karin seem different."

"It is not them who have changed, Skye. It is you who is different. The human side of you is gone and will not return. You are Spirian now until you perish on this Earth and become pure spirit."

"Like Shanuk," I said.

He nodded. "Yes, like dear Shanuk." There was a sadness to his voice.

I wrapped my hand around his. "I feel him with us."

"I do too, my dear." He patted my hand. "I do too."

"I'm sorry I brought my human friends here. I know I should have—"

"Everyone is welcome here at this camp, my dear, human and Spirian alike. You did the right thing."

"I fear for them now."

Case frowned in concentration as if trying to solve a puzzle. "Tell me what happened."

I told him about the four bikers, and showed him what I observed. He seemed pleased with my cleverness in creating an effective escape.

"Yes," he agreed, "your friends are in danger. The Shadows will use them to get to you. It is best if they remain here at camp."

"Sam won't like it."

Case's obsidian eyes glowed with a knowing. "He will

grow to crave it if the Shadows get a hold of him."

"That's what worries me."

Sam was a stubborn man, and one that did not take orders gracefully. He would rebel. Of that I was certain.

"We had best get back," I said.

Chapter 8

The shadowed heart yearns for what it cannot have and is blind to that which is offered.

WHEN I WALKED INTO THE YURT, Maiyun was curled up in her bed, chewing on an old bone. She glanced up at me, wagged her tail, and then continued gnawing with contentment. She was happy to be home, and so was I.

Khalen sat on the couch next to the woman who still wore my robe. He was expecting me to blow up, I could see it in his anxious eyes, glowing gold with apprehension. Whoever the woman was, her feelings for Khalen were not being reciprocated by him and that made my heart sing with appreciative joy as if a fresh new light had filled it.

"Skye," said Khalen. It flowed from his tongue like silk in the breeze. There was undeniable love attached to it. "This is Kiara, an old friend from college."

Kiara smiled at me as if knowing she claimed the prize for beauty. She glanced down at my bare feet and her smile quickly turned to a victorious smirk. "Skye," she said, finally acknowledging my existence.

I smiled back, matching her enthusiasm. "Hi Kiara. It's nice to meet you. I'll leave you two to talk. I need to find my friends."

Khalen stood and met me halfway across the room. He grabbed both my arms with desperation and a want that only I could fully comprehend. His golden eyes bore into me as if willing my soul to join with his.

I reached up and touched his stubbled face. "I love you, Khalen Dunning, no one else."

Tears glistened in his eyes, reflecting the fire-like golden orbs. He opened his mouth as if wanting to speak, and then quickly claimed mine with painful ferocity. He gripped the back of my head as if it would fall away if he let go. Painful as it was, I matched his fervor with my own, craving the taste of him. I wasn't disappointed.

The fire grew with intensity and sparks began to fly toward us. Kiara was miffed.

Khalen stepped away from me, oblivious of Kiara's growing pique. "I'm sorry," he whispered, "my mate." He squeezed my hands as he said those last two words and I knew that he meant them. Union or no, we were united in spirit and always would be.

The fire exploded into a shower of sparks and embers. Khalen waved his hand and extinguished it, never giving Kiara a single glance.

"We'll talk later," I said, glancing over at the angry woman. The robe hung loose about her, revealing more than was necessary or appropriate.

"Sam and Karin are with Eve." He gently kissed my forehead and reluctantly released my hands.

Kiara cleared her throat as I strode past her. "Goodbye, Skye," she said with finality. She had plans to rid Khalen of me, I was certain.

I smiled. "I'm sure we'll see each other again."

"No doubt," she drawled.

I left the yurt feeling more energetic and strong than I had in the past three weeks, despite my lack of nourishment. There was no doubt where that strength originated. It felt good to be home; and this was home— heart and soul.

Before I could reach Eve's yurt, a strong pair of arms wrapped around me and lifted me off the ground. "Ah, she returns," said a familiar voice.

"Ian," I laughed. "Put me down." He did, and then spun me around to face him.

"Aidan is relieved to hear you have come home."

I looked at him questioningly. "Is he?"

Ian smiled and his eyes grew warm. "Yes. He is no fool, Skye. He knew you were out of his reach."

"Well," I said, feeling relieved, "he certainly had me fooled."

"He's stopping by your apartment on his way home and bringing back all your things."

"I appreciate that." I squeezed his arms and smiled apologetically. "I need to talk with my friends. I'll catch up with you later, okay?"

"Okay," he said. "Welcome back, Sister."

My face flushed with heat. He had never called me that before and I doubted that the endearing term would have had the same effect a month ago as it did now. I turned and headed toward Eve's yurt.

She opened it before I could sound off a knock. Her delicate arms wrapped around me and held me so tight I had to hold my breath. "My daughter has returned," she mumbled against my arm.

I wrapped my arms around her and breathed in her scent of lilac and roses. "I have," I answered, "for good."

She led me into the room. "Come, I have prepared some cranberry scones and coffee."

Sam and Karin glanced up at me with a mouthful of scones.

"These are great," Sam said through a muffled mouthful.

I had to laugh. Both of them looked like children in the midst of a candy shop where all was up for grabs. I imagined it had been quite some time since either of them had a home-cooked meal made from natural ingredients.

Case was busy in the far end of the yurt, scolding Pete and another boy I could not recognize in the shadows of the room. Neither of them looked up at me, too intent on what Case had to say.

I sat across from Sam and Karin. Eve sat next to me and poured me a cup of hot coffee. It smelled great. I added some coconut milk and a bit of honey.

Case and the boys came over to join us. When I saw the condition of the boys' faces and arms, my stomach churned.

"Good Lord, what happened to you two?" I asked. They both looked as if they had been attacked by baton-wielding hoodlums.

"We got in a fight," Pete said, holding his crooked nose. "Can you help me?"

Eve moved over and allowed the boy to sit between us. I touched his swollen face and felt the break in his nose and another to his orbital socket. I closed my eyes and allowed the healing vibrations of God to flow through me. Feeling the heat rise in my body, I grounded my bare feet to the wooden floors and imagined the coolness of the earth flowing through me. In a moment, Pete's nose returned to normal, as did the smile on his face.

"Thank you," he said, feeling his restored face. "May I have one now?" he asked Eve, pointing at the tray of scones.

"Yes, Pete, you may have one now."

I healed Thomas next, whose injuries were not quite as severe as Pete's, but were just as painful, I was sure. His arm was cut with something jagged—a rock, I imagined—and his face was cut and bruised, but nothing was broken.

After grabbing two more scones, both boys rushed out of the yurt, jabbing at each other playfully. Case had obviously given them chores to do that would keep them out of trouble for the rest of the day.

I chose a crumpled scone from the serving platter and placed it on my plate. When I glanced up, both Sam and Karin looked at me as if I had grown antlers from my head.

"Better get used to oddities," I said. "You're going to witness far more than I can demonstrate."

"That wasn't odd," said Sam. "That was downright unnatural."

"For you," I corrected. "For me, it is a gift that feels as natural as you breathing air to survive."

Case did his best to describe what Spirians are, having far more patience than I could ever hope to have. Karin reached over and touched me several times but I wasn't sure quite why she had done it. Her intentions were just as garbled as her feeble thoughts.

"Can we become Spirians?" she asked.

"You must be born one," said Case. "You cannot will it to happen."

Sam shook his head back and forth as if trying to urge

his brain into gear. "I always knew you were weird, Skye, I just didn't understand the degree of that weirdness."

"Thanks," I frowned. "I think." I thought now was a good time to bring up their situation, seeing they were already mystified with the gifts that surrounded them. "Can you two stay here for a while?"

Sam stopped mid-sip. "How long of a while, Skye?" He must have heard the change in my tone, betraying my concern. That man knew me far too well.

"A year, maybe two?" The last word squeaked past the lump in my throat.

Sam calmly set his mug down and looked at me intently. "Why?"

Given the moderate tone in that simple inquiry, he may just have well offered me a death sentence should my answer be anything but simple. I cleared my constricting throat and looked to Case for some assistance. He simply smiled with obvious amusement.

"The Shadows at the restaurant saw you and know you are dear to me," I stammered. I took a long sip of coffee, while the right words came to mind. "They will find you and use you and Karin to get to me. I don't want them to hurt you."

Sam's face was unreadable for the first time since I'd known him. It worried me. He looked over at Karin, who continued to eat her scone in silence. She was the type of person who would be happy anywhere that people resided. Sam, on the other hand, was a social bee who craved the busy night life and bustle of the big cities. Camp life was not an option.

"Skye," he said. "You know I love you, gal, but I'm not willing to die for you. If the Shadows want to use me to get to you, they will be sadly disappointed."

Case set his mug down on the scarred pine table. "Can you imagine Karin being used as a slave in the worst possible way?"

Karin swallowed hard, her eyes were as big as the mouth of her mug.

"The police will protect us," said Sam. "I will inform them of what happened and they will place us under protection, especially if you tell me where these Shadows live and who they conspire with. The police will love that information."

Case frowned with frustration. "I'm not convinced that you understand the degree of your situation."

"I have a gun," Sam said, "and I'm not afraid to use it."

Case stood and retrieved something from a locked safe. He loaded the gun full of bullets and handed it to Sam. "Shoot me," he commanded.

Sam's eyes widened with disbelief. "I won't. That's crazy."

"Pretend I'm a Shadow, threatening to take your woman." Case reached over and grabbed Karin's arm. She cried out in pain.

"Don't," Sam yelled. "Leave her alone."

"Shoot me," Case ordered him. "Shoot me now or I will snap her neck." He positioned his hands on either side of Karin's trembling face and began to twist it to the left. Again, Karin cried out.

Sam fired a shot and closed his eyes. When he saw that Case still stood with his hands on Karin's face, Sam fired two more shots, aimed directly at Case's head. All three bullets hovered two inches from where Case and Karin stood, and then fell to the wooden floors with dull thuds.

Sam dropped the gun into his lap. His hands shook

and his face had lost its usual red glow.

Case smoothed Karin's hair then directed her back to the couch. "I'm sorry," he said, "but I had to make you see that you are not dealing with humans here. Nothing will protect you from them apart from other Spirians."

Karin rubbed her arms where Case had grabbed her. I reached over and quickly dispersed her pain and bruises. She started to cry.

"I don't like this," said Sam. He continued to shake his head as if trying to wake from a bad dream.

"I didn't mean to bring you into this," I said. "I'm so sorry." And I was sorry, with all my heart. I should have listened to Case when he warned me about how dangerous it was out there alone without the company of other Spirians. Now I had recklessly placed my good friends in danger.

"The fact remains," said Case. "If you want to live, you must stay here where we can protect you."

Karin gripped Sam's white fists. "I want to stay," she sniffled. "Please."

Sam closed his eyes. "We should have stayed in Oregon," he mumbled against her head.

"There are no mistakes," Case said. "There is nothing you or anyone could do to change where you are at this moment."

"Perfect," Sam muttered. "Not only did I wake up on the wrong side of the bed, I rolled smack dab in the middle of a Kung Fu episode with Master Wang telling me that all is as it should be."

"It's not that bad here, Sam," I offered, trying to assure him. "You might even like it."

His glaring response warned me to stay on my side of the invisible line. I decided it was in my best interest to heed that warning, for now.

"Where will we stay?" asked Karin.

"Our guest house is available," said Eve. "You can stay there until a more permanent home can be built."

"Permanent," Sam uttered. "Great."

Chapter 9

*Beware of those who mean you harm; their strength hides in a
shroud of co-conspirators.*

EVE COOKED A FABULOUS FEAST of roasted leg of lamb,
sautéed peppers and chanterelle mushrooms, and
wild rice with cranberries. Fresh bread accompanied the
meal, along with several bottles of fine red wine.

Khalen invited Kiara to join us, along with Ian, Aidan,
Ember, Jade, and Case's friend, Caleb. Traeger invited
himself, but behaved as promised. Case had asked him to
leave the camp and return only once a week for additional
training. By the looks of it, Case had been harsher on him
than usual this afternoon. I made no effort to heal his cuts
and painful bruises and he never asked.

After enjoying our meal outside by the fire, we
gathered in small groups to chat. It was comforting to
see Karin and Jade getting along so well. Ian had taken
Sam under his wing, so to say, and introduced him to
the skillful art of illusional flying. Judging by the look on
Sam's face, he had found himself a new hobby to replace
his dissolute night life.

Khalen and Aidan were talking on the far side of the fire, while Eve, Ember, Kiara and myself sat on a triangle of logs and shared a bottle of Madeira. Kiara, I learned, stayed in one of the many guest cabins on the far end of camp. She was not happy about the arrangement, but decided to stay all the same.

Case and Caleb were arguing about something, with Traeger interjecting himself into the conversation now and then. The evening marked a moment that would never happen again: Spirians, light and dark, and humans all gathered in peaceful conversation. It was an evening I would not soon forget, and which one day I would long to remember.

I stopped drinking the potent dessert wine when I felt Traeger's thoughts mingle among my own. I glanced over at him and he smiled. He was looking more like Khalen every week and it was creepy how he was adopting some of Khalen's mannerisms. I attributed that to Case's training. Still, it was discomforting having him so close. Unlike Khalen, who drew me in, Traeger had the opposite effect.

Kiara followed the direction of my gaze and smirked. "Eerie, isn't it," she said, "how close they resemble one another?"

"Only in looks," I added.

Kiara's smile broadened. "Hmm, I wonder." She picked up the half-drained bottle of Madeira and carried it over to Traeger. Her sad attempts to gain Khalen's notice were amusing.

"Now there's a deadly combination," said Eve, gesturing toward Traeger and Kiara, who had finally managed to gain Khalen's attention.

He walked over to me and wrapped his arm around my

waist, turning his back to the odd couple. I couldn't see the look on Kiara's face, but I was sure she was frowning. Khalen tensed against me. He had no lingering feelings for the fiery woman he went to college with, yet he did not like seeing her with his brother.

"What's wrong?" I asked him.

"My brother," he retorted, with venom in his voice. "I don't trust him."

I looked up at him and tried to read his face, but the darkness impaired my vision. "Are you sure your ego is not reacting to the amazing effect he has on women?"

"Effect, huh?" The questioning tone in his voice assured me that my choice of words did not go unnoticed.

"Yes," I admitted. "The man has charms that are difficult to ignore."

"And are you drawn to him?"

I shook my head. "No, he is far too predictable for my liking." I looked over at Kiara. "She is not drawn to him either. She is just trying to make you jealous so that she knows you still care for her."

"My taste in women has changed." He kissed the top of my head.

"Hmm," I said, playfully, "tall, dark women with amazing bodies and stunning appearances no longer stoke your fire?"

"I prefer my woman to be short, blonde, sincere, intelligent, gifted, loyal, honest, and barefoot."

"You forgot simple and stubborn—and I am not short."

"Stubborn, I could do without, and simple is something I would never use to describe you, my love."

I laid my head against his warm, broad chest. "I'm tired."

"Let's turn in then, shall we?" He took my hand and led me away from the fire. Maiyun ran up beside us.

In our yurt, he stoked the fire and added a few more logs. He then poured us each a snifter of brandy while I crawled into bed. He handed me my glass, and then sat on the bed beside me.

"Where did you go," I asked, "when you left?" I smelled the potent fire of the brandy and savored its spicy hints. I then took a small sip and allowed it to linger upon my tongue. Clove on fire is what came to mind as it slid down my sensitive throat—E & J Single Vintage, very hard to find.

He sipped his brandy and enjoyed it for a moment before answering. "To my cabin in Grays Harbor."

I didn't know where Grays Harbor was, nor did I know anything about the cabin. "Is that by the ocean?"

He nodded. "When I'm angry, it is the only place where I can cool off without destroying everything around me."

That explained the salt water I had sensed when trying to imagine where he was.

"Skye," he said. "I don't ever want to be that angry again."

His golden green eyes were hypnotic and caused my heartbeat to echo in my ears. "Nor do I."

"I thought I was going to kill you," he said, his lips firm and his jaw tight.

"I felt the same way toward you for giving me away."

He set his brandy down on my end table and placed mine next to it. He took both my hands in his and leaned toward me. "The hurt I saw in your eyes that day as Ian held you close was unbearable. I knew I was the source of that pain and couldn't subject you to more of it. I did what I thought you wanted me to do and set you free."

I stared at him in disbelief. "Set me free? Is that what you thought I wanted?"

"I did at the time."

"What I want, Khalen Dunning, is for you to take me as your own. Make me your wife. I want it to be official and soon. I am ready for this and I want you to be as well. That is what I want." I sat back in a huff, but kept my hands in his.

"My mistake," he said, curling one corner of his mouth. "Forgive me?"

I glared. "Maybe."

"Well, at least I offered you to a man who knows me better than I know myself."

"That you did."

"So, when would you like to make this official?"

"Now," I said.

He laughed and handed me back my brandy. "Not without ceremony, my love. I want to do this right."

I rolled my eyes and took a long sip of the amber drink, allowing it to burn down my throat. "I want you to promise me something," I said.

"Hmm," he hummed, closing his eyes and enjoying his drink.

"Never block me from your thoughts again, ever."

He opened his eyes and considered my request with quiet reflection. "And do you promise the same?"

"I do."

He raised his glass, and clinked mine. "I promise never to block you from my thoughts, ever again, unless it is absolutely necessary." The look on his face left me with some apprehension.

A flood of thoughts entered my mind and my face immediately responded with colorful heat.

Khalen laughed, and then promptly offered more of his thoughts.

"Enough," I cried. "You're horrible."

He leaned over and kissed me soft and slow, his breath laced with sweet brandy and hot against my cheek. "Be careful what you ask for, my love. Be very careful."

We shared affections that evening, but did not join in love. Khalen absolutely refused to make love to me without ceremony. I begged him to change his mind, but he held firm to his decision. My body ached to feel his intimacy, but still he held back with cursed restraint. I felt certain I would go insane with this need far before any ceremony took place.

In the morning, he leaned over to kiss me, but I turned my head.

"What's wrong?" he asked, his brows furrowed with confusion.

"Not without ceremony," I said, still groggy from sleep.

He gently gripped my jaw with his massive hand and pulled my face toward him. He drew near, barely touching my lips, and then smiled. "Very well, my love. Have it your way."

I groaned then rolled over. The man was set on torturing me, I was certain.

Chapter 10

Love is bound with thread that can only be severed by the blade of mistrust.

THAT EVENING KHALEN TOLD CASE and Eve about our plan to unite. Tears rolled down Eve's face. Case's eyes misted over.

"How soon?" he asked.

Khalen squeezed my hand. "Three days. I need to make some arrangements to prepare the house in Union."

Case's smile broadened. "Fabulous idea. Eve and I will prepare your ceremony." His eyes sparkled.

Eve clapped her hands and hopped up and down like a five-year-old child getting her first puppy.

With a roaring voice, Case announced the upcoming ceremony to the clan members that had gathered around multiple fires. Seeing he could speak to each member's mind without words, the announcement was not necessary, but dramatic all the same.

Aidan was the first to congratulate us, followed by Ian, Ember, and Jade. Sam and Karin offered a guarded form of felicitation, not quite certain that a union between two powerful, stubborn souls was such a good idea.

Kiara, too, offered Khalen a hug, and then one to me. "We need to talk," she whispered into my ear.

I followed her over to a log that was away from the crowd that gathered around Khalen and the others.

To Kiara's credit, she kept her intentions well guarded, but readable all the same. She was hurt by our announcement and wanted to try one last effort to salvage what she and Khalen once had long ago.

"Are you sure you know what you're doing, dear?" she asked, stretching her short skirt between the rough log and her thigh.

"Absolutely," I said, amused with how she emptied the tiny rubble from her shoes as if it were clusters of disgusting germs.

"Well, before you make the biggest mistake of your life, I think you should know about Khalen's promiscuous past. History does tend to repeat itself, you know."

"I'm listening," I said, still amused at her fussing with the skirt. I offered her my jacket to sit upon, but she refused.

"Khalen was quite the player in college, you know. A real heart breaker."

"I'm certain," I said. "He's very handsome."

Again she squirmed. I removed my jacket and finally persuaded her to lay it between her and the log.

She shivered and studied me with curiosity. "Why aren't you cold?"

I gestured to the fire. With a look, she stoked it up to a bright blaze to where it was almost too hot.

"That's quite the gift," I commented.

Her teeth chattered. "Yes, it comes in handy at times."

"So, you were telling me about Khalen," I reminded

her.

"Yes," she continued with a renewed spark to her tone. "We were quite the thing, you know. I was on my way to becoming a cosmetic surgeon and he was earning his doctorate in medicine."

I did not reply, which seemed to make her slightly nervous. Unlike most people, I was comfortable with silence.

"Anyway," she continued, clearing her throat. "We were very intimate, he and I. Even as a Spirian, he is well-endowed, I assure you," she smiled as if conjuring the memory sparked an inner excitement.

I had to admit that a measure of jealousy reared its ugly head in my heart. I quickly dispelled it and urged her to continue with what was sure to be torture to my soul.

She continued to graphically illustrate how Khalen had command of a woman's body, and could make her beg for release many times over before he granted it. This, I believed was true, being the sad recipient of that horrid control of his.

"There was a brief moment during our intimacy," she said, staring into the dancing flames, "when I thought he would claim me as his own. He was so close."

Goose bumps formed over my arms as she spoke. I wanted to block her cruel words from my ears, but something forced me to listen with masochistic fascination.

"The pain was so intense, I wanted to back away, but he held me to him. 'Close your eyes,' he told me. 'Keep them closed,' and I did. He pulled out before the union took place. He wanted me though, I felt it. I felt his soul wrap around my own, ready to consume me."

I watched as her body moved with the memory. My

own heart pounded with hers, but hungry for something different. More than anything, I wanted to feel Khalen intimately—more than I wanted my next breath, which felt constricted with an inner need.

"What I'm trying to say, my dear, is that Khalen's heart is reckless and impetuous. You heard what happened to his last mate."

"I did," I assured her, "and if he chooses to take my life as well, at least I know I'll die happy."

She stiffened with that response. I could not see her face, but her energy was collapsing with defeat. Her efforts to ward me away from him were failing and she knew it.

Khalen walked toward us with Maiyun by his side. "Skye, you're freezing. Where's your jacket?"

I hadn't noticed that the fire had died down to embers. Kiara stood and offered me my jacket back.

"Thank you," she said, a hint of sadness in her voice. Not too surprisingly, it didn't match her true feelings.

I took my jacket from her and smiled. "You're welcome," I replied.

Khalen helped me to don it, and then sent me back to our yurt with Maiyun by my side. He stayed to talk with Kiara. He, too, suspected she was up to something and probably wanted to have an exploratory dialogue with her. As promised, he kept his thoughts open to me.

Maiyun expertly led me back to our yurt. I craved a mug of hot cocoa with cayenne pepper and cinnamon honey. It was one of the few things that assured me a good night's rest, although it often prompted some interesting dreams. Tonight I didn't care. I needed something to take my mind from Khalen and our upcoming union.

~Khalen~

I KNEW THAT KIARA'S SADNESS WAS just an act. She never was good at keeping her true motives in check. I played along with her antics to see where she was heading with her charade.

"You okay?" I asked, squeezing her cold hand for the effect I knew it would have on her. She was as weak physically as she was morally.

"Honestly, Khalen, what do you see in that simpleton?"

"Simpleton?" I inquired, feigning innocence—something that the "simple" Skye would see right through.

She rolled her eyes. "She is rather plain, don't you think? I mean, look at her clothes. They look like something she picked up at Value Village, for Christ's sake."

I said nothing.

"Khalen," she said with obvious frustration, "she doesn't even wear shoes. Where did you find her, the Goodwill store?"

"No," I said. "I found her at Starbucks." Even Skye didn't know that I was there that day she asked Gregg for a job. I was standing right behind her and she never knew it. I had engrained her coffee drink in my head, along with her scent, and intriguing simplicity. Skye was real, deep and genuine like the ocean. She had the same strength as well, and the ability to calm the fire in my soul, and the skill to ignite it beyond my control.

"She will bore you to tears within a year, Khalen, I assure you."

"Most women do," I responded, staring into the rising flames of Kiara's temper.

"Did I?" she asked daringly.

"Did you what?" I asked, affecting innocence.

"Bore you to tears?" Again, the flames rose another foot and were becoming quite hot.

"If I said no, would that change anything?"

"It might."

"Then I would be lying."

The fire pit exploded with sparks and embers. "I bored you?" she huffed. "The night you almost claimed me?"

That got my attention. "Claimed you?"

"Yes, you were so close. I felt your soul around my own." She writhed as if conjuring some obscure memory. "You were like a warm blanket, offering protection."

I had to laugh at the absurdity of her dubious view of the truth. "Your memory does you a disservice," I assured her.

"No," she hissed. "It doesn't. I know what I felt."

I stood, having heard enough of her delusions. "And what do you feel now, Kiara?"

She glared back at me. "Sorry for you," she said, "because you're too ignorant to know what is good for you. Remember Valerie?"

I stopped and turned around. "Yes, I do remember her."

"Then perhaps you remember how it ended?"

"With death," I said.

She stood and came toward me. "Exactly. And that is how this union will end for you as well—in death."

"Everyone dies, Kiara, even you."

She laid her hands against my chest. "Yes, but you need someone strong, Khalen. Someone who can stand up to you." She waved her hand toward my yurt. "Not some bimbo, barefooted, bleached blonde who caters to your every wish."

I laughed. "Is that how you see Skye?"

She placed her hands on her ample hips. "It is."

Again, I laughed. "Do yourself a favor then, and don't get her angry."

"Why?" she asked. "What is she going to do, heal me?"

I walked toward my yurt where someone more deserving of my time awaited me. "You can only wish," I said.

Chapter 11

Scattered thoughts lead to scattered intentions.

~ S k y e ~

KIARA HAD LEFT SOME TIME ago that evening. Khalen suspected she had found a decent hotel nearby. Both of us still felt her presence, so she couldn't have gone too far.

I sipped my coffee at the counter while Khalen cooked up some blueberry pancakes and Ian's homemade sausage.

"I can't help feeling that Kiara and Traeger are in tandem about something." I traced the smooth lip of my cup with my index finger.

Khalen glanced over his shoulder. "Oh, I'm most certain of it. There is a reason he canceled his training with Case for next week. At such close proximity, it would be nearly impossible to keep Case from tapping his thoughts."

He presented a plate with two pancakes arranged side by side and a smile-shaped sausage patty below them.

I smiled. He came over to sit beside me, held both my hands, and then bent his head in prayer.

"Father," he said. "Thank you for my beautiful mate. Keep us safe in the days to come, surround us with your protection. Amen."

"Amen," I said.

"I think you should stay home from work this week," he said. "Stay in camp."

I frowned, not really relishing the thought of becoming a prisoner again. "Why?"

"Word is out that our union takes place in three days. The Shadows will try to stop it."

I took a deep breath and tried to formulate my thoughts so they wouldn't come out too harshly. "Their threat to us is constant, my love, union or no."

"Yes, but I would still feel better knowing you were here."

I took a bite of the sausage and relished the blend of seasoned lamb, paprika, basil and tarragon. "Oh, this is good," I commented, assembling another bite. My pancakes were already gone. Khalen had a knack for making them extra fluffy and moist. They did not require any syrup or butter to make them more palatable.

"If we are always together, what could possibly happen?"

"I just have a bad feeling."

I wrapped my hand around his. "Khalen, you cannot wrap me in gauze and expect me to spread my wings. We are protected, never forget that."

He squeezed my hand. "Yes, but that doesn't mean we can be careless."

I took a sip of coffee. "Since when is going to work considered careless?"

"You're not going to budge on this, are you?" he asked, stabbing his last bite of sausage he had sandwiched between two bites of pancake.

"I enjoy my work, and our time together. I promise I won't walk to Starbucks alone this week, if that makes you feel better."

"A bit," he said, "but I'm still apprehensive about you leaving camp."

"Point taken. If anything happens, blame it on me and my careless need to feel productive."

He gathered our plates and headed toward the sink. "I prefer to pray that nothing happens. I'm rather looking forward to our union."

I blushed, having received the thoughts he so willingly shared. "Hmm," I groaned, "these are going to be the longest three days of my life."

A ROAD CREW WAS DOING SOME construction on Highway 3 between Allyn and Belfair. It added another 20 minutes to our drive and left Khalen with an edginess I didn't appreciate. He kept checking his mirrors and suspected every member of the road crew, making them avoid close proximity to our car with a look that threatened to raise blisters on their freezing cold faces. The flagman smiled and eagerly waved us by. Khalen kept his eye on him the entire time until the man was completely out of our sight.

"Aren't you being just a little too paranoid?" I asked.

He kept his eyes on the road. "Every cell in my gut screams this is a bad idea, Skye. I should take you back to the camp and order you to stay put." The harshness in his tone assured me he was serious.

I swallowed back a response, certain it would sound

far too sarcastic for his present mood. I chose to look out my window instead.

By the time we arrived at the office, his nerves were shot and he barely greeted Gregg and Ro as he stormed into his office.

"Tough ride in?" asked Ro.

"He wants me to stay in camp," I explained. Maiyun trotted into my treatment room. She had felt the effects of Khalen's raw mood as well.

Gregg typed something on his keyboard and glanced up at me. "I could clear your schedule."

"No," I said. "I want to work."

"Oh hey," said Ro, "congratulations on your upcoming union. We heard about it from Aidan."

I smiled. "Thanks. I know it's only three days from now, but with Khalen being so paranoid, it will seem much longer, I'm sure."

Ro rubbed my shoulders. "Well, hang in there. Time will pass whether he's paranoid or not." She walked around the counter and glanced at the schedule hanging on the wall. "Both of your schedules are fairly full this week. That should help some."

"Yeah. I better get my room ready." I walked back to the employee lounge to hang my sweater and purse. I typically kept them in Khalen's office, but his door was closed and I knew better than to disturb him.

After turning on my table heater and UV warmer, I returned to the lounge to make myself a cup of joe. Since Khalen didn't stop by Starbucks on the way in, as he usually did, I would have to resort to using the instant packets that cost way more than a small cup of espresso. I added some cocoa and cinnamon powder, along with a dab of honey and milk. It wasn't as satisfying as a latte, but it was better than nothing.

Steve came in and placed his lunch in the fridge. "Hey, Skye," he said, with his usual cheer in his voice.

"Hi, Steve. How's your son?"

I had worked on Toby's arm after he had broken it in three places playing football last week. He was only in junior high, but he was large enough to pass for a sophomore in high school.

"It's great. He said the pain is all gone and he is able to move his fingers around."

I smiled. Steve and the other therapists did not know about my healing capabilities and I preferred to keep it that way. "Well, with any luck, he won't be needing that surgery."

Steve pressed his lips together. "The doc is not too optimistic."

"Well, Khalen is, and I trust him over that surgery-happy orthopedic in Gig Harbor."

"Yeah," he said, "me too."

Ro poked her head through the door. "Steve, your first client is here."

He nodded toward her. "I'll be there in a minute," he said.

I took a long sip of coffee and allowed it to rest on my tongue.

"And the day begins," said Steve. "I'll talk to you later, Skye."

I nodded to him and continued to enjoy my joe before my first client arrived. She was a cancer patient who suffered from a tumor between her clavicle and second rib. The pesky growth had somehow lodged itself among the network of arteries, nerves, and muscles to where it couldn't be removed without complication. In turn, it caused her arm to swell and throb with unbearable pain.

Despite my efforts to rid her of the nasty thing, she continued to suffer. Her body was diseased and I couldn't cure her. I was just as helpless as I was when my family members got sick. My gifts were powerful in their own right, but limited just the same. It was both frustrating and humbling.

Khalen had come out of his office to greet his waiting patient. The smile on his face was inviting but shallow. I knew the difference, but I doubted that Mrs. Tavert observed it. She beamed up at him with tea-stained dentures and followed him into the exam room.

I love you, he said to me in thought. I smiled.

Thank you, I replied. It wasn't exactly an apology, but I appreciated it all the same.

I greeted Jessica in the lobby and led her to my room. She looked much worse today. Her pallor was gray, indicating a lack of energy and will. I closed the door behind us and smiled when Maiyun offered her some comfort.

"Did you have radiation today?" I asked.

She smiled conservatively, as if showing her teeth would cause unwanted ramifications. "Is it that obvious?"

I gestured for her to lie on the table. "How many more treatments do you have left?"

"Five," she replied. She removed her shoes, and then settled onto the table.

I didn't have to ask if the treatments were making any difference. The sight of her swollen, purple-tinted arm and hand were evidence enough. The tumor was growing.

I sat on my stool beside her left arm. I placed one hand on her shoulder and my other around her cold and puffy fingers. Her vibration was low and conserved. She had given up the fight, I could feel it. My heart ached for her and her family. I wanted so badly to tell her to have faith, but I didn't know how.

"I don't think I'm going to make it," she finally said.

I closed my eyes and concentrated on raising her vibration. "You have to," I said. "You have a husband and two wonderful boys depending on you."

Her other hand came up and covered her eyes. "I can't do it anymore, Skye. I just..."

I continued to raise her vibration, knowing it would cause a shift in her consciousness—hopefully a positive one. "Don't give up, Jessica. Your family has not given up on you."

Her body convulsed with stifled tears.

"Let it go," I encouraged her. "Cry and get it all out of your system so that when you emerge from this room, your husband will see that you still have some fight in you. Don't take that from him."

There was more truth to those words than she could possibly know. I remembered seeing Derrick's face when he had lost hope. It was as painful as a searing blade in my heart and nearly as fatal. I felt my own hope fade along with him. I did not want that for Ted, her husband of twenty years.

She released her tears and shook with grief, anger and frustration. She mumbled between her sobs, but the indecipherable words were not important. I removed her pain, and prayed for her recovery. It was and always would be in God's hands. I found peace in knowing that all was as it should be. He was in control, and He had a plan. I might not understand it, but I certainly had faith in it.

She looked at me with glassy brown eyes. Her lower lip trembled. "Do you think I will make it?"

I took a deep breath then slowly released it. "I believe that we make our own choices, Jessica. You must believe that you will make it through this. Healing comes from within, not from external sources."

"I don't know what I believe anymore."

I lightly traced her arm with my fingers toward her heart to encourage her lymphatic fluids to drain. Her swelling was going down and warmth started to fill her fingertips. "Well, I believe your body wants to live and is not giving up quite yet." I smiled.

She smiled as well. "Do you really think so?"

I raised her hand that was no longer purple. "See for yourself. It's better already."

She reached over and touched her hand. "It's warm."

I nodded. "I think you're going to be okay."

"Me too," she said. This time, her smile was genuine and bright.

I helped her off the table, and then led her back to the lobby where her husband was waiting.

The rest of the day was filled with injured shoulders, pulled backs, and one ankle sprain. My last client pulled up with a trailer behind her truck. She walked in looking frazzled and tired.

"Hey Beth," I said. "Who did you bring along?" I gestured toward the trailer that she had parked against the side of the building.

Her face dropped. "My goat, Chad," she said. "We just came from the vet. He said that Chad had broken two cervical vertebrae and should be euthanized."

I frowned. Chad was her best breeding buck and a dear pet. "Do you mind if I take a look at him?"

She shrugged. "I'm not sure what you can do, but sure. You were able to help with Sissy's hip." Sissy was one of her milking does who had fallen out of the trailer last month.

I followed her out of the shop and toward the trailer. The sun was ending its descent, so there was little light left to see with.

"Thank you for taking a look at him," she said, walking in front of me. She opened the trailer door, and then gently led Chad down the ramp. His head hung in an odd angle near the first and second cervical joints. He could not move his head up or down and resisted any movement from side to side.

I placed my hands on either side of his neck and felt the fractures of C1 and C2. He stood very still as I conjured the blue mist and invoked a healing. He then wiggled away from my hand, tossed his head up and leaped toward Beth as if coaxing her to play.

"Oh, dear Lord," she cried. "What did you do? How..."

"His neck was out, that's all."

"But the vet said that his neck was broken."

This was going to be tricky. "I'm sure it looked that way in the x-rays," I said, trying to sound convincing.

"It did," she confirmed. "I saw the fractures myself."

"Well, there you go. I guess the pictures showed some shadows or something."

She shrugged. "Well, he looks better now. That's all I care about." She loaded him up in the trailer and closed the door. "How much do I owe you?"

"We have some does that need to be bred soon. How about if you lend us Chad for a week or two?"

She beamed a bright smile. "Deal. Just say when and I'll haul him over."

"I'll have Ian call you when the does are ready."

Khalen met us just outside the door. The look he gave

me was enough to cause Beth alarm.

"I'll, um, see you inside, okay?" she said, looking at me, and then back to Khalen.

"What's wrong?" I asked.

"I thought we had an agreement," he said, sounding as if his jaw was locked in place. I couldn't see his expression in the dark but the tone in his voice warned me that he wasn't happy.

"Can we go inside, where I can see your face?" I asked.

"You don't need to see my face right now."

"What agreement are you referring to?"

"You said you wouldn't leave the center alone."

"I'm not alone. I was with Beth, and her trailer is right in front of the windows. If anything happened, Gregg and Ro would see."

He gripped my arms and shook me with great restraint. "If anything happened, they wouldn't reach you in time."

"Khalen, I couldn't have Beth bring her goat into the center. You're being—"

He kissed me hard on the mouth. "Please," he growled in my ear, "stay in the center. If you need to leave, come get me and I will escort you." His grip on me drove his point home. He was terrified something had happened to me.

"All right," I said. "I promise." I didn't like how he was acting, but I knew that it was temporary, at least until our union took place.

"What if," he said, holding my face close to his, "your visitor was an illusionist, and not really Beth at all?"

My stomach felt heavy and constricted. I never imagined anything like that ever happening, but I had been a victim of it once, when Sean and his gang tried to kill me. An illusionist could easily lure me away and I would never suspect a thing. I suddenly felt like a dolt. "You're right," I admitted. "I'm sorry."

He pulled me close to his chest. "We are so close, my love. I don't want to lose you."

I squeezed him back. "I'll be more careful, I promise."

Chapter 12

The line that divides light and dark is minuscule against the gray that surrounds it.

-Kiara-

THE CONSTANT HUM FROM THE appliances in the small hotel room was deafening against the silence in my mind. I had purposely removed myself from the endless chatter of Khalen's clan to first find some peace, and to also repair what was left of my shattered heart.

After Valerie, I was certain no other woman could snag Khalen; certainly not some backwoods blonde with bare feet. Just the thought of her sent my temper storming. Other than healing, I failed to see what gifts she could possibly possess that would be any match for my flames.

A knock sounded against the door. It was Traeger, no doubt. He wanted to talk about something. I had a fair idea of what that something was and I wanted nothing to do with it. He was as persistent as his twin, only with a ruthless edge that sharply contrasted with his dull wit.

His looks and charm were definitely alluring, but that was really all he offered.

I opened the door. Traeger stood on the other side wearing a chest-hugging white pullover tucked neatly into a pair of pressed slacks. They fell neatly over his alligator boots with a squared-off toe.

"Come in," I gestured, waving my hand across the tiny entrance to the room. "Welcome to my humble abode."

Traeger walked in and quickly assessed my sad excuse for accommodations. "You know, we have plenty of room for you at my mansion in Hoodsport."

I rolled my eyes. "I'm sure you do." I gestured to a chair in the corner. "Have a seat, Traeger, and get to the point." I walked over to where I had a bottle of Zinfandel breathing. I poured it into a wine glass I had purchased in town, and then sat across from him.

He glanced over at my glass then across the way to where the bottle stood open.

"I have only one glass," I said.

He boldly reached over and took mine from my hand. "I don't mind sharing." He took a long bold sip, swallowed, and then smacked his lips with a bitter expression. "Why don't you let me buy you dinner and perhaps a bottle of real wine, hmm?"

Dinner did sound good, and getting out of this hellhole was even better. I stood and gathered my bag and coat. "You're on."

"While you're at it," he added with a familiar smugness to his voice. "Pack the rest of your things. I will take you back to my place for the night. If you find it less inviting than here, you can return come morning." His smile shone bright and confident.

"I will not bed you," I boldly stated.

He laughed. "Is that what concerns you, my dear?" He stood and walked toward me. "Are you worried that I might lure you into my chamber and take advantage of you?" His face was inches from mine, and his sweet breath feathered over my lips. I had to admit; he had my heart pounding—ruthless bastard.

I stepped back and bumped into the closet. He had obviously honed his skills a tad and had somehow gained a backbone in the process. I didn't remember him ever being so plucky. "You hardly pose a threat, Traeger." My voice betrayed me with a quiver.

He laughed. "Of course not."

He helped gather my things, and then effortlessly carried my bags to his waiting town car. The driver met us, opened the trunk then carefully loaded my bags. Traeger sat beside me in the back, uncomfortably close.

After the driver settled in, Traeger instructed him to take us to a fairly new restaurant in Gig Harbor called Sips. "They'll save us a quiet booth where we can talk," he explained.

Traeger called ahead to reserve the private booth. When we arrived, the waitress flew to him like a fly to dung. It was disgusting to witness his powerful lure in action.

The waitress lowered herself to meet his eyes. Her full bosom nearly popped out of her tight blouse. Auburn ringlets fell loose from her tightly coiled bun and played well against her shiny red lipstick. "Can I get you something to drink, sir?"

I rolled my eyes and sat back against the soft leather seat. The poor young girl had no idea what type of poison she played with. If she did happen to get lucky with Traeger, he would crush her beneath his strength.

Spirians rarely mated with weak-minded humans unless they wanted them dead.

Traeger smiled way too brightly at the young woman and said, "We'll start with two glasses of Pinot Grigio and your fabulous calamari."

"Coming right up," she said, wagging her chest slightly as she rose.

Traeger watched her walk away, his eyes focused on the gentle sway of her ample backside. "Lovely girl," he commented.

I lit the table candle with a thought and coaxed the flame to rise higher than it should go. "For a human," I added.

"Hmm," he replied. "Do I sense a bit of jealousy?"

I scoffed. "Hardly, Traeger. Take her home with you tonight. I'll burn her spent corpse for you in the morning."

"I have more pressing matters to tend to," he said, "and I think you can help."

The waitress returned with our chilled glasses of wine. I took a long sip before asking him about the type of help he expected from me. The cool juice soothed my throat and cooled the fire he stoked with his mere presence. "I'm listening."

Another waitress lowered a plate of calamari steaks before us, and then quickly walked away.

Traeger served a portion for me onto a small plate, and then served himself. He pushed a bowl holding a pungent-smelling sauce toward me. "You'll like this," he said with a menacing smile. "It's hot and spicy."

The way I like my men, I added in thought. It didn't escape his notice. His smile broadened.

"As you know," he began. "Khalen and his new mate-to-be have stirred quite a ruckus among the Shadow clans."

"I can well imagine," I said. "She is hardly his type, wouldn't you say?"

His expression turned to one of mild shock. "She is his equal," he said, "in every sense of the word." He sipped his wine with effort, as if his own words were choking him.

I had to laugh. The image of that barefoot blonde being anything close to Khalen's equal was deniable at best. "The healer?" I inquired, making sure we were talking about the same woman.

His eyes turned emerald with copper specks. "Skye is the legend. If she mates with Khalen, their bond could threaten our kind."

"Our kind?"

"Shadows, my dear."

I sat back away from his hypnotic gaze. "I am not a Shadow, Traeger."

"Not yet," he purred, stroking my thigh with his fingertips. I tried to move away from him but he held me firm, digging his cruel fingers into my flesh until I relaxed. "Bring Skye to me and you can have Khalen all to yourself."

His lure was powerful and I had seriously underestimated him. I was caught in his vortex, swirling helplessly toward the great void that was sure to greet me on the other end. "And what makes you think Skye will come willingly?"

"Oh, she won't, I assure you. She is much stronger than you give her credit for, my dear."

I tapped my fingernail against the side of the wine glass, now dripping with sweat, mirroring my own condition. If I had any sense at all, I would hop on the next plane to England and return home. My all-consuming cosmetic surgery practice was a fine sight better than this current situation.

"No," said Traeger. "It isn't. Your path is here now, helping me. When I have Skye, you can take Khalen and return to your dreary life, but for now, you work with me." It was more of a command than a request.

"And if I refuse?" The words felt like razors in my throat.

He brushed his finger across my lips. "I don't believe you will refuse." My body ached for his touch, though my heart wanted to shrink away. He was commanding—much too commanding for me to resist and he knew it.

"Tell me about Skye," I said, attempting to break the mood.

"She is strong," he said. "She reads your intentions, so you cannot surprise her."

I shook my head. "This is crazy, Traeger. I cannot get close to her without Case and Khalen reading my thoughts."

"Distract them," he said.

I laughed. Distracting those two was as impossible as stopping the ocean from touching the shore. "And how, pray tell, do you propose I do that?"

"We need an illusionist," he said. "I need you to talk to Sean. See if you can solicit his help."

I furrowed my brow. "Why would he be interested in helping you?"

Traeger's eyes grew wide with enthusiasm as if his mind was proposing ideas faster than he could comprehend. "He wants Skye dead," he explained. "He sees her as a threat. If you can convince him that my union with her would strengthen our clan, he might reconsider his idea of killing her and offer his help. They are far removed from the Protected and Case will never know of their involvement until it is too late." He was rambling now, talking in fragments of thoughts that had no beginning or end.

I downed the rest of my wine and finished the last bite of calamari. By the end of the meal, Traeger had the whole thing planned out from beginning to end. I had known many Shadows in my life, but this guy took the prize for being the most sinister. If he had any scruples at all, they were masked beneath a thick shroud of greed, power and lust. I sometimes wondered how he and Khalen were from the same egg.

"Come," said Traeger. "We have much to do." He grabbed my hand and led me hastily out to the car. After settling into my seat, I tried to shrink back away from his touch, but he wouldn't allow it. His grip was firm on my thigh, keeping me pressed against him. He instructed his driver to take us home.

Any chance I once had to escape was gone now. Traeger had me in his clutches and he was not going to let me go. I had often heard about how Shadows claimed one's soul, but I never comprehended the sheer power of their force until now.

Despite my efforts to torch the car, Traeger quenched my flame with ease then countered with his own heat in the pit of my belly. My reaction to his touch widened his smile and fueled his desire to overwhelm me. He was not the same man I had known many years ago. He was stronger now, and much more commanding.

"You will stay with me, tonight," he said as the car stopped in front of a massive stone-faced mansion. His driver opened our door, and then obediently carried my bags to Traeger's chamber.

"I don't think that's a good idea," I said, though I knew my words were nothing more than sprinkles against an established forest blaze.

"Kiara, my lovely. I am the best of your options and you know it."

He led me to the massive room that used to belong to his father. As was customary, he also acquired his father's mates, who were many. I knew that I, too, would soon be counted among those numbers—nothing more than a vessel for potential offspring. It was no secret that mates who did not produce gifted children were severed from the clan through death, along with their non-gifted children.

A wave of power swept over me, giving me courage to fight this destiny. I pulled back from Traeger. "No," I said. "I will not go with you."

He mocked me with laughter. "Kiara," his voice was silky and mimicked Khalen's almost perfectly. "I am Khalen's stronger half. Your gift of flames is no threat to me nor has it ever been to Khalen. How many men can say the same?"

That was true enough. When Khalen left, I had a hard time finding men who could calm my heat. Most of them died trying. But I tried one last gambit. "Traeger, our deal was that you get Skye and I get Khalen."

"Yes," he drawled. "But I have decided that you're more valuable to me as my mate. Khalen will not have you and you know it as well as I do."

He stepped closer to where his mouth was inches from mine. "I will break him," he said, "by taking everything he cares about."

"He doesn't care about me," I stammered, trying to back away from him. He followed me until my back pressed against the wall just outside of his room.

"I do," he said, his sweet breath teasing my mouth open. My heart pounded loudly against my chest and I found it hard to breathe. He wrapped his massive hands around my wrists and raised them above my head against the wall. His smile broadened. I imagined his body yielding to the flames I tried to conjure, but he squelched them just as quickly. His strength excited me and he felt it as well. "Not here," he growled.

He pulled me away from the wall and brought me into his chamber. It had all the amenities of a penthouse suite at the Waldorf Astoria. He sat me down on the oversized bed, and then walked toward the wet bar in the corner. "Can I pour you something to drink, my dear?"

"Sherry," I said, wondering how I ever got myself into this mess. Khalen had told me multiple times how easy it was to fall into the clutches of the Shadows. I never believed him, really. Now that naive disbelief mocked me and there was nothing I could do about it.

Traeger poured a drink and handed the glass to me. He moved more like Khalen than I had remembered. Traeger's braid was not quite as long, but it was as thick and black as his twin's. "I will not unite with you willingly," I said.

With his drink in hand, he sat beside me on the bed. "We shall see." He took a long sip while studying me with his eyes. "I'll make you a deal," he said.

"Another deal?"

He took my drink and set it down on the end table next to his. "I will only take you if you beg me to do so."

I swallowed hard. "That won't happen."

Without touching me, he effortlessly removed my clothes and laid them over the valet in the corner. He then laid me down and held me entranced as he removed his own clothing. His dark smooth skin glistened like satin against the soft light of the room. For a long moment, he just stood there at the foot of the bed, staring at me. His body was ready and pulsing with excitement. I saw his struggle for control. I tried to pull away from his hypnotizing stare, but couldn't.

Slowly, he lay down beside me and caressed my body with his hand. I closed my eyes, driving back the urge to touch him in return. His lips traced a line from my collarbone to the nape of my neck, heightening my sensitivity in their wake. His gentleness was like torture to the heat that needed to vent from my body. Instinctively I moved away from his fiery touch, but he pulled me back and his gentleness turned to mild force.

The delicious torture seemed to last for hours and my strength was giving way to desire. The weight of his body held me firm. There was no escape for me now. I had fallen into his spell and knew if I didn't give him what he wanted, I would perish trying to resist.

"Beg me," he said. "I'll take you further than Khalen ever could."

I did, with reckless abandon, I gave him what he knew I would. I begged him to end the torture, and he did with the skill and finesse of a master. My soul opened up to him and with a sharp ache and a crushing embrace, our union was complete.

Chapter 13

There is strength in numbers and power in deception, but neither can conquer the will of one's heart.

TRAEGER HAD MADE IT VERY clear that I now belonged to him, heart, body and soul. So long as I obeyed, he offered me pleasure beyond my wildest fantasies, but if I went against his wishes, he delivered pain that breached all barriers of tolerance. That pain lingered in my belly as a firm reminder of my position.

His other mates did not take too kindly to me and I didn't care. My gifts were stronger than all of theirs combined. I could remove any number of them without incurring Traeger's wrath. He cared little for any of them. I found pleasure in that and was grateful to share his bed each night.

Today he planned to take me to Sean and his clan. I didn't truly understand my role in Traeger's great plan, but I agreed to accompany him. The ride into Seattle was a silent one. I tried reading his thoughts but he kept me out.

"You will know soon enough, my dear."

I didn't like the distance I sensed in his tone, or the way he kept his hands to himself. I tried to reach out for him but felt his resistance as he pushed me away brusquely.

"What has you so occupied?" I asked, frustration in my tone.

He turned to look at me with an empty gaze. "If we cannot gain Sean's assistance, this plan will fail."

"Why wouldn't he help you? The plan includes his best interests as well."

"He is a bloodsucker. Their needs are—different."

We pulled up to a large stone mansion that looked as if it belonged in the Scottish Highlands. A scrawny looking man, old and human, greeted us at the top of the circular drive. He opened our door and smiled.

"Welcome," he said.

I stepped out, followed by Traeger. He gripped my hand as if I would try to run away. "Say nothing," he warned.

The frail old man led us into the large, open entrance and gestured to a room on the right. "Master Sean will join you in the study."

It was dark in the house, with long tapestries that hung from ceiling to floor. The study was furnished with black ebony tables, a matching desk with brass knobs, and gray leather recliners with a matching love seat. Classical music played in the background, while a small fire warmed the hearth that separated the study from the living space.

Sean, accompanied by two of his minions, entered the room. Everything about him alarmed me. My instincts told me to run and never look back, but I stayed by Traeger's side, obediently. Khalen was right about the Shadows. They removed all that is right in this world and left nothing but confusion and emptiness in its place.

What had I become?

Sean glanced down at me with glowing red eyes. How they became that way was a mystery and I really didn't care to know. I knew little of the bloodsuckers. Rumor had it that they descended from an old gypsy clan in Scotland. Their leader believed that if he drank the blood of the gifted, he would inherit the donor's gift. The theory was never proven so far as I could tell.

Sean's sandy-blond hair was short and well groomed. He had no facial hair nor a single flaw in his black slacks and white pirate-style shirt with billowing sleeves. The man was stuck in a time that didn't fit with current trends, right down to the shiny black shoes with square buckle accents.

"To what do I owe this honor," he said to Traeger, with a shallow bow.

"I believe we have a common interest," Traeger explained.

Sean looked doubtful as he took a seat, and then gestured for us to do the same on the couch across from him. His minions remained standing by the doorway. "I doubt our interests are the same, Traeger." His eyes scanned me from head to toe, making me feel like a mare at auction.

"As you know," Traeger explained, "Khalen will take Skye as his mate in two days' time." His voice projected much more confidence than I knew he felt.

Sean's expression did not reflect whether he already had this information. He simply stared and listened.

"If this happens," Traeger continued, "it could pose a vital threat to our kind."

"Then why did you not kill her when you had the chance?" asked Sean.

"She will be more valuable as my mate," said Traeger. "Her offspring will—"

Sean stood. "There will be no offspring by her," he said, an eerie calm to his voice.

Traeger stood and matched Sean's chilly stare "She is the legend, Sean. I'm sure of it."

Sean scoffed. "All the more reason she should die."

"I will take her as my mate," said Traeger.

Sean shook his head. "Christ, Traeger. Is there a female alive that is spared the fate of being your mate?"

Traeger had many mates, true enough. He prided himself on luring the women and turning them into something they thought they were not— just like me. My stomach lurched as if trying to escape my body. I wrapped my arms around my belly and prayed I wouldn't be sick while the men continued talking.

"Why, Sean, dear fellow, you sound jealous." Traeger smiled.

Sean's expression depicted bitterness, not jealousy. "I'm disgusted at the liberties you consistently display without fail, Traeger. Your gift to lure has left you with ingratitude for all that has meaning."

"That doesn't change the fact that Skye is worth more alive than dead," said Traeger. If Sean's last comment had any blighting power behind it, Traeger's blank expression did not show it.

Sean brought his index finger up to his lips. "True." His sinister eyes glimmered like polished rubies. "If you want her to live, you must surrender her to me."

Traeger smiled. "Very well, and in turn, you will spare her life."

Sean nodded. "Agreed." His eyes returned to me. "And for payment, I will keep your new mate."

Traeger's smile broadened. That was his plan all along. I was dispensable, mere bait to help lure this madman into Traeger's trap. And, his union with me would offer him a direct link to Sean's clan—clever man.

"Keep her for as long as you like," he said. "Lend me your illusionists and I will deliver Skye to you by the end of the week."

I opened my mouth to speak, but Traeger issued a numbing blow. I fell to my knees, the pain in my gut restricting my breath.

"Forgive her," he said. "She has not yet learned obedience."

Sean gestured to his minions to take me out of the room. I did not look back at Traeger. I had made this victory of his all too easy and I knew it. For a moment of pleasure, I had given my soul. I imagined him blazing in flame. He quickly diffused it with a laugh and a wave of his hand.

"I must warn you," said Traeger. "She has a bit of a hot temper about her."

Sean nodded and curled his thin lips into a sinister grin. "Very useful," he said. "I must remember to bind her with a shield lest she get careless."

Chapter 14

What seems apparent is not always the truth. Have faith in what is right and shun the rest, for it is only an illusion.

~ S k y e ~

KHALEN WAS MORE PROTECTIVE TODAY than he had ever been. His edginess convinced me that there was some substance to his fears. I finished sheeting my treatment table for the last time today, and then turned to find him standing in the doorway.

"Your mind is heavy," I said. "You promised to never lock me out of your thoughts and yet I cannot read what troubles you."

Then, a flash of images flooded my mind—nightmares. I saw our camp burned and in ruins. The Escalade was crushed, Maiyun lay still. I grabbed the edge of the table to keep from falling. "Good Lord," I said. "How long have you had these visions?"

He frowned and his lips grew firm. "Since I announced our union."

I shook my head, having a hard time imagining the ruins of our camp, our home. "Khalen," I said. "I'm scared."

He came into the room and wrapped his arms around me. His warm breath brushed the top of my hair as he laid tender kisses along my head. "Don't be," he said. "The Shadows are trying to invoke fear and use it as a doorway. Keep it closed, my love. Do not allow them entrance."

"I want to go home," I said, "and stay there tomorrow."

He squeezed me tightly. "We should unite tonight," he said. "Not wait."

I pulled back from him and stared into his eyes, now misty with fear and desperation. "Is this what you want?"

"Yes," he said, without hesitation. "It is what I want. I don't want to lose you, Skye."

"Union or no," I said, "I am yours and always have been."

"Come," he said, taking my hand. "Let's go home."

We drove in silence, holding hands and keeping our thoughts to ourselves. The night had an eerie buzz to it, like static on an old television. Up ahead, the road crew had a production line consisting of a backhoe, an electrical truck, a dump truck, and a steamroller. A large woman waved a stop sign, indicating she wanted us to wait. Her eyes focused on Khalen. He squeezed my hand. We both felt the coldness emanating from her.

"Don't look at them," he said. "Keep your eyes down."

I did as he asked. It took much longer than expected for the woman to turn the sign and let us pass. She tapped on the car and motioned for us to pass. Khalen accelerated faster than he normally would. His knuckles looked white against the black steering wheel.

As we headed out of town, the road became dark and

void of traffic. "Have Maiyun lie down," he said, "and keep her down."

I instructed her to stay down. She panted heavily as if sensing our anxiety.

Khalen glanced over at me. "If something happens, Skye, you must remember to never surrender to them. I will find you."

I frowned. "Nothing will happen."

His posture stiffened. His eyes grew wide and his arm pressed against my chest as if he were strong enough to hold me back. Two headlights veered into our lane. Khalen drove onto the soft shoulder. The car swerved then skidded sideways. Another set of headlights wavered and then grew larger. The sound of screeching tires preceded the deafening shock of metal crunching against metal, and shattering glass. My body slammed against the door, my head hit the glass. Maiyun yelped, Khalen fell limp. I tried to reach for him, but my hands were heavy and my arms felt numb. Darkness quickly consumed me.

I OPENED MY EYES. VIVID MEMORIES of the accident replayed in my mind, but I felt no pain. I was not in a hospital. The room was dark, but the bed felt large and much too comfortable. A soft down comforter covered my naked body, warm and free from injury. I sat up and tried to focus on anything familiar but it was too dark.

The digital clock beside the bed glowed red with the numbers 3:45am. There was another person in the room, I could feel him. His energy was low and constant. He was asleep. The vibration was unfamiliar. Whoever it was, he was a stranger to me.

Quietly, I swung my legs out of bed and then wrapped the comforter around my body. There was no time to search for my clothes. I needed to leave without waking the man in the room. Judging by the dull vibrations coming from the walls, the room was quite large. I projected my energy outward in hopes of finding the door. My instincts were sharp and on edge. There was furniture in the room. Only one corner felt hollow. That had to be where the door was. I slowly headed toward it, being careful to stay centered. I kept my hearing sharp and trained on the sleeping man behind me. I froze when his breathing changed pace. When a steady rhythm resumed, I continued forward.

The corner was close, I could feel its resistance. I slowed and reached forward. I felt the corner of the wall, and then moved my hand right. I found a picture frame. I then ventured left and felt the edge of a door jam. Moving down and across, I found an obliquely shaped knob that was polished and smooth. Slowly I turned it, praying it wouldn't be locked.

It wasn't. The door opened and I stepped out of the room. Everything was dark, lending no clues as to where I was or what direction to take.

Again, I projected my energy outward, first to the right, and then to the left. The hall was long and narrow in both directions. I chose to go left. Slowly I proceeded, feeling the wall as my own energy bounced against it. There was a runner on the floor. So long as I stayed in the center of it, there was less of a chance that I would run into a low bench or some other type of furniture. In this narrow of a hall, I doubted there would be anything to trip over.

The change in vibration told me that I passed a closed door on the right. I continued on. The hallway opened up to a large room on the left. I heard no sounds coming from it, nor was there any sign of windows on this moonless night. Even if a window was shaded or draped, it would reflect a subtle vibration variance that would distinguish itself from the wall.

This room had furniture, some in the center of the room. It reflected my energy with the percussiveness of hard polished wood. I walked slowly toward the far wall. It seemed the most logical location for a window. I was wrong. If there was a window in this room, it was not along the far wall. The only other wall that made sense was the one to my right.

I turned, being careful not to lose my bearings. It was easy to get turned around in an area that was unfamiliar, especially when you're blind. This wall did not have a window either. What type of room did not have windows? I wondered. Most of the furniture felt like long tables with locked drawers. A file room, perhaps?

I returned to the hall and started heading back toward the room I had been sleeping in. The hall light was switched on. I saw the faint glow from the bulbs but could not make out anything else. Slowly, I backed my way into the dark room and prayed I had not been seen. I stood quietly around the corner and listened for movement. There was none. The light turned off.

Two men were waiting for me at the end of the hallway. I could feel their intentions. I stayed where I was. If they wanted me, they would have to come and get me. After that, I had no clue what to do. Hiding would be useless.

"Skye," Traeger called from down the hall. "Come here." The light in the hall was switched on, though it didn't help much.

I closed my eyes as I rounded the corner and walked toward Traeger. "I should have known that you were behind all this."

"Well," he said, waiting for me to approach him, "I couldn't very well allow you to join with my brother."

"It will happen whether you allow it or not," I replied confidently.

I felt his sting pierce my shield but I held firm and strengthened my guard. His gifts were clearly stronger than my own. I had to find some way to distract him before he brought me to my knees.

"You must be very envious of him," I said. "You look and sound like him more each time I see you." I couldn't see him at this moment, but he may not have picked up on that.

His sting grew stronger. I stopped my approach and forced myself to ignore the pain gripping my insides.

"I do not envy him, my dear. I pity him for not acknowledging what he is."

"What is he?" I asked.

"A Shadow, through and through."

"According to whose standards?"

The stings grew sharper, piercing my feeble wall and my will to ignore the pain. I gasped and swallowed back the urge to cry out.

"Mine," he growled.

He dropped me to my knees. My body trembled, unable to hold back his cruel measure of punishment. Now I cried out in pain, but managed to say: "I will not give you what you want." Each word came out slow and precise. I didn't want to repeat them.

"Oh, you will, my dear. Of that, I am certain." He looked over at the large man on his left. "Take her to my chamber."

It felt like steel belts clamping around my upper arm as I was hauled to my feet and ushered down the corridor.

My other hand gripped the comforter, keeping it in place. The man pushed me into a large room on the right, and then shoved me onto the bed.

"Stay there," he said. I did not recognize his voice. He stood looming above me like an obedient sentry.

I rolled toward the side of the bed and sat up, tightening the comforter around my body. He immediately pushed me down. With my shield, I slammed him against the wall, and then stood. Another stinging dose of electrical current dropped me to the floor as Traeger stepped inside the room. His sentry stood and came after me as if intending to strike me with a fatal blow.

"Stop!" Traeger warned him. "She is not to be harmed."

The man growled down at me, his dark eyes glowing red. I assumed he must be part of Sean's clan. He and Traeger must have joined forces to prevent mine and Khalen's union.

"You are correct, my dear," Traeger confirmed. "You are clever as well as gifted."

The pain eased and I pulled myself up from the floor. "What do you want, Traeger?"

He laughed. "What I want no longer matters." He gestured for his sentry and the other large male to leave the room. They did, closing the door behind them.

Traeger grabbed me and pulled me into his arms. His breath was laced with brandy and perhaps a bit of rum. "Khalen was a fool for not taking you sooner."

"My heart is his, Traeger, and there is nothing you can do to change that."

He slammed his mouth over mine, cutting my lower lip with his sharp incisors. I offered no reaction. While his hands liberally explored my body, I remembered what Derrick had once told me.

"If anyone tries to rape you," he said. "Feign boredom. Men who take women by force are excited by fear, pain, and the fight. If you look and act bored, they will find it hard to stay excited."

"So," I said, between his passionless kisses. "What exactly lures women to you?"

His advances stopped.

"Honestly," I continued. "You're a horrible kisser and your touch is akin to a rhino in a candle shop, feverishly trying to stomp out the flames." I wiped the blood trailing down my lip.

He threw me down on the bed and stripped the comforter from my body. "I will take you tonight whether you are willing or not."

I pursed my lips as if doubting his threat. "Well, this should be entertaining," I said, looking away from his eyes. Inside, I felt like bolting and fighting him, but I knew it would only fuel his lust. I tolerated his painful violation with no reaction.

He slapped my face and forced me to look at him. "You're scared," he said, his voice raspy and deep. "Tonight, you will belong to me." He stood and removed his clothing, allowing it to drop to the floor. My tangled comforter lay around me like spilt milk. My body ached and my stomach threatened to purge my last meal.

"You cannot take what will never be yours," I added. "You are not strong enough and are pathetically inadequate." I looked to his groin while stating that last comment. I had no idea what he looked like in this lighting, nor did I care. I was merely trying to pierce his ego and wound it a bit.

"We shall see," he said, grabbing my legs.

Laugh, a distant voice said. *Laugh hard*. It was Shanuk.

I did as he instructed, trying to imagine something worth laughing about. It was difficult and my laugh came out like a nervous chuckle.

Traeger's reaction, though, prompted a more realistic roar from me. His erection flopped like a limp noodle against my thigh.

"Kind of hard to take me if you can't get it up," I said, still laughing. My face felt the sharp sting of his hand. He slapped me again and my ears began to ring. Anger had replaced his excitement.

"I will enjoy giving you to Sean in the morning," he snarled. He stood from the bed and donned his clothing. He then grabbed my arm and hauled me off the bed and onto my feet. We crossed the room and he flung the door open.

His sentry stood there, probably gawking at my naked form. "Take her," Traeger said. "Chain her to her bed. I'm done with her."

Again, the steel hand clamped around my bruised and tender arm and I was ushered down the hall. The sentry secured metal cuffs to my wrists and secured them to the bed frame. He did not bother pulling the covers over my shivering body. His warm spittle hit my belly then dribbled over my side. He closed the door behind him and I was left alone.

The fear I had been suppressing took hold. I curled up into a ball and allowed the tears to flow from my eyes. My body ached as if it had been dragged behind a truck over gravel. Every nerve felt raw and exposed. I was cold and shivering.

I felt the warmth of Shanuk's presence. *Be strong*, he whispered.

"I'm scared," I whimpered, feeling like a young

child in the midst of a horrid nightmare. Tomorrow I would be given to Sean, the bloodsucker who wanted me dead. Would Khalen know? I remembered how he looked after the accident. The sounds of crunching metal played back in my mind, along with Maiyun's sharp cry. Khalen's limp and bloody form lingered in my memory. He was alive, I felt it, and Maiyun too. "Khalen," I sighed, praying he would hear my thought.

Chapter 15

*When everything you love is annihilated, all that is left is anger
and hate—the demons that consume your soul.*

~ K h a l e n ~

I **FOUND MYSELF IN THE DIRT,** lying in the center of our
camp. My body felt as if it had been crushed. Breathing
was painful. The camp was deserted and dark. The smell
of charred wood, fabric and flesh urged me to stand.
Burnt bodies lay all around me. Every yurt and cottage
was burned to the ground. Even the animals had been
burned. The garden was destroyed. Tattered pieces of the
protective shroud hung like old cobwebs from the trees.
An eerie red circle surrounded the moon as the fog rolled
by.

A sinister laugh echoed off the trees as a form
emerged. Kiara's ruby eyes glistened with vengeance as
she approached. She was flanked by several Shadows with
glowing red eyes—Sean's clan.

"It's all gone," she said. "Everything you love is gone."

After reading her thoughts, I knew she had been turned. Traeger had consumed her, and then traded the remains to Sean. Kiara no longer existed.

"Where's Skye?"

Kiara laughed. "Where she should be, in Traeger's bed."

I dropped to my knees. "No," I growled. "You lie."

Her expression changed to one of pity. She walked toward me. "You fight a losing battle, Khalen. Join us."

"Never," I said. "I will never join you."

She laughed. "You have nothing left, Khalen. What are you fighting for?"

One of the Shadows approached. I recognized him as one of Sean's minions—a gifted bastard with a hunger for death and destruction. "Case and his mate were far too easy to destroy. It was a bit of a disappointment, really," he said, cocking his head to the side as if to judge my reaction.

I felt Shanuk's presence like a warm blanket wrapped around my shoulders. *They're trying to consume you. Ignore their illusion.*

"You want to kill us, don't you?" another Shadow asked. He walked toward me like a hungry hyena measuring its foe.

Rage built inside me, burning my core and dulling my senses. I wanted them all dead. The first man dropped, and then the second one. Kiara laughed with delight. She could feel my weakness.

"Yes, Khalen. Kill them. Kill them all." I dropped the man behind her and felt the heavy darkness that surrounded me. Someone approached me from behind. I turned to find Ian, Aidan, and Case standing like faded figures in a distant dream. Then I collapsed.

I AWOKE IN A STRANGE CABIN that smelled of old carpet and mold. An old man who resembled Grizzly Adams at age ninety turned to look at me. His long gray beard hung to his chest and blended in well with the garb that draped over his shoulders, like a homeless man who wore every scrap of clothing he had collected over several years.

I rubbed my eyes and stretched against the stiffness that came from sleeping on a hard floor. "Where am I?"

"My cabin," the old man said.

I stood and looked around. The log cabin was small, perhaps sixteen by sixteen feet square with one cot, a wood-burning stove, and a chipped basin of dirty water. "How did I get here?"

He shrugged, and then pointed to a folded piece of paper. "They left that."

I opened the folded note, which read:

Your clan is dead, and your woman is claimed. If you want her to live, cooperate. Come to my house in Seattle this evening at 5:00 pm.
~ Sean

I crumpled the note then shoved it into my pocket. It was a lie. If my clan were truly dead, I would feel it. I called upon my father and waited for his reply. I stepped outside the musty cabin and saw nothing but trees.

The old man stared at me as if I was something to fear.

"Where are we?" I asked him.

"My cabin," the old man said again. He was clearly not of sound mind and looked to be blind as well. The Shadows had chosen this cabin wisely, leaving only a sad blind man as a witness. He would no doubt forget the whole thing in an hour or so.

I had to rely on my gifts to find the nearest highway. I turned west and projected my energy out then turned north, east, and then south. My instincts directed me south. *Father*, I projected to Case. *I need you.*

I walked toward an area that looked like a park. As I drew nearer. I recognized it as Belfair State Park. In an hour, I could walk to The Wellness Center where Skye had left her truck. Case had heard me, but he wasn't answering. There must have been a reason.

The walk into town offered me time to think. I knew that Skye had not been claimed. I'm not sure how or why, but I felt it deep in my soul. My pace quickened. She was in danger, no doubt. I needed to come up with a plan, and going to Seattle alone would not be wise. I had to contact Ian, Aidan and Case.

When I got to the center, I tried calling out to Ian and Aidan. Aidan answered first.

Where are you?

In thought, I informed him of the evening's events, my visions, and my feelings in a fraction of a second. In turn, he told me about the attack in camp. Case had the foresight to move the clan to Caleb's land. Ian and Aidan then projected the illusion of people so that the Shadows would believe the clan was destroyed, including Case and Eve.

Case wants you to come to Caleb's first, Aidan sent in thought.

No time, I replied. *I must meet Sean at his house at five pm. That gives me just over two hours to get there.*

No, Case said. *Come here first. Sean will have to wait.*

What if he kills her? I asked.

He won't. Be silent.

Case must have sensed someone listening to our thoughts. That explained why he did not respond to my first calling. We were being tracked.

I willed the locked door of Skye's truck to open, and then tried to sit in the driver's seat. It was adjusted for Skye. I released the adjustment lever and pushed the seat back all the way until my legs could fit under the steering wheel. I touched my finger to the ignition switch and the engine roared to life. Having gifts certainly proved useful at times. I pushed the gear knob to reverse, and then backed the truck up.

The smell of Maiyun's fur was disturbing yet comforting. I wondered what had happened to her and my car. I remembered the accident, but nothing after that.

I put the truck in drive, and pressed the accelerator. The engine revved up then lurched forward like a bucking bronco. Clearly this truck did not like running cold. Even after it warmed up, it drove like a gutless wonder.

Caleb's land resided on the east side of Squaxin Island. Case was wise to move the clan there. With so many elders, the Shadows would have a hard time infiltrating without being noticed. It was nearly an hour-and-a-half away and Skye's truck was hard pressed to go faster than sixty miles per hour.

When I arrived, I was greeted by Case and Ian, who quickly escorted me to Caleb's cabin. My mother wrapped her tiny arms around my waist and gave me a warm hug.

"Thank God you're all right," she said.

"Come," said Case. "There isn't much time." He led us over to a worn leather couch that looked as if it had been brown at one point, but was now a faded tan with blotches of stains and wear. Case pulled over two chairs from the small dining room table. "Tell me what happened last night."

I told him about the accident.

He looked my body over. "No injuries?"

I shook my head. "No, we were under an illusion, I'm sure of it."

Aidan leaned forward. "We found your car in flames off highway 3, just past Allyn."

"Kiara is with them," I said.

Case looked down. "I know."

From his thoughts, I knew that she was dead. Case had killed her. Taking a life was never easy for him. It always left a heaviness in his heart that he couldn't hide.

My brows pressed together. "Where is Traeger?"

"He was staying at a house in Union. But now he is taking Skye to Sean. The illusionists he surrounds himself with make it difficult for us to get near him," said Ian.

"They are going to use her as bait," I said, "to bribe me to join them."

"No," Case said. "They don't want you to join them. They want you dead, and she will die as well."

"I have to meet him tonight," I said.

"Don't worry about their illusionists," said Aidan. "My brother and I will deal with them swift enough."

"It will be dangerous," Case warned. "There are only two of you, and six of them."

"We have been watching them, and how they work," said Ian. "They are sloppy and quick to believe their own illusions. They think their strength lies in numbers, but my brother and I are cunning. We can bring their worst nightmares to life." He said that last part with a gleam in his eyes.

The room was silent. "Sometimes, Ian, you really

concern me," I said.

Case folded his hands and looked as if he were in deep thought. "We are going to have to make them believe they have won—catch them off guard."

I was trying to follow his line of reasoning. How does one fool a fool?

"If they believe you are broken, Khalen," he explained, "they will let their guard down. Of course, that may mean you need to do things you don't approve of."

I studied his obsidian eyes, which were now glowing with rainbow hues. Like Ian, he, too, was starting to concern me. "For example?" I prodded.

"You may have to take some of them down. Can you do that without losing yourself?"

My stomach turned. I couldn't even take a bear down without losing my breakfast. Taking the lives of other Spirians was an entirely different matter. "Are you asking me if I can take a life without losing part of my own?" I shook my head, disgusted with the mere thought of his reasoning. "You of all people should know better than to ask that of me." I stood and looked at Case and Ian as if they were foreign to my clan. What had gotten into them? Were they even my people? I moved the chair at the dining room table to test my gifts. If this were an illusion, the chair would not move. My gifts would be useless. The chair did move, causing everyone but Case to jump.

"This is not an illusion, son. I am not about violence in any sense of the word, but we are at war, and our existence lies in the balance. We cannot allow them to wipe out our kind because we are too proud to take them out first."

"Too proud?" I laughed. "Is that how you see this, Father?"

"Then what would you call it?" he asked. He stood and

began to pace, an action that typically preceded a loss of temper.

I ran my fingers through my hair, trying to think of a better solution.

"The Shadows do not take us seriously, Khalen," Aidan explained, trying to break the reverberating tension between my father and me. "They have infiltrated our camp, and have breached the treaty. What do you think is next?"

"How do I take a life without giving up some of my own?" I asked.

Case grabbed my arms, making them ache. I didn't care. The pain was a welcome change to the gut-wrenching torture of this idea. "You take it for the right reasons," he said, his eyes now boring into mine.

"Is there ever a right reason?"

"Skye is the right reason. They will kill her, and then they will come after you and the rest of us. If we don't stop them now, they will only grow stronger."

I looked over at my mother, whose eyes pleaded with me to comply. For the past seventy years, I have struggled with that side of me they now ask me to unleash. Once untethered, could I rein it back in?

"Yes," said Case. "You can, and you will. Your gifts are strong, my son. You have kept them caged for long enough. Now it is time to use them for the good of us all, and protect what you believe in. There is no other way."

"We will fight them together," said Aidan. "All of us."

"We'll take two cars," said Case. "Keep your thoughts hidden and silent; I have detected listeners who can hear our thoughts. Khalen, you will arrive first. Act defeated as if you truly believe your clan was destroyed. Convince them that you are worn and tired."

I glanced down at my disheveled appearance. My slacks were wrinkled and stunk like the old man's cottage where I woke up. My shirt was torn and just as wrinkled. "That won't be too hard to pull off."

"Let your hair down," said Ian. "It makes you look more gruff and less like your well-groomed self."

I removed the thong securing my braid and allowed my hair to fall over my shoulders. My mother ran her fingers through it to make it look untamed. She stifled a laugh. "Lord," she said. "Skye won't know it's you." She pinched her nose. "Your smell is all wrong."

"Thanks," I replied.

"Ian, Aidan," said Case, "your job is to control the illusionists. Keep them out of our heads. I will wait for Khalen's cue."

"My cue?" I asked with genuine confusion.

"We'll work that out later," Case explained. In all my years, I had never seen such excitement in his eyes. He resembled a high school quarterback about to win the championship game. No one, other than myself, seemed the least bit concerned about the possible consequences of this harebrained scheme, not even my own mother.

Chapter 16

Sometimes, tragedies are blessings in disguise.

-Skye-

THAT NIGHT, I DREAMT OF Khalen and our upcoming union. The dream was shattered, however, when my door swung open. Traeger stepped into the room and released my shackles. His sentry tossed a pile of clothes on the bed.

"Get dressed," said Traeger. "I'm taking you to Sean." A smile tugged at his lips as if revealing a mischievous thought. "We will wait outside your door."

I rubbed my aching wrists and healed the wounds that encircled them. The clothes they left for me were simple: a pair of dark sweatpants and a white, long-sleeved pullover. They didn't bother with undergarments—go figure. Apparently, I was not meant to create a positive impression for this Sean character. My hair was in shambles. I combed my fingers through it, but the snarls were impossible to get through. I needed a stiff brush.

Traeger opened the door. "Come, we're ready for you."

I walked toward him. "Your taste in clothing has changed somewhat since the last time we met," I said, pulling at the baggy shirt and pants.

He showed me a smug smile, clearly amused by my predicament. "It suits you," he said.

His obvious slam to my ego had little effect. I simply smiled back at him. "It does, thank you. They're very comfortable."

"Hmm, I'm sure," he said, grabbing my arm.

He sat next to me in the car, while his sentry took the front seat. Traeger leaned over and whispered in my ear. "You would be wise to keep your sarcasm in check, my dear. Sean is not as gracious with women as I am." He sat back and smiled.

"Is that what you call it?" I said. "Gracious meant something entirely different when I first learned of the word."

He shook my arm, leaving bruises. "You're still alive, aren't you?" he growled, irritated.

His gist came through loud and clear. Sean wanted me dead. It would take nothing to persuade him to do it quickly. Perhaps Traeger was counting on that. I decided to change the subject. "Why did you come to Case for training?" I asked.

His expression changed to one of hurt. "I believed if we understood one another, our clans could unite."

"No matter how vigorously you shake oil and water, it eventually separates," I said.

"Is that how you see our kind? Oil and water?"

"It is."

He huffed. "I see Shadows as pure-grain alcohol, and the Protected as herbs. Both are functional on their own, but together they make powerful medicine."

The look on his face convinced me that he was serious. "Interesting analogy. Do your cohorts feel the same?"

He frowned. "They do not." He wrung his hands together.

"And do you lead them, or do they lead you?"

"My clan is small in comparison to others. I can be overruled. It is best to stick with the masses until I am strong enough to take them over."

"And Case was one way to make you strong?"

"It did make me strong." He looked at me. "One day, you will see that I am the better choice over my brother."

I shook my head. "That won't happen."

He smiled. "We'll see. After today, you may be begging me to be your mate."

"I'd rather die," I said matter-of-factly.

"Oh, you won't die, my dear—far from it."

I frowned, clearly confused. "What does he want with me then?"

"Your blood."

My stomach roiled at the thought of being someone's meal. "And when Khalen comes for me then what?"

"He will be killed, just like the rest of his clan."

"What do you mean?"

"His camp is gone, burned to the ground, along with its inhabitants." The coldness in his voice chilled the air. I shivered. Something about his words felt false, but he believed what he said. The clan was alive, I could feel them. I played along, doing my best to look distraught.

He looked at me and smiled. "He is a weak leader, your Khalen. He failed you all."

"That is your belief," I said, "not my own."

He shrugged. "Suit yourself, my dear."

We sat in silence for some time, which lent me time to think. I kept my thoughts shielded this time. The Shadows, I had observed, were short-sighted thinkers, only keeping a few steps ahead. The Protected, on the other hand, were typically long-term thinkers, envisioning many days ahead. Case and Khalen had a plan, I was sure of it. I hoped I would be around to see it played out.

Traeger's cell phone rang. He answered it with a curt greeting.

I could hear a male's voice on the other end but could not make out the conversation. I had to get better at reading thoughts. It could be helpful at times like these.

"Understood. We are approximately ten minutes away." He paused and listened. "We'll see you then." He pressed a button on his phone then tapped the driver's seat. "Plans have changed. Take us to 510 Emerald Lane, instead."

The driver nodded, and then merged to the right lane. I could not read the exit number, nor did I recognize the landmarks. After several turns down narrow streets, we arrived at a black wrought iron gate. The driver punched in a string of numbers, and then waited for the long gate to slide open. He proceeded up a long, winding driveway toward a large stone house that was three stories tall. It looked like something out of a Hansel and Gretel tale.

Traeger's hand gripped my arm as the car came to a stop. It felt as if he were purposely trying to inflict me with bruises. After wrenching me out of the car, he escorted me to the front door where a pleasant-looking old man waited to greet us. His smile was genuine and inviting.

"Mr. Dunning," he addressed Traeger. "Welcome. Lord Sean is expecting you. He will be arriving shortly."

He gestured that we come inside then led us to a small room on the right. The house was cold, but the hearth was lit and in full flame. Candles provided the only light in the room, offering me little to see by.

Traeger shoved me down on a soft cloth love seat, and then sat beside me. His sentry stood behind us.

"May I pour you some tea?" the butler asked.

"Yes, two," said Traeger. "Thank you."

Traeger handed me a saucer with a steaming cup of tea. The pungent aroma of bergamot oil led me to believe it was Earl Grey. My first sip confirmed my senses. My stomach growled, having been deprived of food all morning.

The butler turned toward me. "May I fetch you something to eat, Madame?"

"No," Traeger answered for me. "The woman is fine."

The butler bowed slightly, turned and left the room.

"Are you planning to starve me to death?" I asked.

"I was ordered to offer you nothing but liquids."

"I see." The tea was hot and flavorful. I took my time sipping it, not really knowing when I would have another chance for such a luxury. I felt like a stray dog being traded for some science experiment.

A man entered the room, but he did so silently as if his feet never touched the ground. Only his cold presence caused me to turn and face him. "Traeger," he said, his voice soft and silky.

Traeger jumped, nearly spilling his tea. He stood and placed his cup and saucer on the tray next to the couch. "Sean, I didn't hear you come in."

"Yes," said Sean. "I like it that way." I felt his eyes turn on me. "Skye, so nice to see you again." His Scottish-Irish accent was soft, but evident. He took my hand in his and pulled me to my feet. All I could see was his shape and piercing ruby eyes. His smell was familiar; he was redolent of red cedar, no doubt from the closet that stored his clothes.

He gathered my tangled hair in his hands and brought it up to his nose. "Does she remain unclaimed?" he asked Traeger.

"She does," he said smugly.

"Impressive," said Sean. "I half-expected you to take this female into your ever-growing harem."

"I offer you first rights," he said.

"Hmm," Sean moaned. "She must be a real spitfire, eh? Too much for you to handle?"

Traeger waved a hand as if to dismiss Sean's comment. "I leave her to you." He started to leave. Sean blocked the doorway for a moment, and then stepped aside to allow Traeger passage.

"Traeger," Sean called. "Thank you for the prize." There was a smile in his voice. I could hear Traeger growl as he left the room.

Sean turned his attention back to me. "Well now, here we are. I see Traeger spent no time preparing you for me." Again, he touched my hair and pulled at my loose clothing. "Charming."

"I know you want me dead, Sean, so be done with it," I blurted, trying to hide the fear from my voice.

"Spitfire, indeed," he said. "The Protected must be lenient with their women, for sure." He grabbed my bruised arm and shook it. " Whereas I am not." His face was inches from mine. The heat of his breath moistened my forehead. "Come," he said. "I will not have you in this pitiful condition."

He ushered me up two flights of stairs, and then down

a long hallway. He opened a door on the left and a woman jumped with surprise.

"Sean, I was not expecting you." Her voice was familiar.

"That is a failing on your part, woman. You should always expect me." He shoved me into the room. "Clean her up, and then bring her to my chamber. Make sure she has shoes on her feet. You have one hour."

The door slammed shut. "Well, well, what do we have here?" the woman said. Again, her voice was someone I knew.

"Kiara?"

"Yes, Skye, it's me. What are you doing here?"

"Traeger brought me."

Kiara snorted. "Well, come on, we haven't much time."

She allowed me the privacy to shower on my own, but spared me the simple pleasure of dressing myself. I raised my arms as a pale blue dress was draped over my head. It tapered to the waist and flared out to my mid calf. She tried to slip a pair of stockings on my legs, but I refused.

"Skye, please. Don't be difficult. He wants you to have shoes."

"Then he can do the deed himself," I said.

"Suit yourself," she said, shaking her head. "Stupid girl." She started brushing my hair. "How did they take you from Khalen?" She brushed it the correct way, starting at the bottom and slowly working her way up to the roots. I noticed the bite marks marring her wrists. One was recent. It looked like she had been scored with a dull crescent-shaped cookie cutter—Sean's incisors, no doubt. Why he and his clan had taken to drinking another's blood was briefly explained to me, but right now, I could not recall what was said.

"I'm not sure," I said, answering her question. "I

remember the car accident and nothing else." I wrapped my hand around her wrist and healed her wound. I then healed her other wrist.

"That is quite a gift you have, Skye. I'm sure you will be a valuable addition to Sean's clan."

"I am not an addition," I assured her. "I am a temporary nuisance that he will soon grow tired of."

Kiara turned me to face her. "Listen, Skye. If you want to live, you must do as Sean and his minions ask of you. They are not kind, nor are they understanding of any female with an attitude."

I shook my head. "What happened to you, Kiara? You are not a Shadow. How did you end up here?"

Kiara told me about Traeger and how he seduced her into believing that she was special. "I am not me, anymore. I am something else." There was a sadness in her voice. "I am a monster at the command of a giant beast with no heart and no room for regrets."

"No one owns you, Kiara, unless you give them power to do so."

She laughed. "When they are done with you, sweet girl, you will sing a different tune." She put the brush down and helped me to stand. "Please wear the shoes, Skye."

"No."

She sighed. "Come on then. Sean waits for you."

Chapter 17

The weather varies as does the tide, ever constant with subtle change. To dance with it is a gift we often take for granted.

~ S k y e ~

SEAN LOOKED DOWN AT MY FEET. "Where are her shoes?"

"My Lord," Kiara stuttered, with a trepidation that was surely out of her former character. "She refused to wear them." Her voice shook with fear.

Sean stood and walked toward us. I could hear Kiara whimper. "I would think," he told her, "that with all your gifts you possess, you could convince her to obey my one simple command."

"I did not want to mar her for you, my Lord." She lowered her eyes and her head.

"It was my choice not to wear them, I said. "If you feel the need to punish someone, let it be me."

His hand gripped my throat with such force, I felt the vertebrae pop. I didn't have time to gasp. I broke his grip with my shield and pushed him back, surprising even myself.

His eyes glowed bright red. My legs collapsed beneath me as he approached. I couldn't move. He looked over at Kiara. "I will deal with you later," he growled.

She hurried out of the room. Sean's attention returned to me. I willed my shield up, but it was weak compared to his debilitating hold on me. He reached for my hand and brought my wrist to his mouth. His sharpened incisors tore into my flesh. My blood flowed in ribbons down my arm as he drank his fill. His saliva felt like acid in my veins. Drawing in my strength, I pulled my arm away from him and stood. I heard him growl deep in his sticky throat.

"I have marked you," he said. "You are mine now."

I covered my wrist and healed the wounds. "I belong to Khalen Dunning," I said, avoiding his eyes.

He reached over and grabbed my wrist. His marks were gone. "The legend is true," he said, "and, you are unclaimed."

"Khalen has claimed me. I belong to him."

"No, the union has not taken place." He reached out and touched my belly. "You will be the mother of our race. I will make you mine."

I wasn't sure how much blood he had taken from me, but my head felt light and dizzy. I had to stay focused. Who knew what this lunatic would try if I passed out.

"Your blood feels strong in my body."

"You're delusional," I said. "A sickness without a cause."

Again, he tried to bite my wrist. I yanked it away. His eyes captured my attention, and I looked away, knowing that was how he paralyzed me the first time.

"Skye," he said, drawing my attention. "Look at me."

I felt like an insect in a cage with a hungry spider, fighting against the web in which he tried to encase me. His hands gripped me harder this time. I couldn't shake them free. I tried using my shield but my body was weak.

"I want to taste you again." He sounded drunk. His grip loosened and I pulled my arm free and backed away from him. He stumbled toward me. I avoided staring into his eyes. He stumbled then fell, reaching out toward my foot. I backed up.

Skye, run, I heard Shanuk say. *Run*. I did, rushing out of the room and slamming the door behind me. I fumbled my way to the stairs and carefully made my way down them. The butler addressed me at the bottom step.

"Madame, can I help you?"

"I need some air," I gasped. "I need to go outside."

He took my hand and led me to the front door. I ran outside, burst through the partially-closed gate and kept going. I had no idea where I was or where I was heading. I just wanted to get away from that bloodsucking lunatic.

It was bright enough outside for me to see shapes, but the sun was already beginning its descent. I had no money or any way to contact Khalen, unless he was close enough to hear my thoughts. I continued to run down the street. I would have to find a secure place to hide, but where? My energy level was far too low. My head felt as if it were suspended on a thin string that was about to snap. I stopped running and leaned against a large cedar. I was out of breath and my world was spinning.

A car was coming. Part of me wanted to throw myself before it and beg for help, while the rational side of me reasoned that I would seem like a madwoman coming down from a long and steady high. The car slowed as it passed me; I sensed a human female inside. At first she intended to stop, but something about my face caused her to change her mind. I must look like something awful, I thought. I felt pale and cold. She continued driving by.

I walked, trying to stay out of obvious sight. On the left, there was a trail that led into the forest, probably a community nature walk. I decided to head toward it. If I was going to collapse, I wanted it to be in an area where I wouldn't be found. I needed time to recover. My sugar levels were dangerously low. What I needed was food, but with no money, finding sustenance would be difficult. Right now, I wanted to lie down and sleep.

I stayed off the trail and wandered into the thick of the woods. Not the best idea for a blind woman, but the only option I had. I spotted a fallen tree up ahead with what looked to be chanterelle mushrooms growing around it. Their lily-like shape and pale yellow color were distinctive. I tore a small piece off and tasted it to ensure myself they were not jack-o-lanterns, the poisonous chanterelle lookalikes. The subtle fruity aroma and peppery aftertaste on my tongue was a delightful confirmation.

I preferred to have my chanterelles sautéed, but seeing there was no pan or fire to be had, eating them raw was a palatable alternative. I indulged myself until I felt somewhat normal again. Still, I was very sleepy. The sun was falling over the edge of the hills, making it difficult to see much of anything. I curled up between the fallen tree and a few standing ones and allowed myself to drift asleep.

- K h a l e n -

A IDAN OFFERED ME HIS TRUCK, but I decided to drive Skye's vehicle, instead, gutless as it was. The stereo looked as if it were the factory original, analog knobs and all. I turned on the radio and a CD began to play. She had been listening to The Calling. Their song, *Wherever You Will Go*, began to play. The lyrics reflected my thoughts exactly.

If I had made her mine, I would be able to track her, find her, protect her. As it was, we were both blind. I had to be close enough to read her thoughts and she could be anywhere by now. Traeger had been wise not to bring her to a location of our knowing. The treaty was breached, trampled, and tossed to the wind now, and there was absolutely nothing stopping either side, Shadow or Protected, from treading on each other's land.

Things were about to get ugly. My rage was primed and dangerous now. I needed Shanuk's wisdom, his guidance in all this. Case was emotionally entangled in this web and I knew that his actions were questionable. He seemed very eager to begin this fight, and that confused me.

The last time we had to engage in such a battle was when the treaty was established two hundred years ago. Before that treaty was agreed upon, there were many deaths on both sides of the Spirian race, to the point where the largest clan consisted of twenty-three members. Spirian men were forced to take human wives, which reduced the chance of having gifted children. Spirian women, of course, cannot have children with human males.

Eve was human, but her union with my Spirian father offered her many of the Spirian benefits, such as slow aging, and mind-tapping capabilities. Giving birth to

Spirian children, however, was risky and often resulted in the mother's death. Why that happened was never understood, especially by me.

The fact that Skye had such strong Spirian traits led me to believe that her parents were both Spirian, but she didn't like talking about either of them for some reason. If they were Spirian, they may not have known it, or never joined a clan. That would have made them susceptible to many dangers, including illness. Skye mentioned that her entire family died from cancer, a common killer of Spirians who were left to live without the benefit of a clan.

Clan living not only provided protection, it enabled the members to re-energize their life force by being around one another. That constant hum of energy is often unbearable for most humans, which is why Sam and Karin had to leave. It was making them nauseous. Case had suggested that they return to Oregon for their own safety. Sam was eager to comply.

I had to admit, when they left, things became rather dull. Sam was quite a character and his wife was equally entertaining. It was easy to see why Skye had enjoyed their company so much. She was sad to see them leave, but understood the reason.

Skye was close, I could feel her as I took the turnoff for Seattle Center. Her thoughts were weak and incoherent, but present all the same. I called out to her, but there was no definite answer. I may have been too far for her to hear me. Her telepathic gifts were not strong yet. I needed to be much closer to her.

The narrow roads that led me to Sean's house left me with a claustrophobic feeling. I preferred more space, and not the confinement the city had to offer. To some, the closeness provided a sense of security and community. To me, it was suffocating.

I parked the Dakota on the street and walked up the long driveway. I didn't bother with the gate; I easily hopped over the top. It was only 9 feet high and my adrenaline needed some release.

I rang the bell and waited for the door to open. The look on the old butler's face was one of alarm and surprise. He glanced over at the closed gate and eyed me speculatively with large brown eyes.

"May I help you, Sir?"

"I'm here to see Sean. He's expecting me."

The butler looked up at me, gawking at my size. Bloodsuckers did not grow especially large, and few of them were over 6 feet tall. I'm sure I provided quite a sight to this frail old man of 5 feet.

"May I ask your name?"

"Khalen Dunning."

"Oh," he stepped aside, "please, Lord Dunning, come inside."

It had been a long time since I had been called Lord. It was an old-fashioned term that had been dropped many years ago. In Europe, the title was expected, but not so much in the Americas. Then again, Sean always had been stuck a century back. Even his home and clothing reflected it.

"The Master is at his other residence. I will inform him of your arrival." He led me to the tearoom where a cozy fire burned. I helped myself to a glass of brandy. The bloodsuckers were sick and demented in their practices but they had excellent taste.

Skye was not here, nor had she ever been. The butler had mentioned that Sean was at his other residence. I was unaware he had another one. When the butler returned to ask if I wanted tea or something to eat, I probed his thoughts and discovered the location of Sean's other home.

"I'm fine," I said, holding up my brandy. "I hope you don't mind."

The butler shook his head; the scant layer of white hair that covered it stayed firm to his scalp with the help of ample amounts of gel. "Of course not, Sir. Master Sean will be arriving in ten minutes."

"Good to know, thank you." I wanted to tell Case to scope out the other residence, but did not want to risk being eavesdropped on by a local listener. This clan was littered with them.

"Khalen?" Kiara's voice came from behind. I turned to find her standing at the bottom of the circular staircase. Her eyes were red and she had lost much of her natural color. The dark burgundy dress she wore made her look washed out and gray. I thought Case had taken her life, and apparently, so did he.

I walked toward her. "Kiara, what have you done?" I reached for her left arm and glanced down at her wrist. She had been marked by both Traeger and Sean. Claimed first by Traeger, no doubt.

"Everything you said was true," she said. "They take everything away—care, love, and even joy. Nothing is left but fear, pain, and the will to survive."

I frowned. "Why?" I shook my head. "Why did you allow them to take you, Kiara? You are of pure Spirian blood. Any Spirian high-blood male would have taken you as a mate."

She laughed. "Not you."

"We weren't a good match, Kiara, and you know that. I know you felt it. What we had for one another was lust, nothing more."

She looked down, and then away. Tears began to fill her eyes. "I felt more," she said, turning away from me.

"Case saw you in camp. Were you a part of its destruction?"

She sniffled then looked up at me. "Yes, under Sean's command."

I turned away from her and walked toward the tearoom. She grabbed my arm.

"Help me," she said.

"How? You belong to them now. There is nothing I can do."

"Take my life, Khalen. Do it now."

"No. I won't."

The front door opened and Sean walked inside. He saw Kiara take her hand off my arm and his eyes grew bright as rubies. "Why are you here, Kiara?"

"I thought I would wait for you here, my Lord." She fell to her knees and cried out in pain. The pleading look in her eyes was unbearable, though taking her life now would end badly for everyone, including me.

"Get up," Sean ordered her. "Return to Nick immediately and inform him that your previous punishment was not effective. Tell him to triple it, and do it downstairs. I don't want to hear your screams."

Again, she looked at me, which earned her another harsh reprimand. When she was able to stand, she ran down the hall. It was hard watching her get punished. I wanted to toss the bloodsucker against the wall and rip his head off, but coming between a man and his mate was way out of line. Sean would have his comeuppance soon enough.

"Khalen," he said, "So nice of you to come."

"Where is she?" I asked, not wanting to hear any more of his pompous small talk.

His arrogant laugh made my blood boil. "You don't waste time, do you, my friend?"

"No, I don't, and I am a far sight from being your friend." I drank the last of my brandy, partly to give my mind something else to think about other than killing the bloodsucker, and partly to calm my nerves.

"Let's just say she is no longer your concern."

"She is my mate!" I growled.

He carefully took the brandy snifter out of my hand. "Yes, well let's discuss that, shall we?" He led the way back to the tearoom, and then set the snifter down on the serving table. He gestured for me to sit on the couch while he sat across from me in a high-back chair.

"Khalen," he began, "we both know that the woman is unclaimed." His dark eyes began to glow. I looked away.

"The woman is mine, Sean. Tell me where she is."

"Join us," he said, a smile raised on his face, "and the woman is yours."

"I won't join you, and she is already mine. I will find her with or without your help."

Sean laughed. "Khalen, dear boy. Your clan is dead, including your father and mother. The only family you have left is Traeger, and God knows he can't lead a clan. He's too busy claiming every halfling with two legs."

I felt the hum in the room, and Sean's minions gathering. I stood and poured myself another brandy. "We both know how war ends between our clans, Sean. Is that really what you want?"

"War? Are you planning to take on my lot singlehandedly, dear boy?" He stood and walked out of the tearoom. Standing in the foyer were nearly twenty of

Sean's clan. If Case had a plan, he better make good of it quick. The hum in the room grew louder.

I stayed in the tearoom and faced the dark, red-eyed lot before me. More of them gathered outside. I felt Case, Ian, and Aidan. They stayed in the shadows where they wouldn't be detected. I suddenly felt like a lion trapped in a cage of hungry hyenas. Sean's clan had grown considerably. He must have joined forces with the neighboring clans.

I wondered if I had dropped Sean where he stood, would the others attack or stand down?

Wait, Shanuk's voice rang in my head. *He will weaken you too much.*

The minions in the foyer shimmied and blurred. Ian and Aidan were breaking through the illusion. Sean's numbers were not that great, so his illusion created more of a threat than there really was.

He stepped toward me. His cold hand traced a line down my arm. I grabbed his wrist, twisted it and brought him down to his knees. My anger was nearing its tolerance and his touch was a nudge in the danger zone.

He smiled as he gave into the pain. "Your Shadow side is showing," he sneered.

I twisted his wrist further, wanting to see the pain on his face. He wasn't going to show it. "Tell me where she is."

"Her blood is sweet," he said, his eyes distant in thought, "intoxicating."

When my intention shifted to breaking his arm, two of the sentries pulled me away from him. I shoved them backward, my anger rising beyond my control. Glasses and bottles started flying off the shelves toward Sean, powered by my thoughts. He easily flung them away, laughing.

Gain control of yourself, Shanuk warned. *They are trying to turn you. Remember who you are.*

I forced my thoughts to calm down, to think more like a leader and not some riled teen in a schoolyard in the midst of thugs. After my third deep breath, my anger subsided and my mind was starting to clear.

"I will not join you," I said, "and you refuse to give me Skye. Where does that leave us?"

Sean kicked the broken glass away from his feet and then met my eyes. "It leaves you with two choices, dear boy. Seeing you no longer have a clan of your own, and I have the only thing you want, you can either join us, or die."

There was a commotion outside that drew his attention. Case was making his way toward the house, making quick work of anyone who tried to stop him. He let himself in and approached us. His eyes were black obsidian. To touch him now would be like touching a bolt of lightning, as the poor blokes outside likely realized.

The look on Sean's face was a cross between surprise and doubt. Sean looked over at the twins standing in the foyer. They both shook their heads, confirming that Case was not an illusion.

"I saw you die," said Sean.

"You saw nothing," Case countered. "We simply allowed you to see what you wanted to see. Our clan is alive and well, I assure you."

I wasn't sure why Case had revealed that information, but I didn't doubt his wisdom. He had survived these wars for over a century. I was too young to remember how the other one ended.

Sean's expression betrayed a hint of concern, but

upheld a confident facade. "The Shadows are strong, Case, much stronger than your feeble clan of halflings. If war is what you are suggesting, you will lose."

"We will take what is ours," said Case. "If a Shadow breaches our previous treaty, we will kill him or her without council."

"The woman is not yours," said Sean. "She is unclaimed. Since she is currently in my possession, that makes her mine for now."

"You don't know where she is, do you?" Case said. It had to have been a guess, since Sean's thoughts had been unreadable.

I suddenly glimpsed an image of a thick, cold forest. Beads of sweat glistened against my forehead. I felt weak and uncomfortably warm. Wherever Skye was, she was sick and in need of help. Case must have known that before he came in.

"Enough of this," I said. "Treaty or no, I will protect what is ours, without hesitation. The Spirian rules will be kept. No one shall be claimed unless there is mutual consent. Women will be given a choice."

"That is your law, Khalen, not ours," spat Sean.

I met his cold red stare. "No," I roared. "It is the Spirian law. Shadows are not exempt, nor have they ever been."

I didn't want to waste time with all this, not when Skye needed help.

"And if we don't comply?" asked Sean. He looked at my father, and then at Ian and Aidan who were holding his horde in a misty illusion. Sean was on his own and sadly outnumbered. He was formidable, but not stupid. He would not stand in our way—not now.

"Your mates will die," I assured him. Then I turned

to leave. To take the life of a halfling was nothing for me, though I didn't relish the thought. I knew, in my heart, it had to be done. These women were mere shells of what they once were. The Shadows had taken human women as if they were candy, turning them into something they never wanted to be.

Case followed me out of the room. When we stepped outside, the minions offered us a wide berth. Ian and Aidan joined us as we reached the cars we had parked on the street.

"She's in trouble," I said. "I need to find her."

"I know," said Case, "but how? She is too far away to read her mind clearly and we don't know what direction to take."

"I think I do," I said. "Follow me."

I drove toward Sean's other residence, keeping my mind open and sharp. If she were near, I would hear her and feel her. I stopped at a footpath leading into a thick patch of woods. I parked the car and walked toward the path.

"Yes," said Case. "This is it."

As we ran down the path, the feeling became stronger. My knees felt weak, my chest heavy and warm. In my mind, I saw a fallen tree with yellow mushrooms all around it. Case must have seen it as well. He scanned the area.

"Reach out," he told me. "You can find her."

Like sonar, I projected my energy outward, turning slowly until I felt a strong draw. "This way," I said, running deeper into the woods. The floor was thick with fallen branches and thick brush, but I trudged through it, ignoring the pain in my legs as they endured the bruising bites of sharp branches and thorny vines. In the distance, I saw the fallen tree and yellow mushrooms. Skye was nowhere in sight. I continued to move forward.

Then I spotted her blonde locks, barely visible, among the fallen leaves. She had nestled herself along the backside of the fallen log to remain out of sight. I brushed the damp hair from her face, hot and flush with fever.

"God, she's burning up," I said, lifting her into my arms. "Let's bring her to the center." Case led the way back to the cars.

Ian and Aidan held the door open as we approached. I laid Skye down on the back seat of the Dakota, and then crawled in next to her, placing her head on my lap. I tossed the keys to Case who was getting into the driver's seat.

"We're taking her to the center," he told Aidan. "Return to camp. Tell everyone to be on alert. I have a feeling all hell is about to break loose."

"It already has," I grumbled, lifting Skye's hand to my lips. I traced the marks on her wrists where she tried to heal them. She must have been too weak to heal them completely. The scars were barely visible but present just the same. If it were possible, I would rid this planet of every one of those bloodsuckers, and all who served them. If I did, though, I would become a Shadow, just like the lot of them, and that would hardly serve our purpose.

Taking a life to protect another was one thing. Wiping out an entire clan was a self-serving notion born purely from hatred. If I saw them near Skye again, however, death would be inevitable. I kissed the scars that marred her wrist. She was shivering and damp.

"Turn the heat up, father."

Case turned the dial toward the thick red lines and then increased the flow. "That was a bold statement you made to Sean," he said. "Are you intending to keep your word?"

I met his eyes in the rearview mirror. "You know I am."

He smiled. "Shanuk said this day would come."

"The Shadows have been allowed to run ungoverned for far too long," I said, pushing down the anger that welled in my gut.

"You controlled yourself quite well back there," said Case. "I half-expected to find a line of corpses when I came through the door."

"You can thank Shanuk for that," I said.

-Traeger-

MY CELL PHONE VIBRATED AND began playing the distorted tones of a jazzy tune. I checked caller ID, and then pressed the answer key. "What is it, Sean? Is the fiery lass giving you some grief?"

"Where is she?" His voice seethed on the other end. "Did you take her?"

My face grew numb, as if a blizzard had just whipped across it. "Take her? What are you talking about?"

"The female is gone. She's blind and couldn't have gone far. My minions have combed the area and there is no trace of her. My listeners cannot even pick up any calls of distress from her."

"Did you drink from her?"

"Of course, you idiot. Don't you think I thought about that? I pick up nothing from her; it's as if a cloak has been draped around her."

"Khalen," I growled. "He's shielded her, I'm sure of it."

"Find her, Traeger, and bring her back."

"Bring her back yourself, Sean. I'm done doing your bidding."

"Traeger, you fool. You know what it means if they join."

"Then perhaps you should have kept her on a shorter leash, Sean. I have larger issues to consider right now."

"Like what?"

"My brother and Case."

"Their clan is weakened. I hardly see them as a threat to us. If our clans unite, we can easily take them down."

"You ignorantly underestimate their strength, Sean. I believe it is time to get Victor involved." The silence on the other end of the phone confirmed my belief that Victor, the Shadow leader of the Pacific Northwest, would act unpredictably. Bringing this situation to our regional leader was akin to hanging out our soiled sheets for all to see. We allowed this situation to get out of hand, and there would be hell to pay and then some.

"I fail to see why Victor would have an interest in this," Sean replied with hesitance. "Our clans are small in comparison to those in Oregon and Montana. Insignificant, really."

I gritted my teeth with impatience. "You underestimate the momentum of this problem, Sean. For God's sake, do you not feel our control slipping away? Khalen has issued a threat. He does not do so with hollow intent. He will follow through."

"Then we'll take him down. Unlike you, Traeger, I have not lost my nerve or my impulse to protect what is mine." There was a long pause. "Talk to him yourself. If he does have his precious Skye, he will be more interested in keeping her safe over his threat to trim our mates."

"We shall see," I growled then pressed the end button.

That damn female had changed everything, I thought. Before she came, Khalen had refused his place of full leadership, causing his father to oversee things. Now that Khalen had something to fight for, he would be ruthless in his ruling, I was sure. And with Case backing him, Khalen would be unstoppable.

Chapter 18

Pride is an anchor to the soul. In deep water, it is best to sever your pride or risk drowning.

I LAID SKYE DOWN ON THE exam table and began hooking her up to an IV with electrolytes. I dripped a homeopathic remedy of belladonna along her gums for the fever, and covered her with several blankets. When she finally stopped shivering, I removed her clothing and cleaned her with lukewarm water and a sponge. I wanted to bring her fever down slowly, without causing her body more stress.

Case stood by and offered assistance by fetching clean water, towels, and anything else that I asked for.

I added a few more drops of belladonna to her gums, brushed the hair from her forehead, and sighed. "Come on, Skye. Come back to me."

Case placed his hand on my shoulder. "She's strong, Son. She'll be all right."

"She is strong," I confirmed. "But right now, she is very weak. Her pulse is barely palpable. That bastard has a sick thirst for blood. It's a miracle she made it as far as she had."

"Go and get cleaned up. I will stay with her."

I looked down at my wet clothing, stained and torn from our trek through the woods. I was hesitant to leave her, but knew she would be out for quite some time until her body rehydrated. I pointed to another bag of electrolytes on the table. "If she runs low, give her another bag."

Case waved his hand at me. "Go, I'll take care of her."

I glanced back at Skye lying quietly on the exam table. Her blonde hair, still matted and littered with debris, cascaded off the table, nearly touching the floor. When I returned, I would have to brush that mess out and braid it for her before she woke. She despised being dirty and seeing her hair that way would make her feel uncomfortable.

"I'll be upstairs," I said. "Let me know if anything changes."

"My thoughts are open to you," Case said. "If she awakes, you'll know."

I had clean clothing in my office. I grabbed a few things and headed up to Skye's apartment where I could shower.

The door to her place was open. Aidan had cleaned it when he gathered the rest of her possessions. Perhaps he didn't latch the door completely when he left? My instincts were sharp. I felt a presence, but it wasn't human or Spirian. A creature, maybe?

Skye's scent lingered in the tiny space along with Maiyun's. I wondered what had happened to the dog. No one had seen her. If she was caught inside the car, she would be dead by now.

My heart felt heavy with the thought. Of all the dogs I

had encountered in my lifetime, she was one that I didn't mind being around. I found it hard to believe that she was gone. She was too smart to allow the Shadows to trick her. Unlike humans and Spirians, animals were not prone to illusions. They saw only the truth of things, nothing more. If she were alive, she would find her way back to us, somehow.

I discarded my dirty clothes, and headed for the shower. My stomach growled loudly. I hadn't eaten for several hours, but despite my body's protest, I was not really hungry. I just wanted to get back to Skye.

I rushed through the shower, and roughly shaved my face and brushed my teeth. I donned the clothes I had brought up with me, and tossed the old ones into a bag. I braided my hair and secured it with a strip of cloth.

A scratching sound under the bed caught my attention. Cautiously, I knelt down and peered beneath the old wood frame. Two brown eyes peered back at me, hazy and sunken with fear and neglect. A low growl sounded in her throat.

"Maiyun, it's all right, girl. Come out here." She didn't budge. When I reached out for her, she growled louder. "Hey, it's me. Relax."

How she managed to crawl under this bed frame was a mystery. It barely cleared one foot from the floor. I lifted the frame and called her out again. "Come on, Maiyun, this thing is heavy." I used my energy to keep the frame up as I reached under to grab her.

She scurried out from her hiding place and curled up in the corner of the room. Her fur was rumpled, dry, and her sunken body looked as if she hadn't had a decent meal for several days. I dropped the bed and walked over to her. "Hey, it's all right."

She released a low, tired growl, and then looked away. The side of her head was swollen and her face had a trickle of dried blood caked to the side of her ear and jowl. "Good God, what happened to you?" I reached out, ignoring her warnings and scratched the uninjured side of her head. Her eyes closed and she seemed to relax some. "Come on. Let's get you something to eat. I have some soup in the kitchen downstairs."

I grabbed my bag and called her to follow me. With hesitance, she stood and followed me out of the apartment.

I returned to the exam room to find Case with one hand on Skye's forehead and another on her shoulder. Her color was better, and her shivering had ceased. He had replaced the IV bag.

"Has she..."

Case shook his head. "Her thoughts are quiet and guarded. She must have been terrified."

Maiyun came around the corner and wagged her tail when she recognized the quiet form lying on the table. Even though it was against all her training, she raised her front legs up onto the table and nuzzled against Skye's throat. Gently, I guided her down. "Later, girl. Let's get you cleaned up first and fed, shall we?"

"Where was she?" Case asked.

"Cowering under the bed. Judging by the soot in her fur, she must have made it back to camp and found the place burned. She came to the only other place that offered comfort."

I led Maiyun back to the kitchen and offered her some leftover beef and barley soup. I then began the arduous task of cleaning her up. I decided the best idea was to take her back to the apartment and give her a proper bath.

I returned to Case. "I need to bathe her upstairs. I'll

be back shortly."

Case stood. "No, I'll take care of it. You stay with Skye." He took Maiyun's collar and led her from the room. Her reluctance to go was understandable; she didn't want to be taken from Skye.

"Go with Case," I said. We'll be here when you get back."

She obeyed with hesitance. I heard Case talk to her softly as he took her back to the apartment. He was even less of a dog man than I was, yet he showed honorable patience with Maiyun.

I turned my attention back to Skye, giving her a kiss on her forehead. The fever had subsided. She released a low moan. "Khalen?"

"I'm here, Skye. Open your eyes."

"I feel drunk," she said, "and weak."

"You need food. Can you drink something for me?"

She frowned then slowly tried to sit. "Stay down for now. I'll be back to help you."

I came back with a glass of cranberry juice. Her eyes were closed again. I set the juice on the table and gently shook her. "Skye, wake up, love."

Her eyes opened again, and she frowned. "I want to sit. My head is pounding."

I lifted the upper half of the exam table, and propped her up with pillows. She groaned and rubbed her temples.

I handed her the glass of juice. "Here, drink this. It will help. Sip it slowly."

Her hand shook as she took her first sip. "What happened?" she asked.

"How much do you remember?"

She took another sip and reflected on her memories as if none of it made sense to her. "After the accident, I woke up in a strange house. I tried to find my way out but it was too dark and unfamiliar."

She told me how Traeger tried to claim her but couldn't perform due to her cruel ridicule of his physique and lack of finesse. She seemed embarrassed by her actions, but grateful for the knowledge her late husband left her with all the same. She then talked about Sean, and Kiara.

"He drank my blood," she said, shaking her head as if trying to purge the awful memory from her mind. "It was crazy. The more he drank, the more intoxicated he became. He finally reached a point where he couldn't tell if I was there or not. I was able to run out of the house and down the street. After that, I remember bits and pieces. I was so hungry and weak. All I wanted to do was sleep."

"We found you in the woods, cold, shivering and damp," I explained. "Sean must have taken a lot of your blood. You were extremely dehydrated."

"He was trying to mark me as his but I healed the wounds." She touched her wrists and frowned. "Hmm," she said. "I didn't do a very thorough job of it."

I removed her hand from her wrists. "Later, my love. Right now, you need to rebuild your strength."

I heard the front door chime open. "I know someone who will love to see you."

Maiyun trotted into the room and eagerly placed her damp front paws on the table. She licked and nuzzled Skye, making her laugh with delight. It was like watching a playful puppy lavishing love over a giggling little girl.

I took the spilling juice from her hand. Seeing the two of them together, I would never know that each of them were in the midst of recovery. Every ounce of their energy was instantly restored upon their reunion. Maiyun's tail wagged so violently that I had to move things out of her way before she knocked them over.

Case walked around the corner. "Nice to have you back, Skye."

She beamed at him, her eyes sparkling with bits of silver. "Case." She reached out for him. He gripped her hand, and then leaned over to offer a hug. Maiyun laid her head on Skye's thigh. Her rear legs were shaking from weakness and excitement.

"Come on, Maiyun. Let's get you some more food." I urged her down and led her into the kitchen for another meal. I found some cooked lamb, potatoes and eggs in the fridge. I mixed them all up in a bowl and offered it to her. She didn't waste time.

I went to my office and took my sweater off the hanger behind my door. It would look more like a dress on Skye, I was certain. It was all the clothing I had for her. I tossed the blue dress she had on in the waste bin.

When I returned to the room, I found her and Case in a quiet discussion. The exertion from her reunion with Maiyun had caused her color to pale a bit. I touched her hands. They were damp and cold. "How are you feeling?"

She smiled. "Always the doctor," she mused. "I'm fine, just hungry and weak."

I pulled the sweater over her head and guided her arms through the sleeves. "I'm taking you home." Then I remembered we no longer had a home. It had been burned to the ground.

She must have noticed my angered expression and tapped my thoughts. "Burned?" she asked. "How? Why?" Her hand covered her mouth as if an image just clarified the horror of it all. "Oh God. The clan—"

"They're all right," I said, hugging her close to my chest and cradling her head. "They're staying at Caleb's until we can rebuild."

"Take her to the Union house, son. It's stocked with food and has been made ready for you," said Case. "Eve is on her way. She wants to see Skye."

Maiyun had returned to offer Skye more attention. "She's injured," Skye observed. When she placed her hand over Maiyun's jaw, I gently removed it.

"Skye, please. You are not strong enough yet. Her injuries can wait."

She rolled her eyes. "Sorry, girl. You'll just have to suffer until my doctor releases me from perpetual rest."

The front door opened, and all three of us stiffened. We could feel the visitor was not Eve. "Stay here," I told her, adding emphasis with my eyes. She smiled up at me in return, stubborn to the end.

Case reached Traeger before me. "This is not neutral ground, Traeger, and you are no longer welcome among us," Case warned.

Traeger's eyes narrowed. "The treaty no longer exists. I was told that Khalen has threatened the lives of our mates."

I met his cold stare. "You heard correctly," I said. Case positioned himself between me and my brother. The hum in the room increased, along with my anger.

"You have no right, brother, to force your beliefs down our throats." Traeger clenched his fists and I could feel his stinging blows on the periphery of my shield. I easily shunted them aside.

"They are not my beliefs, Traeger. That is the Spirian law, one set by God Himself. I have merely proposed that we uphold that law and stop acting like careless anarchists."

Traeger tried to come closer to me but Case held him

back.

Traeger growled. "If God wants to enforce such a law, leave it to Him to do so."

Case interjected, "You weaken your own race by taking so many ungifted mates, Traeger. Your clan has few gifted members, and even they are weak. I assume that is why you had to join forces with Sean. Think about the implications of your actions, Traeger. Do you really believe that Sean will not take you down soon enough? If you are as wise as I believe you are, you would strengthen your clan. Choose your most gifted mate, and release the others to other males of your clan. That is your best option." Case shifted his eyes to Khalen. "I back my son's decision on this and will support his efforts."

Traeger's jaw tightened and flexed. "Leaving me with only one mate will do little to change the strength of my clan. The other males in my clan are worthless and you know it. Giving them a mate of worth is a waste of good female flesh. I'm sure you understand what your threat means." His voice, aimed at me, was deep and laced with vengeance. It was clear he did not hold the same respect toward me as he did my father. That would have to change.

"We do," I said. "Unfortunately, both sides will lose."

"You will lose, brother." Traeger's eyes shifted to something behind me. I turned to see Skye walking down the hall. I placed my arm out to keep her behind me.

"You can't protect her forever."

"He won't have to," said Skye. "You are not a threat to me or to our clan, Traeger. You have your own clan to lead; you best concentrate on finding order in it, or risk losing everything."

"Brave and bold words you speak from behind the shield of your leaders, woman."

Skye tried to find her way around my arm, but I held firm. "You have said what you wanted to say, Traeger, now leave and never return."

"Oh, I will return, brother. On that you can certainly depend." After staring long and hard at Skye, he gave Case a parting glance, being careful to remove the warning from his hazel eyes. The respect was evident.

Case focused on the man as he closed the door. "This is getting messy," he said. "We need to unite the clans and increase our numbers."

I nodded in agreement. "I will no longer accept the Shadows' lax attitude toward our laws," I warned.

Case pursed his lips. "Many lives will be lost."

"I see no other way, Father."

Case breathed deep and shook his head. "Nor do I, Son, nor do I."

Skye leaned against the wall, her legs beginning to buckle. I caught her arm. "Did I not ask you to stay put?" I lifted her up and carried her to the lobby then set her down in a chair.

"I don't like being told what to do," she said.

Case said nothing, but his expression clearly displayed the relief of knowing she was my problem to deal with and not his.

"Skye, it is imperative that you obey me not only as your mate, but as your clan leader. Understood?"

"Obey?" she said. "Like a dog?"

"No," I countered. "Like a female who respects the wishes of her mate."

"And will you also obey my wishes?" Her brow was arched to emphasize the power of her inquiry.

"If your commands are for my safety or the safety of others, yes, I will obey."

She frowned. "Good enough." She brought her hands to her temples and started to rub them. I knew this conversation was not over in her mind, but she lacked the energy to continue right now.

"Would you like to lie down until Eve gets here?" I asked.

She nodded. I lifted her into my arms and carried her to her treatment room where it was dark and comfortable. I laid her down, and then covered her with the spare blanket she kept folded under her table. I gave her a pillow, and then kissed her gently on the forehead. "Sleep now. I'll wake you when Eve arrives."

She nodded and closed her eyes. Maiyun curled up on the floor beside her. I closed the door and returned to the lobby where Case was waiting. He looked deep in thought. I sat down beside him.

I remained silent, studying his expression, which fluctuated between anger, sadness and concern. He was thinking about Shanuk. I saw visions of war nearly one-hundred years ago. Shanuk looked much younger back then. He fought with such control, and fatal accuracy. No energy was wasted with injury. With each killing, he kept his emotions in check, protecting his soul. Case was sharing this vision with me on purpose, almost pushing the images into my mind and linking their significance.

"When you take a life, Khalen, you cannot give up any part of your own," he said. "The Shadows will use that weakness against you, offering their pawns to rob your strength. When you are too spent to fight, they will take you down."

"How did he do it, father, take a life with no emotion?"

"He separated himself from his gift. You must remove your need for anger to spark your gift."

I laughed. "A gift, or a curse?"

"That depends on how it is used. When a father punishes his son, he does it with love in his heart and leaves anger out of it. Use your gift to honor the love of our Holy Father and not so much to punish those who dishonor the law."

I twisted my hands together, fighting the side of me that still felt the shadows in my soul. "How does taking a life honor the Father?"

"When a lion kills his prey, does he do so with guilt in his heart?"

"I am not a lion, nor are the Shadows my prey."

Case smiled. "Very well then, when a mother bear kills the lion for threatening her cubs, is she remorseful?"

I found his logic disturbing, yet there was a thread of truth to it. "Anger runs deep in my veins. When invoked, it almost becomes impossible to tame."

"Yes," said Case, placing his hands over mine to still them. "That is the gateway the Shadows are counting on opening in you. Purge that anger from your soul and fill it with light. Always remember the light. It will guide you out of the darkest of places."

I nodded, needing to ponder that for a while. "I wish Shanuk were here."

Case gestured to the surrounding air. "He is all around us, Son. All you need to do is call his name."

We sat quietly together until I remembered how Kiara had asked me to end her life. I wanted to release her from her binds, but my instincts warned me to stay out of it. "Kiara is alive," I said.

Case seemed surprised with the information. "Is she now?"

"Only her illusion was killed, no doubt with many

others."

Case shook his head. "Damn illusionists."

"She begged me to take her life."

He looked at me questioningly. "And?"

"I said no."

"She is a purebred, Khalen. Her offspring will strengthen their numbers."

"She is good, Father, not a Shadow. Traeger tricked her and then sold her to Sean. What if her offspring inherits her goodness?"

"What if they don't?"

I looked off in the distance, thinking about my brother and the number of women he had destroyed. "Our numbers dwindle. Spirians are all but extinct. It seems pointless to take the life of one when there is a chance to increase our numbers."

"Agreed," he said. "But we have become careless in our attempts to increase our numbers. We have taken inappropriate mates and have weakened the Spirian blood. To grow our numbers, we must produce pure-blooded offspring. It is the only way."

"Kiara is good," I reminded him.

"She has made her choice, Khalen."

"Then we will take her children and raise them as Protected."

Case knew that I spoke from pure emotion. I couldn't take the children any more than God could force us to follow him. The choice had to be ours and ours alone.

"End her misery, Khalen."

I stood and crossed the room. "This is an unbearable burden to bear."

"It is the burden of a leader, and one for which you are well suited."

Eve pulled up in their white Volvo. When she walked into the Center, she glanced at Case, and then at me. "Bad timing?"

Case laughed. "Your arrival is never bad timing, my dear." He pulled her into him for a crushing hug. She returned his fervor of affection, and then turned to me. I hugged her and breathed in her comforting scent of lilac and sandalwood.

"Mother," I said against the top of her head.

"I understand that it ended well?"

"Your son laid the gauntlet down and shocked the hell out of the Shadows."

A smile stretched across her face. "Did you now? Good on you, I say. It's about time those Shadows have someone to answer to."

"Good or no," said Khalen. "The loss will be great."

She rubbed my arm. "Sometimes you must prune many branches to save the tree."

"Now you sound like Shanuk," I said with a smile.

She shrugged and turned away. "He said it once, many years ago. I can't remember why." She looked around, and then spun to face me. "Where is my daughter?"

"Sleeping," I said. Her endearing term for my future mate warmed my soul. It sounded good on her lips. "She is worn out."

Eve frowned. "Is she all right?"

"Yes, just tired and weak. Sean nearly sucked her dry. He would have finished the job if she hadn't pulled away from him," I explained.

"Can I see her?"

I nodded then led the way to Skye's room. I opened the door slowly as not to disturb her. Maiyun jumped up and growled.

"It's all right, girl," I said.

Eve leaned over and checked Skye's forehead. "Lord, she's warm."

I checked as well then smiled. Her skin was dry and not hot with fever. "She's always this warm when she sleeps." As I expected, her feet were hanging out of the covers.

Skye opened her eyes and smiled when she recognized Eve. "Hi," she said, her voice groggy with sleep, and then tried to sit up. I offered some assistance. Skye rubbed her eyes.

"How are you feeling?" Eve asked.

"Better now that I've had some rest." She started to stand. I grabbed her arm, still not confident in her level of strength. The two women hugged each other.

"I heard that you had a bit of excitement during my absence?" said Skye.

"Just a bit," my mum replied.

"Come," I said. "Let's get you into the lobby where you can see a little better."

Eve grabbed Skye's arm and I allowed her to lead her out to the lobby.

"I'm taking her to the Union home," I said.

Eve beamed us both a smile. "That's wonderful. I'm sure you'll be much more comfortable there. I have supplies stashed in the shed."

"I'm afraid our celebration will have to wait, Mother."

"Oh, no bother. We will have it when the time is right."

Case took my arm and led me aside. "Do not wait for the celebration to join with her, son."

"Yes, I understand," I assured him. "As soon as she is strong enough, I will make her my own."

"Excellent, my boy. May God bless you both with many children." He slapped me on the back and laughed then placed his arm around Eve. "Come, my mate. We have much to do, and Khalen is eager to bring Skye home."

Eve gave Skye and me one last hug then handed the car keys to Case. We watched them drive away before I lifted Skye into my arms and carried her out to the truck. Maiyun followed us out.

"I can walk, Sir," she said.

"You can also allow me to care for you. It is not an order, just a simple request." I added that last part in hopes of gaining her cooperation. I sat her in the truck, started the engine, and turned the heat on high. "I'll be right back. I just need to lock the place up."

"I'm not going anywhere."

I opened the back door for Maiyun then hurried to lock up the Center. When I came back, Skye smiled at me.

"It feels good to be back in my truck again," she said, scratching Maiyun under her chin.

"Don't get too used to it. My first order of business is to buy us another car."

She looked incredulous. "What's wrong with this one?"

"It's gutless, old, and smells like wet dog."

"I like it," she said flatly.

I shook my head. It was no use arguing with her. Before she got to know me, she was much easier to control with mock intimidation.

Chapter 19

The contradiction between a gift and a curse lingers within the division of good and evil.

-Skye-

KHALEN INSISTED ON CARRYING ME into the massive home that nestled along the shore of the Hood Canal. It was only 20 minutes west from the cottage I had rented last year. The large gray stones that formed the outer walls gave the place a castle-like feel. The plush reclining chair he lowered me into surrounded me like a soft leather pillow. I was ordered to stay put while he settled us in.

The living room, where I now sat, was flooded with full-spectrum lights. The polished wooden floors were rich with dark hues, playing nicely against the lighter colored rugs with light beige fringe. The walls displayed original oil paintings of what looked to be Indians and wolves. The kitchen off to the left was large enough to entertain a small army. He promised to show me the rest of the house later, after we ate. I could get used to this, I thought, staring out at the Hood Canal through large picture windows. I was tempted to wander outside, but Khalen made me promise to stay where I was.

Maiyun strode through the door behind him, gripping a bag by its handle with her teeth. "Take it to the kitchen, Maiyun," he told her.

She eagerly complied, and then came to offer me some affection. "Good girl," I said, scratching behind her soft ears. "Go on and help Khalen, now."

Maiyun rushed off to follow Khalen back outside. They came back with another load of bags. "Those weren't all in the truck," I said, as he made his way back to what I assumed was the bedroom.

"No, Eve placed them in the storage shed for us."

"Are we moving in for good?" I was very tempted to stand up and help them bring in the next load.

"For a while," he said over his shoulder. I watched as he and Maiyun went back outside. This time, they came back with bags of food and placed them in the kitchen.

When they left to get another load, I couldn't help myself. I had to at least put the food away—do something. Khalen came back, placed another load of bags on the counter, lifted me effortlessly into his arms, and then carried me back to the chair and plopped me down.

"Did I not ask you to stay here?"

"You did, but I'm fine, Khalen, please let me help. I'm feeling much better now."

His eyes narrowed. "Skye, for once, please do as I ask. It is a small request, not too difficult, and it would make me feel so much happier if you would oblige me."

It was not a demand, but a request—one that would make him happy. Well, he knew how to manipulate me,

I'd give him that. "Fine," I sighed. "If it makes you happy. I will oblige you, but I cannot help feeling rather useless."

He leaned down and planted a slow and lingering kiss on my lips. "You are definitely not useless. I just need you to build up your strength for what is to come." He raised his brows as if trying to pique my interest.

Part of me felt a wave of excitement, while the practical side of me cruelly splashed images of Derrick in my mind. I once promised him that there would be no other. He had laughed at that feeble promise, and I remember getting mad at him for it. He was right, though. Life was unpredictable, and to make such a promise was like spitting into the wind—it was likely to come right back at you as an insult.

"Did you happen to bring any wine?" I asked, as he began putting away the food. Maiyun was busy chowing down on the huge bowl of kibble he had poured for her.

He held up a bottle of Barolo. "Purchased from Giovanni Nardoni himself."

I had no idea what that meant, but I was sure it meant that the wine was good, and probably expensive. "Perfect," I said. "I'm parched."

Khalen picked out a glass from the cupboard, and then filled it with water. He carried it over to me. "Drink this, it's better for you right now."

"Khalen—"

He brought his hand up. "You'll have your wine, my love. I just need to let it breathe."

I drank the water. Its sweet, crisp flavor was refreshing and he was right. It was what my body most needed right now, apart from food. My stomach roared so loud that Maiyun looked up at me from her bowl.

Khalen brought over a cutting board loaded with

slices of cheese and fruit. "Here," he said, "this will tide you over until dinner is ready."

I arose from the chair, picked up my glass of water and cutting board, and then followed him to the kitchen. I set my things down on the counter and took a seat on the stool. "I'm still sitting," I said, smiling up at him.

His frown didn't soften. "I will have to do something about your stubbornness," he said, "and blatant disobedience."

"Yeah, well, good luck with that." I scoffed.

He looked up at me, and then continued to chop the tops off a bunch of carrots. "Luck will have nothing to do with it," he said. With another slam of his blade, he managed to sever the root of an innocent onion.

Suddenly, the sweet goat brie in my mouth tasted bitter. "I was lonely over there," I said, trying my best to seem unaffected by his anger. He was one of the few men who could ever intimidate me, next to Case and Shanuk.

He looked up at me as if to say that didn't matter, and then concentrated again on the onion under his blade.

I started to stand.

"Stay put," he growled. "I need you to rest and allow your body to recuperate."

I sat back down and nibbled on a slice of parmesan. I watched as he carefully decanted the Borolo into a beautiful crystal carafe, whose shape resembled that of an elegant swan. He then took out a bottle of Pinot Grigio from the fridge and twisted the cap open. He poured two glasses then slid one before me. "Thank you," I said with a smile.

"Wait," he said, grabbing his own glass. He then walked around the counter and stood before me. I had never realized his full strength until now. His body hummed with it and his woodsy scent was intoxicating. I looked up at him. His chest was twice the width of my own, and I was not a small woman by any measure. He pushed his glass toward me.

I lifted mine and gently pinged it against his. He bent down and softly pressed his lips to mine. "Tonight," he whispered, "I make you mine." The last part came out as a throaty growl. My stomach twisted with anticipation and perhaps a bit of fear. I swallowed hard, and then took a sip of my wine to remove the dryness in my throat.

He smiled. "This is the first time I have witnessed fear in you, my love."

I raised my chin, the way my mother always taught me to do when I wanted to appear strong and in control. "I'm not afraid."

This made him laugh. He tossed a carrot chunk over to Maiyun. The meat he had been cooking in a pan started to sizzle. He turned the colorful meat concoctions over, and then continued making the salad. The meat in the pan resembled pinwheels of red and white. They smelled like steak and gorgonzola cheese with some basil mixed in.

"What are we having?" I asked.

"Gorgonzola steak with sautéed mushrooms and artichoke hearts, poppy seed salad, and mum's dark molasses bread."

My stomach growled with anticipation. "Sounds fabulous." I finished my cheese and my last sip of wine. My fingers were no longer tingling and I was beginning to feel more human again. My hair was another matter. I combed my fingers through it, trying to remove the debris of leaves and twigs from its tangled masses.

Khalen turned the burner down then disappeared into

the bedroom. He returned with a brush. "Turn around," he said. He grabbed a towel from the counter and laid it onto the floor to catch the debris. Then, with gentle skill, he knelt down and started brushing the tips of my hair that hung down past the seat of the stool.

"I should just cut it off," I said.

"No, I like it long." He continued working his way up. His slow and caring strokes felt good against my back. "It's soft, yet strong, like fine silk."

"It's dirty and needs a good washing," I said.

"Later," he replied, standing so he could continue working toward my head. "Your showers are much too hot and it wouldn't be good for you right now. Trust me, you're going to need your strength for tonight."

I turned to face him. He smiled and turned me back around.

"I was married at one time, you know," I said. "It's really not that big of a deal." My words were meant to assure myself more than him.

"It will be much different, I assure you, my love." He finished brushing my hair, and then retreated back to the bedroom, taking the towel full of debris with him.

"In what way?" I asked, hoping to gain a firmer insight other than what Eve had revealed.

He came back and brushed a soft kiss across my head. "Soon enough, Skye."

I sighed, frustrated with the looming fear of not knowing what to expect. Khalen, on the other hand, was enjoying my anxiety way too much.

Chapter 20

*When fire unites with metal, a magical alchemy occurs, creating
an object of enduring strength.*

DINNER WAS FABULOUS, BUT IT paled in comparison
to the Borolo. Drinking that fine red juice was like
treating my taste buds to a symphony of flavor. The fruity
balance coated my tongue with a sweet zing, while the
spicy finish left a delightful tang in my throat.

Three hours later, the bottle of wine was spent, the
meal was consumed, and the sun had set. We conversed
well into the evening, laughing and turning serious again
when the focus drew back to the clan and its recent
misfortune.

Khalen ordered me to stay where I was as he cleaned
the kitchen. He then drew me a warm bath, not hot, and
poured me a glass of brandy, letting it warm slowly over
a gentle flame. He expertly removed my clothing then
guided me into the tub. I closed my eyes and sank deep
into the water. Worried that I might burn myself with the
brandy warmer, he removed the glass from over the flame,
extinguished the fire, and then set the brandy beside me

on the wide ledge of the tub. "Take your time," he said, kissing the top of my head.

He left to shower in the adjoining room. Since little steam escaped the doorway, I assumed his shower was lukewarm if not cold. I sat up and took a small sip of my warm brandy. It did much more to warm me up than the lukewarm bath water. I rinsed my hair under the tap, and then proceeded to dry off.

I noticed a small bottle of oil on the counter. I placed a drop onto my palm and rubbed my hands together. Aromas of rosewood, cedar wood, cypress and frankincense greeted me with familiarity. It was the essential oil blend that I called Calm Spirit. Khalen had mentioned many times how much he enjoyed it. I smoothed the oil over my skin, breathing in the relaxing fragrance. I added a little bit to my hair as well. It would make brushing it out easier.

Khalen had laid out a white silky wrap for me to wear. It smelled sweet, like tea roses, and felt delightful on my skin. The purple slippers he left for me were inviting, with soft and fuzzy uppers and pillowy soft soles, but I left them where they were and padded my way out to the living room with my brandy in hand.

Maiyun had just finished another bowl of food and lay comfortably by the sliding glass door. I placed my brandy on the table and sat beside her. Khalen had installed full-spectrum lights, but not enough to reveal the details of the walls and furniture. The view outside was too black for me to see, though I could hear the gentle lap of the water against rocks, frogs croaking, and what sounded like a seal with a hoarse throat in the distance.

I ran my hand through Maiyun's fur. It was soft and clean. I laid my head on her chest and closed my eyes. Her slow and rhythmic breathing shadowed the sound of her strong heartbeat.

I awoke sometime later to find Khalen sitting on the couch and smiling down at me, holding a snifter of brandy. Maiyun was still sound asleep. I carefully scooted out from under her heavy paw and sat next to Khalen on the couch.

"How long was I sleeping?" I asked, still a bit groggy.

He glanced up at the wall where I assumed was a clock. "About two hours."

My right hip ached from having to endure the hardwood floor for so long. The rug I had curled up on provided little cushioning. I rubbed my hip encouraging blood to the area.

"You smell great," he said, pulling me closer to him. He laughed. "Relax, Skye. You're stiff as a fence board."

Realizing that I had been holding my breath, I inhaled deeply. "Just a little nervous, I suppose."

"We can wait another day if it would help," he said, clearly disappointed with the idea.

"No," I said, shaking my head. "I want this. It's just been so long since I..."

He cradled me in his arms and brushed the damp hair from my face. "Yes, it's been some time for me as well." With one smooth movement, he picked me up in his arms and carried me into the bedroom. Several candles flickered against the wall and soft music played in the background—Beethoven's Moonlight Sonata. I swallowed back the lump in my throat, my face pressed against the smooth hard muscles of his chest.

He laid me down then gracefully rolled beside me. "You are so beautiful," he whispered, his fingers pulling at the ties that held my robe together. I reached up and untied the single belt that secured his robe. He shed the robe quickly and tossed it to the floor. The candles did little to illuminate his massive shape. To see him, I would have to use my hands.

He groaned as I traced the contours of his chest, abdomen and hips. He grabbed both my hands and held them above my head. "Your touch is going to drive me over the edge, my love. Tonight I need to stay in control."

He explored my body with his hands, making me gasp with anticipation and pleasure. His breath feathered over my skin, increasing in tempo and heat. Slowly he moved above me, his weight pressing down on my hips. I wanted to thoroughly immerse myself with him, but he took his time.

He pressed his mouth over mine, his breathing intense and laced with longing. His sweet tongue caressed mine, countering the sharp pain of his teeth against my lips. My eyes dilated.

I wanted to feel him completely. I wanted to draw him into my soul.

He brushed the hair from my face and feathered tender kisses over my mouth and forehead. I struggled to see his face but couldn't. His eyes began to glow like molten gold. As the pain intensified, I closed my eyes.

"Open your eyes, Skye," he said. "Stay focused on me."

I did, biting back the wave of pleasure and pain in the center of my belly. His eyes held mine captive. I cried out. Never had I felt so complete. The feeling was intense, yet my body craved more of him. He held me firm with his body, and his mesmerizing eyes. I tried to look away, but he demanded my attention. I felt my body opening to him in a way that I could never describe with words. I was hollow inside and he filled me completely.

He remained deep in my core and held himself there. I couldn't breathe. For a moment, I felt as if time were still. My heart seemed to swell and the pain in my belly was gripping until an explosion of heat filled me. His heartbeat synced with mine. I felt his own pain as he held his position.

A cry escaped my lips as tears ran down my face. He rolled over, pulling me with him. My hair cascaded over his chest and shoulders. The pain eased a bit, but the evidence of its apex remained. Every breath seemed to be an effort as he brought me down for another long kiss.

We relaxed against one another. Our breathing slowed and our hearts beat as one. "Now," he whispered. "You are mine." He wiped the sweat from his brow and pressed his dampened fingers against the underside of my left wrist.

It burned like acid against my skin. I tried to pull away but he held me firm. "Shh," he said. "It only lasts for a minute. It'll be over soon, my love. Be still."

When the burning subsided, he lifted his fingers from my wrist and collapsed with exhaustion beside me. Still he didn't let me go, crushing me to him as if I would disappear.

"It's never been like that," I said.

He brushed the hair from my face and cupped my cheek. "With Derrick?" he asked.

I closed my eyes and nodded.

"He was human, not Spirian." He gently guided my weary head down to his chest and cradled me until sleep consumed us both.

I WOKE UP TO FIND KHALEN on the deck in his robe, sipping a cup of coffee and staring down at the beach below. I wrapped my arms around his waist and hugged him. The pain in my belly gripped me like a lingering cramp.

"Good morning, Love," he said. I stood beside him and smiled at his focused interest. Maiyun was playing with the shore birds. I kept my hand on my belly, trying to ease the pain but not really wanting to relieve it all together.

He placed his hand over mine and smiled. "This pain, you cannot remove."

I frowned. "Not that I really want to, but why?"

"I have awoken something that has been sleeping in you for over 45 years. Your body is shifting in response. The pain will pass soon enough." He took my left hand, turned it over, and then pressed his warm lips over my wrist.

My eyes widened when I saw a unique design etched with surreal color in my skin. I didn't recognize the design, nor could I name the colors that it bore. I remembered the burning pain as he touched me there last night. "What is it?" I asked.

"My mark," he said. "It tells other males that you belong to me."

I rubbed the tender spot and marveled at the crispness of the raised design, unlike any tattoo I had ever seen. The details were lost to my eyes, but my fingers detected an intricate pattern of infinity with a patterned circle in the center. "What is it?"

He traced his finger over the pattern on my wrist. "Two dragons that represent our clan family. The subtle variations in the dragons' color and shape depict where the clan originated and its leader. The blue water dragon represents yin or female energy. The red fire dragon represents yang, or male energy. Neither of them rise above the other. They are equal."

I smiled.

"Yeah," he said, "I thought you would like that part. The yin and yang symbol is a universal representation of balance, the ebb and flow of opposites. The shape of the joined dragons forms the symbol of infinity, God, our Father—the beginning and end of all things.

"In the dragons' mouth is the Celtic knot that symbolizes symmetry. The image shows the infinite dance of life's balance. The dragons are dancing with one another, each flowing into the other's realm, respecting each other's space but joined in one continuous union.

"The symbol as a whole, represents a union of two souls bound by God for all eternity—an infinite dance of love and balance."

"Why dragons?" I asked. "It seems odd to associate something so sacred with frightening creatures."

An endearing laugh escaped his lips. "Dragons," he explained, "are mythical creatures that have symbolized everything from luck, protection, magic, and evil. In all cases, they are powerful, mysterious, and sadly misjudged. They can look fierce but harness the purest of hearts. They can kill with a single breath, or protect with a love that honors God. They are the epitome of yin and yang—the perfect reflection of the human spirit. I can remove it, if you prefer." His golden eyes searched mine.

"No," I said. "I like it there." I wrapped my arms around him and buried my face against his chest. "I feel as if a hundred different voices are screaming in my mind."

He chuckled. "Yes, you hear the clan. You are connected now through me. In time, you will learn to tune them out. My voice, however, you will not. Even if we are miles apart, I merely need to think your name and you will hear me as if I were right there next to you."

"Can you hear my thoughts as well?" I asked.

"Every one of them," he said, kissing the top of my head. "You wonder if the pain will be as intense as it was last night, every time we make love."

My face grew red. I did not want to look up at him. "Will it?" I asked.

"No. The first time is the worst."

I looked down at the mark on my wrist. I didn't remember seeing one similar to it on Eve's wrist.

"She is human," he said, reading my thoughts. "They cannot be marked."

I looked up at him. "Human?"

"Yes, there were very few Spirian women left and we were forced to take human mates to rebuild our kind." He took my hand and led me inside.

I sat at the breakfast counter while he poured me a cup of coffee. "What happened?"

He stirred in the cream, and then set the steaming cup before me before refreshing his own cup and joining me at the counter. "The Shadows infiltrated our camps and stole our women. Most of the females refused to give in to their ways and were killed. Those who were spared were used as breeders, and passed from one male to another like cattle. This is why their numbers outweigh our own."

I shuddered with the thought of being used as breeding stock. I allowed the coffee to soothe my thoughts and warm my throat. "Does Eve have children?"

Khalen shook his head. "No. She was pregnant once and nearly died giving birth to her son. It was then we realized that human women were not well suited to birthing Spirian offspring. If the child was mostly human, few complications arose, but if the child had gifts, the mother typically lost her life while giving birth. Case refused to impregnate her again."

I frowned. "Refused? How can he refuse?"

Khalen sipped his coffee, his eyes a golden green. His robe fell open at his chest and my previous hunger for him stirred. "Spirian women are always fertile. It is the male who determines when the woman becomes pregnant. We can even determine the sex of the child."

Again, my hand fell upon my aching belly. "Derrick and I tried for years. I wanted his child more than anything."

"He was human," said Khalen. "He could not impregnate a Spirian female."

"But his energy radiated like yours."

"Because of his closeness to you," he explained. "Like Eve, he took on certain Spirian traits, but he was not Spirian. Eve can read thoughts, but that is her only gift. The same holds true for Ember and her sisters. If your friends, Sam and Karin, could have stood the constant hum from the camp, they too, would have developed the power to read thoughts. Once they left camp for more than a month or so, that gift would dissolve."

"Is that why Ian won't take Jade as a mate? Because she is human?"

Khalen nodded then pressed his brows together as if in deep thought. "Ian and Aidan are illusionists and hold a high status in the clan. When they are ready to take a mate, it must be one that equals their status, which is difficult to find."

"But your father took a human mate. I don't understand."

"He did, and is unable to continue his line because of it. Our kind is endangered, Skye. We must take steps to ensure we survive or this world will be run by the

Shadows."

"My parents were not Spirians," I said. "They didn't have gifts."

Khalen stood and walked into the kitchen. He opened the refrigerator door and pulled out a package of sausage and a carton of eggs. "They may not have known. When Spirians live outside of a clan, they tend to die young and some never realize their potential." He took out a pan and began heating it before adding crumbles of sausage. "Your own gifts were sleeping until Shanuk came to your side. He drew you toward us, which enabled you to grow your skills and strengthen your inner spirit."

I remembered feeling empty and tired inside, as if a part of me had given up this life. Shanuk had restored my inner fire and my passion for survival. He, no doubt, played a role in the events that brought me to Belfair as well. "So, if Shanuk had not found me, what would have happened?"

He cracked some eggs in a bowl, added a few spices and milk then began beating the mixture until it became frothy. "Either the Shadows would have found you, or you would get sick and die."

My stomach twisted with the thought. I sipped my coffee in silence and concentrated on the pain gripping my gut. It felt as if my uterus was contracting, the way it did when I was a young teen. "I would like to have a son," I quietly said.

He smiled then looked up at the sliding glass door where Maiyun waited to be let in. Khalen willed the door open, waited for Maiyun to enter, and then closed it again. He made it look so easy. His attention returned to me. "Your first two will be girls, your third will be a boy."

"Only three?" I questioned, playfully.

His smile broadened as if enjoying this new power he had over me. "Many more than three," he said.

I felt doubtful, despite the claims he had made. I did not want to get my hopes up too high. On the surface, it felt as if the Father had given me a new lease on life. Deep inside, however, I felt as if I had fallen into my deepest fantasy, which could end with a single twitch.

Chapter 21

The blind are not spared the vivid beauty of this world; they simply see things on a different level.

I STROKED THE STRONG LINES OF my mate's chest and abdomen. "Khalen?"

"Hmm," he responded, his eyes closed and his expression content with the peace that follows passionate love.

"Is it possible to use our gifts in the midst of an illusion?"

He opened his eyes. "No."

"Why is that?" I moved my fingers lightly over his chest. He grabbed my hand and pulled it away with a groan.

"Honestly, Skye, your touch is going to kill me."

I would not get my answer from him until another round of passionate intimacy. As promised, the pain was not as harsh, but the intensity had not diminished one bit. In my wildest dreams, I had not imagined such intimacy being this fulfilling. I thought no one could compare to what I had with Derrick, but I was ignorantly wrong.

Khalen had a way of making me feel as if the entire world no longer existed. All that mattered was the way he felt inside me and how my soul sang with complete fulfillment. The more he loved me, the more my body craved him.

"You never answered my question," I reminded him, after he had some time to recover.

He looked at me with languid eyes and held both my hands in one of his. "These hands are lethal," he said, and then brought them up to his lips. "When we are in an illusion," he explained, "we cannot call upon the truth, the Father's power."

"But why?" I asked. "It doesn't make sense." I propped myself up on one elbow, my hair cascading around my shoulders. He played with the strands that rested upon his chest.

"Because," he sighed with frustration, "we are under the influence of an illusionist. They make us see what they want us to believe. Do you think they would allow us to use our gifts in their own illusion?"

"There must be some way to protect ourselves," I said. "I cannot believe that we become nothing but victims in the spell of an illusion."

I traced a line down his chest toward his stomach. He grabbed my hand and brought it to his lips, taking a deep breath and squeezing my hand tightly. "God, woman. Can you not control your own power?" It sounded more like a growl than a question.

We didn't accomplish much that day, or most of the evening, either. The dinner he planned to make did not happen, and we barely left the bed for longer than three minutes. I was famished, but not for food. I wanted more of him. Judging by his performance, I was certain he felt the same way about me. Though he complained before each round, he didn't seem too upset with the outcome.

He rolled out of bed, hitting the floor with a thud. I leaned over to check his condition. "Are you okay?" I asked.

He raised his hand. "I'm fine." He stood and donned a pair of sweatpants before leaving the room. I decided now would be a good time to clean myself up. I padded my way to the bathroom and rinsed myself off with a cool cloth. By the time I returned to bed, Khalen had walked in with a tray of fruit and cheese and two glasses of wine. I smiled as my stomach growled with approval.

"I think I know how your husband died," he said, crawling back into bed beside me.

"You do?" I asked, thinking he must have read my mind.

"Yes. Overexertion."

I frowned. "No, he died of cancer."

Khalen laughed. "Well, I will soon die of utter exhaustion if I don't get some nourishment."

The feeling I had at the moment was enough to fuel me for the next millennium, if not longer. I was charged, happy, and more content than I had been in years. The cheese, pears and wine before me simply added to the delicious life I felt inside.

"I will have to teach you to protect yourself," he said, his brows furrowed with concentration.

"From what?" I asked. "Now that you have claimed me officially, the Shadows should have no interest in me."

"You carry our child, Skye. They will have plenty of interest in you."

I stopped chewing. The words he spoke felt like a cruel promise with no delivery date. I looked down at my stomach. It looked the same. Of course it did, I reminded myself. The babe was less than a day old. "What are you saying, Khalen?"

"You're pregnant with our daughter, Skye. I have waged war on the Shadows, and that makes you a target."

I considered taking a long sip of my wine, and then set the glass down. I was pregnant, and shouldn't be drinking.

"Skye, I tell you you're a target for the Shadows, and you worry about what one drink will do to the young?"

I nodded, "Yeah, I do. The Shadows will just have to take a number and get in line. Right now, this little girl is my main concern."

"The good Lord won't even help the poor Shadow that stands between you and that child," he said, lifting his glass for a toast.

I clinked his glass then gave him a long, lingering kiss on his lips. He set our glasses down, swallowed a slice of salami, and then made love to me one more time. I loved the way he took command of the situation. Once I revved that engine of his, he was unstoppable. Even if I wanted to, I couldn't cease his momentum, and that was what fueled my own and induced me to give him whatever he wanted. I was helpless under his command and he knew it.

The doorbell woke us from our sleep. "It's Ian," we both said at the same time. Khalen jumped out of bed and slid his sweatpants on. I looked all over for my wrap then suddenly felt it hit me in the face. I donned it quickly.

Khalen checked to ensure I was covered appropriately, and then opened the door.

The look on Ian's face was a cross between bemusement and shock. "I half expected Skye to be more worn out than you, brother," he said, stepping into the entranceway. "By the looks of it, she's getting the better part of the bargain."

But his thoughts belied his outward cheer. "The Shadows stalk the camp," I said. "They're waiting for our return."

Ian leaned back against the wall and folded his hands as if waiting for me to continue.

"What?" I said.

Ian smiled. "I think I liked you better when you were telepathically deaf."

I narrowed my eyes at him. "So," I said, "what are they planning?"

When I saw the image that he revealed to me, I had to lean against the wall to keep from collapsing. "Oh, God, no!"

Khalen pulled me against him. "Skye, relax. We will be ready for them." He looked over at Ian. "Tell Case to be prepared. Skye and I will come home tomorrow. I need everyone to act unalarmed and prepare for our ceremony. The Shadows will attack when we do not expect them. I want to be ready."

Ian nodded. "Brilliant." He gave me a warm and lingering hug. He slapped Khalen on the shoulder. "Keep your strength, brother."

Khalen closed the door behind him then turned to face me. "It begins," he said.

"We expected nothing less," I added. "The gauntlet was tossed, and it was retrieved. Let the games begin."

"I wish it were a game," he said. "Shanuk warned me of this day, but I refused to listen." He slammed the heel of his fist against the wall. "I didn't want to believe."

I brushed my hand down his back. "Save that anger for the enemy," I said. "Right now, we need to eat and continue on with our evening."

He turned to face me, looking far too serious. "I'm afraid I've placed you in danger, my love."

"These are dangerous times. What you have done is given me something to fight for." I placed one hand over my belly and the other against his strong jaw. "The Shadows don't have a prayer.

Chapter 22

Peace is God's way of letting you know that you are on the right path.

WHEN KHALEN AND I ARRIVED at the camp, we were greeted with fierce enthusiasm. Eve hugged me tightly with tears rolling down her face. Case placed his hand over my belly and smiled at his son.

"Well done," said Case.

Caleb came over next and offered me a warm embrace. "Welcome home, child."

I looked around at the half-pitched yurts and temporary shelters that had been built since the attack. There were only two yurts that stood complete.

"We were able to finish yours and Case's homes, but have not yet completed the others. My brother's clan will come later this afternoon to offer assistance."

I kissed the back of his hand. "Thank you."

Case took Khalen aside and looked far too serious to calm my curiosity. I heard them both as if they were standing right in front of me. Khalen was trying to convince him to take me away and keep me safe until peace was restored. Case reminded him that he was stronger with me by his side.

"She cannot fight," said Khalen.

"She can learn," said Case.

Both of them knew I was listening, so I added a few thoughts of my own. "I can fight," I assured them. They both turned and looked at me. I smiled sweetly, and then left to join Eve and the other ladies.

Case blocked me from his thoughts, but Khalen kept his promise and left himself open to me. I would catch up with him later. Right now, I needed some female time. I nestled myself between Eve and Ember and allowed the warmth of the fire to ease my aching bones. Each of them placed their arms around me.

"I missed this," I said, closing my eyes and taking in the silence diffused with quiet conversation, crackling fires, and the sound of footsteps treading upon the soft ground.

"It's addicting, isn't it?" said Eve. "Now you understand why we live this way, in clans, in yurts, away from civilization."

"Yes," I said. "I understand." Although staying in the comfortable cabin on the Hood Canal was enjoyable, it lacked the connection to nature and the sense of community. Neighbors stayed in their own enclosures, hidden from sight and from any chance of conversation. I curled my toes around the dirt beneath my feet. It felt good.

I looked around at the other fires where people gathered and laughed as they shared stories and thoughts. This was home. This is what I wanted. I looked over at the two standing yurts. "I feel bad that ours are the only ones standing," I said.

Eve smiled. "It is customary to build the homes of the clan leader and elders first," she explained. "The others will be up in no time, especially with help."

"It already looks so much better than the last time I saw it through Khalen's eyes."

Eve took my left hand and rolled it over. She traced Khalen's mark on my wrist with her finger. There was sadness in her eyes.

From her thoughts, I knew that she could not bear the mark of Case, for she was not a Spirian woman; she was human. Instead she wore the traditional ring on her left hand. I wanted to comfort her, but didn't know how.

She shook her head. "Don't feel sorry for me, my dear. I am very happy with my life and the choices I have made."

"You are sad for Case," I said.

She nodded, confirming that I had read her correctly. "He wanted to help strengthen the clan with his offspring. It was too late when we discovered that human females rarely survived the birth, and the children were rarely gifted."

"What about the children? Are they more human or Spirian?" I asked.

"Some are more human, some more Spirian. In all cases, they are sterile." The sadness in her voice made my heart ache with an emptiness I hadn't felt for many years.

I thought about the time I was taken to Traeger's mansion—when I had inadvertently broken the treaty between the Shadows and the Protected. It seemed so long ago, yet it had only been seven months. There were so many women under Traeger's claim who were not gifted, and Seth, the one son he toted around like a well-trained dog.

"He has more," said Eve, reading my thoughts. "None of them are gifted."

I remembered how Sarah, one of the non-gifted slaves, described herself and the others as "disposable," and frowned. To Traeger and the other Spirian males, they were disposable—sterile and ungifted. Their only use was for pleasure and dispersing anger. My stomach twisted with the image of Sarah's disfigured hand, a product of Talon's rage. I would make it a point to free those women.

"Eve, how is it that you and Ember can tolerate the energy in this camp, but Sam and Karin could not?"

She smiled. "Once you are claimed by a Spirian male, you crave the energy just like any other Spirian. Without it, we become diseased and die."

"Is that why Jade and Ember's other sisters live elsewhere and only come here to visit?"

Eve nodded. "Yes. Neither of them have been claimed, and therefore, they cannot handle the energy for long periods of time."

"But Jade can read thoughts?" I mentioned, clearly confused.

"You become like those you hang around," she said, smiling. "One cannot live among the gifted for long before developing their own."

"Then why can't you become a Spirian?"

Eve laughed. "You have to be born one, Skye."

"Why? If you can develop gifts by being around Spirians, why can't you acquire other aspects?"

Her brows pressed together in thought. "We just don't."

I remembered my parents and how they differed from other people. They kept to themselves and tried very hard to blend in, but they never really did. If they had gifts, they kept them well hidden. What if there were others who had Spirian traits but never allowed them to manifest?

"I need to help the ladies with the meal and prepare for your ceremony," said Eve, looking toward the direction of our yurts. Ember was calling for her in thought.

"Can I help?" I asked.

She placed her hand on my shoulder. "Yes, you can relax and allow us to do this for you and Khalen."

Ian and Aidan were walking toward me, both with smiles stretched across their perfect faces. They were talking about how different Khalen looked today compared to the last several years. Aidan reached toward me, and then lifted me off the ground to spin me around. His strength never failed to amaze me.

"Ah, lass, you're looking good."

"Well, if you keep spinning me around, I'm going to look green and pale."

He set me down then pulled me into his chest. "So, how does it feel to be claimed, finally?"

"Noisy," I said. "I can hear everyone talking and it sounds like I'm surrounded by a crowd of excited people."

"In time, you will learn to turn that off," said Ian, pulling me away from his brother for a hug of his own.

They sat with me on a log by the fire. Ian poked at the embers a bit before adding another two logs. I could feel the presence of Shadows, but they kept a good distance away. "What's the plan?" I asked, knowing they knew my thoughts.

"They will be drawn in by the ceremony," said Ian. "Their illusionists will hide their numbers, and the others will swarm down upon us." He made it sound so casual as if the attack were nothing more than a play on a football field.

"Why can't we use our gifts when we are in an illusion?" I asked.

"Because the energy we project is altered. You would have to get into our minds and control the energy we emit."

"Khalen and Case can do that."

Aidan shook his head. "No, lass, they can't. An illusionist can alter their energy so quickly it is difficult to grasp it. Like a dream that happens in mere seconds but leaves hours of memories."

"Is there anything we can do to protect ourselves in an illusion?"

Ian frowned with concentration. "Shielding, perhaps."

I shook my head. "I tried, it didn't work when Sean and his clan came for my throat last fall."

In an instant, I found myself standing in a field of bright yellow flowers. Ian stood before me, Aidan behind me. "Form your shield, Skye," said Ian as he advanced toward me.

It was like trying to fold sheets in the water. My shield swam around me then faded.

"No, Skye," Aidan said. "Build your shield from within, project it past your physical body."

With every breath, I felt my shield grow strong within me. I allowed it to expand past my body and felt the heat of it as it wavered. It hummed as Aidan reached out to touch me. "Make it stronger," he said. "More dense."

Ian flicked his hand and my shield dissipated like smoke in the wind. My confidence went with it.

"No," said Ian. "Remember, what you see in an illusion is false. Do not allow me to alter your truth."

My efforts were easily thwarted by their skills. It was

difficult to believe in myself when they defeated me so easily. I felt like a small child trying to tackle a couple of bulls. Ian shook, and then morphed into a large red wolf with red glowing eyes. He came toward me and swiped my leg with his powerful paw. The pain nearly brought me to my knees.

"Shield him," said Aidan. "Block him out. Remember what is real."

I closed my eyes and took a deep breath, assuring myself that this illusion wasn't real and I was in control. I felt Ian's canine breath feather across my face. My shield grew thick and dense, blocking out the heat of his breath. I felt his paw brush against my leg. I imagined a strong connection with the earth and the heavens. Nothing else mattered except this connection. My shield grew stronger until all I could hear was the hum of the white light surrounding me.

Suddenly, everything went quiet and I found myself on the ground with Case and Khalen looking down at me. Ian and Aidan sounded distressed and out of breath. "That was amazing," I said, unable to hold my enthusiasm. Case and Khalen stared at the two men behind me. I turned to find Ian and Aidan standing in shredded clothes and showing dark bruising along their bodies.

"You two are lucky to be standing," said Case.

"I've never experienced anything like it," said Aidan. "She had the force of a lightning bolt." He stumbled back and fell against the log. I reached out for him. His ribs were broken and his belly felt soft and warm. The healing came quick and effortlessly.

Ian was in much worse shape. His lungs were affected by the blast and he couldn't take a full breath. I healed that first, and then proceeded to heal his ribs and tissue.

Instead of feeling drained and worn, I felt energized. My hands were warm but not hot.

"She blasted out of our illusion," Ian explained. "We didn't get a chance to release it."

"Skye, what did you feel when this happened?" Case asked.

I told him about the incredible white light and the power it projected. I sent him images of my memory and he winced. I then healed the wounds on my legs.

"Did you have control over it?" he asked.

I shook my head. "I was just trying to form my shield in the midst of an illusion. I wanted to know if it could be done."

"Yes, well, I think we have Shanuk to thank for Ian and Aidan's life. There is no other excuse for why you two survived that blast." He looked at me with his intense obsidian eyes. "Please, Skye, no more experimenting unless Khalen or an elder is with you. Your union with Khalen has made you strong and we have not unveiled your full potential."

Now my hands were shaking. The coldness from the Shadows dissipated. "They're gone," I said. "I don't feel them anymore."

Khalen frowned. "They left when they saw the blast of white light."

My head felt a sudden wave of dizziness and my body went soft. Khalen caught me before I collapsed. Case held both my feet until the dizziness subsided.

"Thank you," I said. "I feel better now." Case continued to hold my feet. "Will they be back?" I asked, returning their attention back to the Shadows.

"Probably not tonight," said Case.

I looked back at Ian and Aidan, who still looked a

bit stunned. It was the first time I saw them off guard. I tried to stand with Khalen's help. "Are you two all right?" I asked, unable to read either of their thoughts.

Aidan sat down on the log. "It happened so fast," he said. "It felt as if a thousand bolts of lightning slammed into me, knocking me senseless."

"To me it felt more like a Mack truck slamming into my chest and then the shock of electric eels stinging my body," said Ian, taking a seat next to his brother.

Khalen guided me to the log and urged me to sit. "The Shadows won't attack tonight," he said. "I need to speak with my brother."

I stood. "I'm coming with."

He placed his hands on my arms. "No, my love. Not this time. I have a message to deliver, nothing more. I'll be back by sundown, I promise." His eyes turned gold as he stared at me. "Stay here." It was said as a warning, and the power of his words sent chills down my spine. He hugged me close then turned to leave.

Case watched him go with pride in his eyes. He pursed his lips then turned to join the other men by the fire. Was I the only one uncomfortable about this? The only thoughts Case offered me were ones of praise for Khalen. He was happy about his son's decision. Khalen assured me all was all right in thought, but nothing more.

You promised, I reminded him, never to lock me out.

I'm letting him know that we will not tolerate any Shadow's presence on this island. I'm claiming the island as our own. He won't like it, but he is not strong enough to challenge me tonight. I just want to give him something to ponder for a while.

And what if he has reinforcements? I asked

We may need to postpone our ceremony.

Chapter 23

The only thing as powerful as a prayer is the ability to relinquish the expected outcome.

I PACED BETWEEN THE TWO standing yurts. The sun had been setting for quite some time and still there was no sign of Khalen. As promised, he kept his thoughts open to me. He had issued his warning to Traeger, and then his thoughts went silent.

"Skye, lass, he'll be all right," Aidan assured me.

"Can I borrow your jeep?" I asked.

He laughed in response. "The sun is going down, Skye, you won't be able to see a thing in twenty minutes. It takes that long just to get off the island."

"I don't care. I need to find him. Something's wrong."

"I'd offer to drive you, lass, but Khalen warned you to stay in camp."

I grabbed his arms. "Something is wrong. I'm not going to just leave him." I headed toward the jeep that was parked at the far end of the drive. Maiyun trotted alongside, keeping pace with me. When I reached the door of the jeep, my body dropped to the ground and I doubled over in pain. It felt as if someone had zapped me with a taser gun. I cried out.

Aidan pulled me back. "When Khalen issues a warning, lass, you best heed it."

The pain subsided and I was finally able to breathe again. "He wouldn't dare bind me here," I said. Again I reached for the door handle and fell to my knees.

Aidan pulled me back. "Blimey, lass, are you daft?"

Khalen, I called out in thought. *Where are you?*

I saw images flash back to me. Khalen was surrounded by Shadows, but very much in control. He was not in danger. I breathed a sigh of relief. The images left and I could no longer feel him. "Why does he do that?" I asked.

Aidan helped me to my feet and brushed the dirt from my legs. "He's using his energy for other things, lass, nothing more. Don't get your feathers all in a ruff." He turned me to face him, his green eyes intense and deep. "He's a strong man, Skye. Have faith in him."

I nodded. "Yes, he is a strong man."

"Come," he said, leading me toward the central fire. "I have tea warming on the flames."

Khalen returned several hours after sunset. He did not look pleased. Judging by his dark thoughts, the meeting did not go well. Case met him at the drive entrance, where I could not go due to Khalen's cursed boundary he had placed upon me. In thought, I let him know just how happy I was about it, too. His return thought of— *Tough*— was enough to drive my anger over the edge.

I carefully placed my teacup down on the log and walked toward our yurt. I had not seen it since we had returned to camp. The door was different, plain, with no window. The insides were different as well. The floor was honey-colored, and the fireplace was faced with wood instead of stone. The kitchen was in the same location, but the black granite counters had been replaced with cheap laminate with a dark green hue. The cupboards were made of pine, and the bed was much smaller than the oversized king Khalen once had. The clever accordion-style closets were also missing. I sighed and made my way toward the bed. The stiff comforter was a far cry from my soft purple blanket. Still, this was much nicer than some of the tents the others had to stay in.

Someone had taken the care to install full-spectrum lights and start a warm fire. I felt very blessed to have such a supportive clan who ensured we had a warm place to stay. This wasn't at all like our familiar yurt, but it was warm, safe and comfortable.

Khalen came in like a storm, intent on giving me a hug. I stayed on the bed and hugged a pillow to my belly. "Aidan told me about your attempt to leave," he dared to say with a smile.

I tossed the pillow at him. He easily blocked it and cast it aside as he advanced. "I told you, Mate, that I would enforce my wishes."

"Wishes or demands?" I asked, turning my head away from him. I was happy to have him home, but I did not want to receive his affections right now while my temper still flared.

When his weight pressed down on the corner of the mattress, I felt my shield go up. I honestly did not want to have him near me. He effortlessly cast my shield aside with a hearty laugh that only served to fuel my anger. "Your spirit amuses me," he said.

He gently gripped my chin and pulled me around to face him. "I do not issue a warning that I cannot back," he dared to say.

Union

"I don't obey," I countered.

"I know," he said, smiling. "And that is your choice."

"Ugh," I pulled away from him, but he caught me and pulled me back and pinned me beneath him. "Never do that to me again," I seethed.

"Oh, I will, my love, I assure you." He was enjoying my anger far too much. When his lips pressed down on mine, I was very tempted to bite his off. My every attempt to urge him off me was fruitless. He was not budging. "I would take you right now, Love, but our ceremony awaits."

He lifted himself off me, and then effortlessly pulled me up from the bed. "Try and look as if you love me, will you?"

"I do love you," I growled.

"Excellent," he said, opening the door to the yurt and leading me outside.

His mood was almost as irritating as his petty victory over my stubbornness. Funny how he chose to back up his warnings after we were joined. I was sure I would have had second thoughts if he had done it sooner. He grabbed my hand and gave it a firm squeeze as if hearing my thoughts and reminding me that I was indeed his now, second thoughts or no.

He returned my glare with a smile that glowed with triumph. He was purposely trying to fuel my anger and prevented me from pulling my hand away from his.

Case obviously sensed my plight and a smile formed over his face as well. Spirian men, I decided, were nothing but gloating, self-satisfied jingoists.

Eve approached us and reached for my other hand. "Come, we must get you ready."

Khalen released my hand. *Have fun*, he added in thought.

I glared back at him and assured him that this issue was not resolved. In turn, he said that he would be disappointed if it were.

"You've only been joined for less than a week and you two are already at it with one another?" asked Eve as she led me toward her yurt. When I told her about what he did, she laughed. "Oh, that's just the beginning, my dear."

My eyes grew wide. "What do you mean?"

She patted my hand. "Let's just say that you would be better off giving him what he wants."

"Well, apparently, he wants a fight. I'm more than willing to give him a ride worth his ticket."

Again, she laughed. "Okay, close your eyes."

"Um—Eve, I'm blind and the sun's gone down. What do you think I'll see?"

"Close them anyway," she said. "Please," she added.

I did as she asked and allowed her to guide me across the threshold. The furniture arrangement was different from their last yurt. There was much more space judging by the open echo of sound.

"Okay," said Eve, "open them." The enthusiasm in her voice reminded me of a young girl showing off a puppy. Ember stood before me holding what looked like a dress with sparkling objects dappling the neckline. "Well, what do you think?"

"It's beautiful," I replied, reaching out to touch the fabric, hoping to gain a better idea of what it was.

"You can't see it, can you?" said Eve.

Ember slapped her forehead. "I forgot the light bulbs," she said, running toward the kitchen. She hung the dress up on a hook, and then bustled around the room replacing the regular bulbs with full-spectrum ones. "There," she said, securing the last one in place, "better?"

I smiled. "Much better, thanks." I walked over to the cream-colored dress and marveled at its delicate beauty. The fabric was soft as cotton, but much more refined.

"Khalen said that the fabric had to be soft, so I chose the softest fabric I knew for a dress," Eve explained.

"What is it?" I asked.

"Brushed silk lined with cashmere. The dressmakers said that it couldn't be done, but given enough money, it certainly was. Khalen said that only natural materials could be used, nothing synthetic."

I smiled, warmed by the thought that he knew me so well and had ensured that I would enjoy the feel of the dress, even at an exorbitant cost. My anger toward him dissolved. The silky ribbons that fell from the waist glided like delicate streams of water as I let them filter through my fingers. They were cobalt blue, and played well with the myriad of colors that shone from the shiny dots lining the soft, round neckline and flaring three-quarter sleeves.

"Australian opal," said Eve. "They represent health and fertility."

I smiled back at her and patted my tummy. "No problem with that one," I said, still having a hard time believing that I even carried an embryo. I wanted so badly to believe it, though, I didn't mind playing along with the game. After all, how could Khalen possibly know that I was pregnant so soon? I showed no signs, nor did I feel any different.

The design of the dress was simple, which made it appropriate for other occasions. Khalen not only thought about my comfort, but my sense of practicality as well. He knew that buying me a dress that could only be worn once would not make me happy, so he chose a design that catered to many events—not that we went out much, but that could change.

Eve held my hand and led me over to a chair in the center of the room. Ember stood armed with a natural boar-bristle brush. "Come on, we need to fix your hair," she said, patting the chair. "Khalen wants it down and loose."

"And does Khalen always get what he wants?" I inquired.

"Yes," they both said in unison.

"I'm afraid he does," Eve added. "He can be very persuasive when he sets his mind on something."

I had experienced quite a bit of that trait myself. "Well," I said. "He better get used to being disappointed."

"This should be an interesting year," said Eve, patting my arm. "I'll pray for you, my dear."

Ember removed the band holding my braid, and then began separating the strands. "Your hair is like silk," she said. "It's so soft." She ran the brush through it as if she were brushing strands of gold.

Eve retrieved delicate strings of strung opals from a rosewood box. "These are for your hair," she said, her eyes sparkling with joy. The tops of each string had a sturdy yet tiny clip that could easily grip a small clump of hair and still be cleverly concealed. The clip resembled a long narrow bead made of gold that opened lengthwise. Inside was a soft cushion of silicone that served to grip the strands that were closed between the bead.

"I've never seen anything like this," I said, genuinely impressed with the crafty design.

"Khalen designed it, and then paid someone to cast them. He wanted them made of 14K gold, but it proved to be too soft, so he had to settle for a gold blend."

My eyes widened. "He's crazy," I exclaimed.

Eve smiled. "He's in love."

Ember finished brushing my hair, and then both ladies worked diligently on adorning it with the beautiful strings of opal. Eve lifted another string from the box. It was different from the others. The beads were still opalescent yet red in color, like fire. "These," she said, "are fire opals, very rare. They represent protection. He wanted them placed on your left side, closest to your heart as a vow of his protection."

"I feel like a national treasure to him as it is," I said.

Eve patted my hand. "You are to him," she said. "Honestly, I have never seen my son so wrapped up in another being. Until this day," she said, "I don't believe he understood what love truly is."

I remembered the painful sting of his boundary earlier today and frowned. "He has an odd way of showing it, sometimes."

It took another hour of unbearable fussing before I was ready to leave the yurt. Khalen knew that I didn't like synthetic makeup, so my face was powdered with mineral clays, my eyes were dusted with powdered blue stone, and my lips glowed with a blend of oils that brought out their natural color. I hardly recognized myself and wondered if Khalen would approve.

The dress hung on my body perfectly and flared gently from my waist to the bottoms of my knees. I was grateful that Khalen had not chosen a pair of shoes to go with the dress. My feet were left blissfully bare.

We walked out of the yurt. The camp had been transformed with light. Torches formed a large circle near the central fire. Khalen was nowhere in sight, but I could feel his energy so I knew he was close. Eve led me toward the circle of light and offered both my hands to Case. He held them firmly while looking into my eyes. His glowed like rainbow obsidian in bright sunlight. It was the only thing I could see.

"Shanuk wanted to perform this ceremony, himself," he said. "He wrote the vows he wanted for you both. I would like to use them tonight, if you agree."

"Of course," I said, not really understanding what I was agreeing to. Seeing I loved the old man, and he had played a vital role in my life and its current direction, I felt I had nothing to fear.

Drums began to beat, slow and rhythmic with the melodic songs of frogs and crickets. The camp was quiet, with only the soft breaths of the clan audible as they waited. The fire crackled and my feet felt comforted by the warm earth beneath them. I could feel Khalen as he silently walked up behind me and took his place by my side. Instead of standing on my right, he took his place on my left—a Spirian tradition, Eve had explained, that signified the man's protection of his mate's heart above all else. The woman stood on the right to signify the strength and stability she provided to her mate.

He wore a black suit accented with a gold cummerbund and an ornate silk tie that was fastened with a decorative brooch. His white silk shirt contrasted his dark skin and jet-black hair, neatly braided and tied in gold. He was stunning against the light of the fire. I looked down and smiled. His feet were bare.

Case took both my hands and arranged my left on top of my right, and then placed them between Khalen's. We stood facing one another. His hands felt warm over mine, and protective. "I offer this woman to you, Khalen Dunning, to be your mate for life. Do you agree to bind her to your soul and journey through this life together as one until death?"

"I do," he said, his golden eyes boring deep into mine.

"Skye Taylor, do you agree to offer yourself to this man and share your soul and life journey until death?"

"I do," I said, my voice a bit shaky. I wondered if Derrick could see me now and what he would think if he were here. Would he be angry, sad, hurt?

Khalen squeezed my hand, offering his own kind of comfort.

Case held up his right hand and turned to Khalen. Khalen pressed the palm of his left hand against it. "By repeating these vows, Khalen Dunning, you form a pact with God to uphold the sanctity of marriage defined by the Spirian laws. If you agree with this, repeat after me."

Khalen nodded in agreement.

"I, Khalen Dunning, agree to claim this woman, Skye Taylor, as my lifetime mate. I vow to keep her safe, and provide for her needs. Her heart is mine to protect and her body is mine to bless with children. Together we vow to strengthen the clan and uphold the Spirian laws. With her by my side, I accept the position of clan leader and vow to fulfill my duty until death."

Khalen repeated each word with authority and pride as if he had rehearsed them a hundred times. Now, it was my turn to repeat my vows. My knees were shaking and my throat felt tight and small.

Case raised his left hand. Khalen lifted my right hand and placed the palm against Case's. He then held my left hand. "I, Skye Taylor," Case began. "Vow to love, honor, obey, and respect my husband."

I nearly choked on that one word, "obey." I should have known Shanuk would add that in there. I heard Khalen silently chuckle when I spoke the word. He was

Rowena Portch

obviously enjoying my plight.

"I accept my position as the clan leader's mate and will stand beside him in all matters. My heart and body willingly belong to Khalen Dunning until death."

I repeated the words knowing that I belonged to him without even speaking the vows. He had my heart from the beginning.

Case reached for my left hand and turned it over to expose Khalen's mark. He produced a clear crystal that looked flawless in the firelight. It was attached to a silver chain. He said a few words in a language I did not recognize, and then laid the crystal over my tender skin, just below Khalen's mark. With a slow, deliberate stroke, he drew a line of blood. He repeated the same thing on Khalen's right arm. After saying another phrase in Gaelic, he bound our wounds together with a red silk ribbon.

The need to heal the wounds was difficult to ignore, but both Case and Khalen's silent warning to leave them be was a stronger deterrent.

"Your blood is one, as are your souls, united for life in love, faith, and honor. May the Father bless your union and your souls in this life and beyond." He raised both his arms and addressed the clan. "As clan elder, I honor this union and deem it official and pure." He placed the crystal in Khalen's hand then turned us around to face the clan. "I present your official clan leader and his mate, Khalen and Skye Dunning."

The clan roared and cheered as Khalen draped the crystal pendant over my head then leaned me back and claimed my lips with obvious possession. "Now," he said with a smile. "It is official."

"Am I going to like this?" I asked, feeling a bit apprehensive.

His smile turned serious now and his eyes softened. "I'll make sure that you do, my love." He brushed my cheek.

Chapter 24

Leadership is not so much to rule as it is to guide and provide
direction down the path that benefits the whole.

AFTER DANCING SEVERAL DANCES WITH Khalen, Ian,
Aidan, Case, Gregg and Caleb, I was grateful for a
little rest time by the fire. Maiyun had given up early and
had retired to the yurt shortly after the dancing began.
Khalen continued to dance, looking happier than I had
ever seen him.

So much had happened during the last few days, it all
seemed like a blur. Part of me wondered if it was all real or
just another dream. I felt the tiny wound on my left wrist
and wondered if Valerie had endured the same.

"No," said Eve, taking a seat beside me. "There was
never a ceremony for them because Case and Shanuk did
not honor the union."

I lifted the small crystal that now hung on my neck
and turned it around in my hand. "This is pretty," I said.

"It belonged to Shanuk's wife, Calla. It's a blue
Herkimer diamond, or something like that. Shanuk
wanted you to have it. It was also used to bind their

union."

I held it tight in my hand and said a silent thank you to the old man. His presence was strong during the ceremony, and lingered well after. "I miss him," I said.

Eve nodded. "We all do, my dear." She placed her hand over mine. "He thought highly of you to offer such a gift. For years, he had planned to take that crystal with him to the grave."

"I hope I don't disappoint him," I said.

"I don't believe you will."

"There's my mate," Khalen said from behind. He had been dancing with every female in camp. Where he found the energy, I would never know. By the looks of him, he could easily last another two hours. "Come dance with me, love."

Eve smiled as I stood and followed him to the circle of lights. His hold on me was commanding and firm. I felt confident waltzing among the clan members, knowing he would not allow us to collide with anyone. I hadn't danced in years, but he made it seem easy with his clear directions and smooth transitions.

"You make me very proud, Skye," he said, pulling me close to his chest.

"It's the bare feet, right?"

He laughed. "No, not the bare feet."

"Why then?" I asked.

He smiled, and right away, I knew I would not appreciate what he was about to say.

He lifted the string of fire opals from my hair. His smile broadened. "For vowing you would obey me," he said.

A low growl escaped my lips. "There are conditions to that vow, you understand."

"I don't believe Shanuk defined them in the vows," he countered.

"You're right, he didn't, because he wanted to leave that up to me."

He swung me around so quickly, I lost my balance. He steadied me then pulled me against him. "Well," he said. "We have a lifetime to figure it out."

"So," I said, changing the subject, "who did you give our red ribbon to?" It was traditional for the groom to offer the binding ribbon to the man he chose to care for me should anything happen to Khalen—my guardian angel, in effect.

"Aidan is your templar."

"Good choice." A templar, as it was explained to me, was the man who had first rights to assume me as a mate should anything happen to Khalen. If my templar already had a mate, he would choose a suitable man to take his place.

"Yes, well, I couldn't very well trust Ian to keep his hands off you, now could I?"

"Perhaps not," I agreed, "but you can definitely trust that I won't allow another man to touch me, regardless of who he is."

"That I do, my love. That I do." He held me tight as we made our way gracefully out of the circle. "I believe it's time to consummate our union," he said, taking my hand and leading me back to our yurt.

"Um, I believe we've already done that, lover," I giggled, "several times over, if I remember correctly."

"Yes," he said, grinning with mischief laced in his golden eyes, "but tonight, it is official and I will treat it as such."

Union

UNTIL LAST NIGHT, I HADN'T known that a soul could be bound to another more than once, but now, I knew better. This time, our union was much more intense and deep. I felt Khalen's blood as it coursed through his veins. I felt each breath as he lay beside me, his eyes closed and soft against the candlelight that lingered on. I imagined the strong lines of his jaw and the smooth texture of his skin, wishing I could see him here in the darkness. My hands ached to caress him, but I didn't want him to wake. Carefully I edged my legs out from under the covers and began to sit up.

His strong hand curled around my arm as he pulled me back against him. "Where are you going, my sweet?" he whispered into my ear.

"I can't sleep," I said. "I was going to go for a walk."

He groaned. "It's too early in the morning," he said, wrapping his arm around me and holding me tight. "I think I know of a way to help you sleep," he said with a grin in his voice. How he had any energy left after last night eluded me.

SEVERAL HOURS LATER, I ROSE to the smell of fresh coffee and breakfast. I glanced across the room at Eve and Case sitting at the breakfast counter talking quietly over their cups of joe. The fire had been stoked. I jostled Khalen awake.

"Again, my love?"

Case laughed, causing Khalen to sit bolt upright in bed, tossing the soft blanket over my body. "Bloody hell, do you not honor our privacy?" he growled. He stepped out of bed and donned his pants.

"It's near noon, my boy," said Case. "We figured you needed some nourishment at the very least."

Khalen walked over and took a swig of his father's coffee. "Noon, you say?"

"Yes, noon."

I smiled at the three of them. "Thank you for thinking of us," I said. I looked around for my clothes, but they were nowhere in sight. Khalen picked up his white dress shirt and walked it over to me. He then glared back at his parents.

"Do you mind?" he asked, waiting for them to turn around. He stood guard as I donned his shirt and stood away from the bed. The end of his shirt fell to the top of my knees. It was soft and silky, revealing my body a bit too much for my comfort. He grabbed a pair of my pants from the suitcase we had yet to unpack and handed them to me. After he ensured that I was presentable, he kissed me slow and deliberately, released a deep throaty growl then reluctantly led me to the breakfast counter where his parents sat waiting.

My stomach growled, having not eaten anything since earlier the previous evening. Khalen held my hand as we said prayers, and then we dug into the hearty meal of fried potatoes, scrambled eggs and blueberry pancakes. I typically didn't inhale my food, but this morning, it felt as if I couldn't get it down my throat fast enough. My plate was empty before Khalen had finished half of his portion.

"Did you have enough to eat, dear?" Eve asked. Her brows knit together with concern.

I felt the blood rush to my face. "Yes, thank you." Khalen slid his plate in front of me and I shook my head. "I'm all right, really."

He slid it back in front of him and continued eating. I stood and served everyone another cup of coffee before setting the kettle on the flame to brew another pot. Case stared at me with concern etched in his expression.

"Come here," he said, gesturing for me to stand before him. I did and nearly jumped when he placed his warm hand over my belly. His concern did not soften.

Khalen followed his point of interest and mirrored his father's concern.

"What?" I said. "Is something wrong?"

Eve covered her mouth and her eyes began to moisten. I read Khalen's thoughts and suddenly felt very ill. My little daughter had a twin. Both Khalen and Case were concerned about the dangers of a Spirian carrying and delivering twins; according to their disturbing thoughts, the chance of surviving the ordeal was rare at best.

I ran from the yurt and headed straight for the woods to purge my breakfast. Seeing it was much too soon for morning sickness to occur, I was sure it was the shock that caused my breakfast to unsettle. As far back as I could remember, I never heard of our family ever having twins anywhere in the bloodline. How could this have happened? Khalen, Case and Eve came out toward me as I wiped my mouth clean with the napkin still clutched in my hand. Maiyun ran up to greet me first.

I heard Case tell Khalen that one of the embryos would have to be removed. My back stiffened. "No," I said, as soon as they were close enough to hear me. "I absolutely won't allow that."

Khalen frowned. "Skye, it's too dangerous. If we remove one of them now, both you and the other baby stand a greater chance of survival."

I placed my hand protectively over my belly. "Please, Khalen, I'm begging you. Don't take one of them from me." I knew that anger would not sway his mind, nor would threats. Hurting me, on the other hand, was something he couldn't do.

"Skye," Case reasoned, "the chances of you or the young surviving the birth is very low. Please be reasonable."

I looked over at Eve, whose eyes pleaded with me to listen to the men. There was also something else in her expression—desperation with a hint of support.

"Where is your faith?" I asked them all. "Are we in control or is our Father?"

Case raised his hands and rolled his eyes. Khalen's fists clenched tight by his side and his jaw stiffened. Eve simply smiled. Finally, Case shook his head with resignation. "She's all yours, Son."

Khalen gripped my arms and looked deep into my eyes. "Skye, I won't risk losing you."

My eyes narrowed. "So, to save me, you take the life of one of your daughters?"

His lips grew firm. I heard the battle inside his head. "Yes," he said. "To save you, I would."

"Well, I'm not willing to do the same."

We stood there, staring each other down for what seemed like several minutes. His golden-green eyes flickered with frustration, anger and remorse. I could feel the way his insides torqued and twisted with emotion. He released my arms and walked away. I knew better than to follow him. His anger had risen too high and he was fighting for control.

"You ask a lot of him," said Case.

I placed my hand on his arm and met his black gaze. "It will be all right, Case. I know it. My daughters and I will survive."

"I pray you're right," he said, sadly walking away.

Eve took my hand. "Come, let's get you something to calm that belly of yours."

"Why is carrying twins so dangerous for Spirians?" I asked her as she led me back to our yurt. The kettle was screaming when we stepped inside. I had forgotten to take it off the flame before I fled outside. I lifted the kettle and poured it into the French press.

"The gestation period for Spirians is longer than it is for humans," she said. "It is twelve months, not nine, so the babies grow much larger before they are born." She picked an apple from the basket on the counter and began cutting it in thin slices.

"Twelve months? Why so long?" I asked, pouring us each a fresh cup of coffee.

"Like all Spirians, the baby ages much slower, especially if she's a purebred. You and Khalen are both purebreds, so the babies will be as well. Khalen is worried that you won't go full term, or if you do, you won't be able to deliver them without severe complications."

"Eve, I feel good about this. I really do. It would be helpful to have you in my corner on this one." I sat beside her and nibbled on the apple slices. The pains in my stomach began to settle.

"I'll stand beside you on this, my dear, but God help us all if anything happens to you or the young."

I looked at her with disbelief. Had she not heard a word I said? "Eve, nothing will happen. I'm going to be fine."

Maiyun came up to me and placed her head on my lap. She, too, looked worried, no doubt having picked up on Khalen's foul mood. I scratched behind her ear. "It's okay, Maiyun. Dad is just a worrywart." I slid Khalen's uneaten meal in front of me and started in with the eggs. He wasn't going to finish them and I was very hungry.

"Eve," I said between bites, and hoping to change the

subject, "I want to ask Khalen to free the women from Traeger's care. Do you suppose they could come live here if that happens?"

"How many are we talking about?" She took a sip of her coffee.

"Fifteen, maybe twenty. I'm not really sure."

Eve thought for a moment. "Are any of them Spirians?"

I shook my head. "No, they are all halflings from what I could tell, uneducated and completely ignorant about life."

Eve looked as if she had just swallowed a bitter pill. "Hmm, you might be able to convince him to free the ladies, but he will not allow them to stay here."

I took a sip of my coffee. "Can they survive without being around other Spirians?"

Eve shook her head sadly. "Not for long, I'm afraid. Halflings are not known to live past the age of thirty. Most of them get sick and die much younger."

My shoulders sank. I thought about sweet Sarah and the other women. What chance did they have at living a normal life? My anger toward Traeger grew. "Does Traeger know?"

"Yes, he knows." She placed her hand on my arm and looked me in the eyes. "Skye, do not allow your anger to swell inside you. The Shadows look for that doorway and use it to get in your head."

"If he knows then why does he continue to sire more of them?" The anger in my voice surprised me. I had not felt this strongly about something since a time many years ago, when I rescued wild horses that were illegally trapped; strange how it seemed like several lifetimes ago.

"Shadows are not known for their integrity, Skye. They take pleasure in owning things, including women.

To Traeger, the more women he owns, the more powerful he feels. Each one is like a conquest to him, a prize of sorts."

I noticed she was frowning now while staring into her coffee. "What?" I asked. Her thoughts were all over the place and difficult to decipher.

"I think Traeger's inability to have you so easily is what makes him want you so badly. You are a challenge for him—one he cannot resist or deny."

"And you're afraid that he will want to claim me now more than ever because I carry Khalen's children?" I thought back on Valerie and how he convinced her to abort Khalen's son. Now Eve's thoughts made sense.

"I do," she said, "and I'm sure Khalen is aware of that danger as well."

"Honestly," I sighed. "I wish you all had more faith in me. I am not a weak woman and Traeger does not attract me in the least." It was time to change the subject again. "It is hard for me to believe that a human cannot develop into a Spirian."

"We thought it was possible, a long time ago," she said sadly. "The pineal gland can develop and grow, but the body remains human. That is why we cannot get pregnant without severe complications." She placed her hand over her belly as if remembering her own misgivings. "Our children, if they do happen to survive, suffer the most."

A cold chill ran up my spine. A Shadow was near. My back stiffened. Maiyun growled and ran toward the door.

"Stay here," said Eve, as I followed Maiyun to the door.

I turned to face her. "I will not hide from them," I said firmly. I opened the door and saw Traeger and his son Seth stepping out of the black Lincoln. Traeger's hair was tied neatly in a braid, just like Khalen's. I walked out to meet him.

"Skye," he said, bowing his head. "You're looking lovely."

I glared. "What are you doing here?" I asked.

His eyes scanned me from head to toe, and then rested on my belly. A creepy smile stretched over his face. "You're with child," he said. Thank God he only saw the one.

"You were warned to stay off the island. What is so important that you risk your miserable life?"

He laughed. "So bold, for a mere female. You sound as if you stand a chance against me, a lead male, far stronger than yourself."

I laughed back. "Your self-professed importance does not make you strong, Traeger, it makes you pathetic."

He blasted a wave of energy toward me, meant to bring me down to my knees. I easily deflected his blast and directed it into the earth. I grew my shield around me and felt it hum. I had two young ones to protect now, which made me just as lethal as Khalen—or so I thought.

Traeger stepped toward me with menace in his eyes. He didn't get too far before he slammed onto his back and gripped his throat. Khalen walked up behind me. "You dare look at my mate again, brother, and I will strip your life from your miserable bones."

Maiyun pressed against my legs, and then lay down beside me.

"We come to make a truce," Seth said, standing calmly with his hands at his sides. His eyes were softer since the last time we met, not at all like his father's.

Khalen released his hold on Traeger. "Stay down," Khalen warned him.

Traeger tried to stand then yelped with pain as a shock

coursed through him. "Let me stand," he roared. "I am a clan leader, not a subordinate." He glanced over at me. "Like your mate," he sneered.

Khalen placed his arm around my waist and drew me to him. "In my eyes and the eyes of this clan, she is my equal. You will stay where you are, in the dirt. Now tell me what you have come here to say."

"As my son disrespectfully blurted," he spat, "I have come to seek a truce with you."

"I'm listening," said Khalen.

"We will honor the treaty last spoken by our fathers."

"No," said Khalen. "You have dishonored that treaty and have tainted the Spirian ethos with your promiscuous ways. I have given you two weeks to decide on one mate. She must be of pure blood. The others must be released."

"That is not the way of the Shadows," said Traeger. "We have our own rules."

"Not any longer," Khalen warned. "For years, we have allowed you to run wild, taking any woman you saw fit. Our race is weakened because of you, and the humans suffer. No good comes from what you have done."

"Very good," said Traeger. "I will release the women and choose only one."

I watched his energy fluctuate and dim. "He lies," I said. "He intends to hide his women."

Khalen smiled and Traeger growled. "She knows nothing," he said.

"Get back in your car, Traeger. Warn the other clans that I will be visiting in two weeks' time. All humans and halflings must be freed or I will free them for you."

Khalen pulled his bind from Traeger, who stood and brushed the dirt from his pants, no longer shiny and black. "Get in the car," he barked at his son.

Seth looked over at Khalen. "I wish to stay here, if it is all right with you." He bowed, showing Khalen that he respected his position.

Khalen considered the request for a moment then nodded. *What are his intentions?* he asked me, in thought.

They are good, I assured him.

"You will not!" Traeger yelled at his son. "I demand you to get in the car." He cast a piercing blow at his son. Khalen dispelled it, willed the car door open, and then pushed Traeger with great force into the vehicle. The door slammed shut.

Khalen looked at the driver. "Drive," he ordered.

The driver nodded nervously, jammed the car into gear, and sped away, leaving Seth in a plume of dust.

Chapter 25

Change is inevitable. Without it, we would fester like a stagnant pond.

KHALEN AND **I** BOTH LOOKED at Seth, who stood like a statue staring after the car. He had always been an odd bird, never really fitting into his father's world. He had no gifts that were evident, nor did he exhibit a violent nature.

Khalen jostled me. "Skye, lower your shield, you're making my entire body sting."

I had forgotten all about it. The hum faded as I pulled my energy back in. My hands began to shake a bit, both from fear and adrenaline. I imagined Seth was shaking as well. Here he stood in the midst of our clan with no gifts to offer, his heart pumping Shadow blood.

Case approached us. "I cannot hear his thoughts, son, can you?"

Khalen shook his head.

"He wants us to train him," I said. "He wants to become Protected."

Both Khalen and Case looked at me with questioning

eyes. "You can read him?" asked Khalen.

"Of course, just look at him."

Seth smiled as he approached us. "Uncle, she is correct. I've come to ask for your help, and in turn, I offer you my loyalty."

"What is your purpose?" asked Case, clearly not convinced that any son of Traeger's was trustworthy.

Seth met his eyes, his own softened. "To learn from you—become like you."

"There is more that you are not telling us," I said. His energy fluctuated as if he had something to hide. Whatever it was, he kept it well hidden.

He looked over at Khalen. "The other clans will try to provoke you into killing your brother."

Khalen's eyes narrowed. He had multiple opportunities to take Traeger's life, but never did. "For what purpose?"

Seth's eyes turned cold, almost dull. "To kill you. You cannot take the life of your twin without sacrificing your own. If Traeger dies, you die. Your blood is the same."

Case's eyes narrowed. "How do you know this?"

"My grandfather told me. It was the only reason he did not kill Khalen when he decided to leave the clan. Killing Khalen would mean killing his twin." He looked at Khalen. "You know it as well, which is why you allow Traeger to live. If he were any other Shadow, you would have taken his life without question for threatening your mate."

Khalen frowned. His thoughts were rampant with disbelief. His knuckles turned white with anger. I could feel the hum radiating from his body.

"You can break the bond," I said to Seth. "You know what to do." His energy changed. He tried pulling it in and keeping me out but it was too late and he felt it.

His eyes narrowed. "You're very perceptive for a female. How is it that you can read me when Case and Khalen cannot?"

"Your intentions are clear. I feel them," I said. "You have many gifts, but your mother has warned you to keep them hidden from Traeger. Why?"

Seth stepped forward, shaking. "She doesn't want me to be like them." His young innocence was pulling on my heartstrings. He couldn't be more than twenty, maybe even younger. His body was strong and stout as his uncle's, and he carried the same strong jaw line. He was not quite as tall as Khalen, but near enough. His dark eyes were like those of a nocturnal predator and had an unnerving yellow glow.

"And what do you want?" asked Khalen.

"I want to save my mother and my sister but that's not possible so I am here alone."

"Why are you afraid?" I asked. "There is so much fear in you."

Images flashed in my mind. I saw his mother and sister, a young girl, writhing on the floor before Traeger. Another man twisting their necks. I shut my eyes and winced. I grabbed Khalen's arm. "We have to save them," I mumbled.

Khalen had been reading my thoughts. He looked at Seth. "You see premonitions."

"They don't always come true," he said. "I see only days in advance. Father will question my mother about me. When she refuses to tell him anything, he will kill her and my sister. Then he will go mad."

"This is not good," said Case.

"The Seattle clan is stronger than you think," Seth explained.

"And you're afraid," I guessed, "because if you help sever the bond between Khalen and Traeger, the Shadows will know and will target you?"

"I believe I am dead either way," he said. "Breaking off from the Shadows is treason. It will not be dismissed or forgotten."

"Then why did you do it?" asked Khalen.

Seth cocked his head like a confused dog. "Why did you?"

Khalen drew his brows in. "I had my reasons."

"Come," said Case. "Let's take this inside." He led the way back to his yurt. Eve went to the kitchen to assemble a few things to nibble on, and some hot tea, while Khalen, Seth, Case and I sat on the floor near the fire pit.

"You risk a lot coming to us," said Case. "I'm curious about your motive."

Seth rolled his eyes in frustration. "I've already explained all that."

"Explain it again," said Khalen.

Not wanting to hear the same tired story, I stood and went to help Eve with the snacks and tea.

Seth explained once again how he wanted to become Protected, but his voice wavered. He wasn't lying, but he wasn't telling the entire truth, either. I knew what Khalen and Case were trying to do. By getting him to talk about something that seemed mundane, his defenses would drop and his mind could be read. She had seen the two men do it numerous times. They operated like a pack of wolves, ready to pounce when the poor victim was weak and confused. Ian and Aidan would no doubt get into this mess as well when they returned from work.

Eve carried a platter of cookies, vegetables and sliced apples, while I carried the tray of tea. My stomach roared, causing all three men to look up at me. My face blushed.

I sat next to Khalen, who felt compelled to hand me one cookie after another. I preferred to eat the carrots and jicama, despite his persistence. Suddenly he stood and started to pace. The images that flooded his mind were disturbing and caused my stomach to turn. I pushed my food away and stood as well. He had been reading Seth's mind, trying to figure out how to sever the bond between him and his brother. The method was less than favorable.

"Explain," Khalen finally said, having not been able to make sense of the scrambled images in his mind.

"Explain what?" asked Seth. Apparently, reading thoughts was not one of his gifts.

"How do you sever the bond?" Khalen growled.

Seth frowned, clearly confused by Khalen's impatience. He stuffed a cookie into his mouth and struggled to chew it with any dignity. After seeing the anger rise in Khalen's face, he quickly washed everything down with a gulp of tea.

"Both of you must be in the same room. I put you to sleep, and then separate him from you and you from him. Sometimes, remnants of each of you remain."

"Remnants?" Khalen inquired.

"Yes, you assume some of his traits and he assumes some of yours." He said it so matter-of-factly that I wanted to laugh in response.

"No," said Khalen. "That is unacceptable."

"So," I tried to confirm, "my mate may lose a part of himself and gain another aspect from Traeger?"

Seth nodded. "Exactly."

Case observed the exchange with an immense display of calm. "I want to hear worst-case and best-case scenarios."

Seth shrugged. "Worst case, Khalen would lose his gifts and gain one or more of Traeger's. He would take on Traeger's personality and mannerisms. Best case, Khalen would lose one or two gifts and gain a few from Traeger. Khalen would keep his personality and show hints of Traeger's."

"Have you done this before?" asked Case.

Seth looked down and broke a cookie in half. "No one has done it successfully."

"Wait," I said. "We don't even know if what Seth is saying is true. How do we know that if one twin dies, the other will follow? Case, you didn't even know about this. Don't you find that odd?"

"It is true," Seth said, defensive now. "I swear it."

"But you haven't seen it," Khalen said.

"No, I haven't, but my mother has assured me that she has seen it, and also witnessed her own mother performing the severing of two other twins, one of whom was dying."

"I need to speak with your mother," said Khalen. "Can you bring her here?"

Seth's eyes grew wide as walnuts. "Here? You want me to bring her here?"

Khalen stared at him, obviously feeling no need to repeat his request. "You wanted to save her."

"Save her, yes, but not by risking all our lives. Going back to my father's home is suicide."

Khalen stepped toward him, his eyes gold and bright. "Staying here is suicide as well, I assure you."

"I'd do as he says," said Case. "He is not one to issue idle threats."

Khalen tossed him the keys to the Dodge. "Here, take our truck. I expect you back here by tomorrow morning."

"And if I don't make it back?"

Khalen laughed. "You can keep the truck."

I slapped him on the arm. "You most certainly cannot. I want my truck back."

Seth smiled for the first time since I had known him. "I'll bring it back." He left apprehensively, but feeling much more relaxed than when he came.

"He'll make a good addition to the clan," said Case. "He reminds me of you in your younger days."

"He has many gifts, but few of them are developed," I added.

"Now how is it," Khalen inquired with a smug expression, "that you could read his thoughts, but we couldn't?"

I smiled and glanced over at Eve, who already knew the answer. "Women's intuition, my love. I read his body language and filled in the blanks. It was the only way to get him to talk."

Case laughed. "Brilliant."

Eve handed her husband a steaming cup of tea. "So what do you plan to do with his mother and sister when they return?"

Case took a sip of his tea and thought for a moment. "That will have to be their choice. But allowing them to stay here invites trouble. Traeger will have every right to reclaim his mate and daughter. Seth is old enough to make his own choices."

"Can't we protect them?" I asked.

Khalen shook his head. "Sunjia belongs to Traeger. We have no right to keep her from him. To sever her bond, she would have to die."

I swallowed hard, fighting to keep the meager amount of food in my belly. The life of a Spirian was so absolute. It was no wonder there were so few of us left.

"If the bond between you and your brother can be severed," I said, "why can't a union between two souls?"

"It's never been done," said Case. "We have meddled too far into what the Father has deemed to be the way of our people, and we've nearly wiped out our kind as a result. When we question the Father's ways, we begin to make our own kind of laws without really knowing what the long-term ramifications may be."

I thought about that for a moment and images of my mother and father flashed in my mind. In their belief, those who had gifts were evil and thought of as witches or as pagan. They showed no signs of having gifts of their own, but for me to be pure Spirian, they had to have at least one gift. I wondered if they knew they were Spirians. Something must have drawn them together. Something must have convinced them that gifts were evil. Man-made religion, I deduced. Somehow we dismissed the fact that Jesus himself had amazing gifts.

"We need to return to the basics," said Khalen. "It is the only way to ensure our kind does not fade."

"Agreed," said Case.

"A meeting of the elders is required," Khalen decided. "Spirian leaders from all clans must gather and agree to a common plan for this to work."

Case nodded. "We can meet in two months."

"Where?" asked Khalen. "The energy that will be emitted is sure to draw attention."

"Away from the poles," said Case. "Somewhere near the equator where the concentration of the energy will have fewer effects."

"What about Arcadie's place in Brazil?" said Khalen. "It's near the equator, away from dense populations, and large enough to accommodate everyone."

"I'll contact him," Case agreed.

Eve quietly gathered the dishes from the room and carried them into the kitchen. The men's plans made her uneasy. Her mouth was tight and her eyes were distant in thought.

"Hey," I said to her in the kitchen, "you okay?"

She glanced up at Case and Khalen, and nodded. "What they do is necessary but dangerous," she quietly replied.

"Dangerous?" I asked.

"You have felt the energy in this room when Case and Khalen disagree."

"Yes," I said, nodding, remembering the event very well. The buzz had been nearly deafening, and the pressure in the room unbearable. I felt as if I were sinking into the depths of the ocean with no end in sight. I had to leave the room that night.

"Now," said Eve, "imagine over one hundred clan leaders, all very strong and gifted, meeting and trying to come toward a common goal."

I shivered.

"Their energy will be felt for miles. I assure you, many earthquakes will be reported that night."

Chapter 26

The choices of our past lay the foundation of our future.

LATE THAT EVENING, SETH RETURNED with his mother and sister. Sunjia was a beautiful woman, dark, exotic, and delicately balanced on a tiny frame. She was not shapely as she was refined. She held herself as if she pumped royal blood through her veins. Her dark eyes matched her son's, but they lacked the golden hue and she kept them looking down.

Her daughter, however, had blue eyes, the color of the deep sea. She looked to be around nine or ten years old, stood a good five-feet tall, and had her mother's tiny frame. Her long brown hair flowed gracefully down to her waist. She held her head high and had no problems looking directly at me and the others. I had expected her to be as submissive as her mother; she clearly was not.

Case invited them into his yurt, where we all gathered. Ian and Aidan had not yet returned home. Khalen assured me that they were fine and were probably seeking female affection.

"Can I get you something to drink?" asked Eve.

The little girl shook her head. Sunjia looked up a bit apprehensively, "A glass of red wine, if you have it." Her voice was soft and gentle. She took the glass from Eve with shaking hands. Maiyun came close to offer her comfort.

"Don't be afraid," I assured her. "We are not here to hurt you."

She took a long sip of her wine, and then set the glass down on the floor beside her. Neither she nor her daughter were accustomed to sitting on the floor, and their dresses made it even more awkward. Unfortunately, the furniture that Case had ordered had not been delivered yet. It would have made more sense to meet in our yurt, but Case had said no for whatever reason he had.

"Has Seth told you why we brought you here?" asked Case.

She nodded, never meeting his eyes. Her submissiveness infuriated me. "He has."

"Is it true about the fate of twins?" Khalen asked, impatiently. The woman's submissive behavior was clearly wearing on his nerves as well.

I walked over to her and placed my hand on her shoulder. "Sunjia, there is no need for you to fear us."

She took another long sip of her wine. "It is not you I fear," she said with a mild Brazilian accent. "Seth has chosen wisely to come here. It was upon my request that he did so. I only wish Tria and I could also stay. For me, it is too late. My soul is dark and empty; there is nothing left to save. Tria, however, is good like her brother." She was talking now as if in a trance. Her eyes were distant; her finger traced the edge of the wine glass.

"Traeger's father turned the clan dark—ignored the Spirian laws and made his own. He corrupted Traeger until he became a different man than the one I was promised to. I knew if I produced ungifted children, he would stop siring them with me. I told my children to keep their gifts hidden. I don't want this life for them. The Shadows have strayed too far from the way. They are a different breed of Spirian now." Her jaw clenched with tension. "A dark cult that worships anarchy."

"That will soon change," Khalen assured her. "Can you help sever the bond between me and my brother?"

Her eyes studied his. "Give me your hand," she said. Against Khalen's, hers looked like a young child's. He allowed her to fold her tiny fingers around his. She closed her eyes. "Hmm," she mumbled. "You are the stronger twin. Your gifts are—intriguing." She released his hand and took a deep breath. "Traeger knows I'm here," she said. "He's in my thoughts. I feel his anger." She downed the rest of her wine.

"Come, Mother, let's get you home," Seth said, holding his hand out to her.

"I don't want to go back," Tria said, her voice strong and defiant.

Sunjia closed her eyes and pressed both hands against the sides of her head as if it ached with indecision. "We are out of time." She looked up at Khalen. "Listen to me. Do not separate your soul from your brother's. You are strong and can survive his death, but you cannot be the one who kills him. He knows that, so be careful." Her eyes shifted to her daughter. She took both her hands. "Tria, dear. You are under claiming age. Your father must determine your fate. If you stay, he will kill you, I'm sure of it. Your only chance to survive is to go with him when he comes to collect us."

Tria pulled her hands back. "No, I will not! Uncle Khalen left when he was young."

"Things were different then," Sunjia explained. "The Shadows do not tolerate treason. Even your brother is risking his life."

"I don't care," she said, storming over to Khalen's side. "Please, uncle, please say I can stay here with Seth."

Khalen looked over at me. I could feel the pain that tore at his heart. Taking his brother's children was wrong on several levels. "What if I took Traeger's life?" I asked. "Would that not free you all?"

"No," Sunjia said, shaking her hands as if trying to free them from dirt. "You are too close to Khalen. Traeger must die at the hands of another clan, not from anyone here or Khalen may die."

Traeger was close, we could all feel his presence. This time he had company. "Skye," Case said. "You and Eve take Tria and Sunjia back to your yurt and stay there. Understand?"

I nodded. Khalen grabbed my arm and turned me around. His eyes bore into mine as if I would disappear if he didn't remember every detail of my face. "We'll be all right," I assured him. "Stay safe." He pressed his lips upon mine, and then held me close.

"Stay in our yurt," he whispered.

"I will," I promised. "See you soon." I followed Eve and the other two out the door and hurried back to our yurt with Maiyun close by my side. She didn't like leaving Khalen any more than I did. She kept looking back at him as he watched us retreat to our yurt. I closed the door and tried to calm my pounding heart.

"He will know where we are," said Sunjia. "There is no sense in hiding."

"We are not hiding," Eve explained. "Case is removing us from the line of fire."

Sunjia's eyes widened. "There are so many of them," she said. "More than Case and Khalen can handle alone.

"You underestimate their abilities," I said. I heard Case and Khalen call for Caleb, Ian, and Aidan. Caleb would bring Drew, his older brother, I was certain. I smiled as each of them responded with excitement and enthusiasm. There was nothing the men liked more than a hearty Spirian battle.

"Sunjia," I instructed, trying to give her something other than worrying to do. "Stoke the fire and add another log. It's getting cold in here." The coldness, though, came from her and her daughter, not the lack of heat. "Tria," I addressed the young girl, "Perhaps you can help Eve make some cocoa?"

Eve glanced at me approvingly. With shaky hands, she began pulling mugs from the shelf. "Come, dear, you can stir the milk." She filled a saucepan with goat milk and set the flame to medium heat.

The Shadows were here; their presence was numbing. Through thought, Case and Khalen had warned the rest of the clan to stay hidden. The fires had been extinguished and the camp looked deserted and cold. Caleb and his brother Drew arrived first. Ian and Aidan were only minutes away. Traeger and his mob were coming down the driveway in seven vehicles.

I'm scared, I thought to Khalen.

Don't be. Their numbers are many, but their skill is weak, he replied. *Please, keep yourself safe.*

You too, I replied.

Sunjia gripped her stomach and fell to the floor. I rushed to her side. Sunjia cried out in pain. Her daughter came running. I tried to remove the pain, but something kept pushing me out. My shield dissolved before it could form. Eve turned off the stove before coming to help.

The front door slammed open. A man I didn't recognize stood on the threshold with three other men behind him. I built my shield around us, but the first man easily dispelled it.

Maiyun growled then stepped between me and the four men. The first man waved his hand and sent her flying across the room. She hit the wall with a loud thump and a sharp yelp.

"Maiyun!" I yelled. There was no response. She lay unconscious in a heap.

"Stay together," I told the ladies.

The first man reached out to grab my arm then jumped back with slew of cuss words streaming from his mouth.

"Leave us," I warned. "There is nothing here that belongs to you." I felt the hum around my body grow stronger. I projected it out and around us all.

The other three men surrounded us. One of them reached over and grabbed Eve. She cried out as he pulled her away from our circle. My shield wobbled from the breach, but held firm.

"Remove your shield," the first man said, "or Tim here will remove the human's head."

The man named Tim gripped the back of Eve's skull with one hand, while the other hand clamped over her forehead. Eve cried out in pain.

"No!" I said. "Don't, please." I pulled my shield in. Again, the first man tried to reach for me and was severely burned for his efforts.

"Damn it! I said remove your shield."

"I did," I stood from Sunjia and moved back. Tim slowly twisted Eve's head. A blast of energy flew from my hand and pushed him back against the wall. Eve dropped to the floor. A shock pierced my back, bringing me to my knees. I drove the charge to the ground, stood and faced the man who had cast it. He cast another. I deflected it back to him, biting back the sting in my hands. His next cast was much stronger and pushed me back. I felt its sting as it tested my shield. Another man reached out for me then jumped back grabbing his hand.

"Grab her," the first man yelled.

Ian and Aidan burst through the door. A deafening hum surrounded me then everything went blank as if I had just stepped into a white room surrounded with bright light. The brothers had zapped me into an illusion of protection. In this place, I knew that time could vanish in seconds, as if I were in a dream. In this place, I could not distinguish what was happening outside of the illusion, nor could I alter it in any way. That was the brothers' intentions, I was sure. Nothing but the hum reverberated in my ears, and the ground beneath my feet felt cool and smooth. They wanted me out of harm's way.

Suddenly the hum stopped, and the white room vanished, leaving me on the floor of the yurt, next to Sunjia and her wailing daughter. Eve lay still on the floor, while Ian and Aidan dragged four bodies across the floor and tossed them outside. "Stay here," Aidan called back as he and his brother hurried to help Case and Khalen.

I crawled over to where Eve lay very still. Her neck hung at an odd angle, and her breathing was very shallow. "Eve," I said. "Be very still."

"I can't feel anything," she said.

I placed my hands on either side of her neck and focused on the bones. The C2 and C3 vertebrae had been snapped clean. With just a little more force, her spinal cord would have been severed and she would be dead. I held her neck steady and waited for the bones to mend. Slowly, her fingers began to move, and then her toes. I waited for the healing to complete, and then helped her to her feet. She was unsteady, so I guided her to the couch and helped her sit.

"Please," Tria called out. "Help my mom."

The powerful blows that Sunjia had sustained caused her to bleed internally. She lay doubled over in pain. "Sunjia," I said. "I'm going to take the pain away." I placed my hands on her belly. My hands vibrated as if they rested on snare drums played hard and fast. The energy that attacked her was still in full force. It was as if a hundred electrical leads were clamped to her skin, sending blinding amounts of voltage into her body. I felt the sting as it entered my body then a sharp pain to my gut that forced my hands away.

"Skye, what's wrong?" Eve asked.

My hands were shaking, yet each time I tried to touch Sunjia, the shock of her was too great. "Someone is shielding her," I explained.

"Please, help her," Tria cried. "She's dying."

I built my own shield and then tried touching her again. The pain was intense, but not unbearable. To stop the vicious attack on her body, I would have to extend my shield to include her. She jerked violently beneath my hands.

"Please," I begged the Father. "Help me save her." The stings grew stronger. I pushed them to the ground, trying to ignore the burning pain of their bite.

Maiyun whined. She had been tossed like a rag doll against the wall and probably suffered from broken bones. "Hang on, Maiyun. I'm coming."

My efforts did nothing to ease Sunjia's pain, nor did it

offer healing. I was fighting against a force much stronger than my own. I removed my hands. Sunjia writhed in pain. I felt helpless. Then suddenly, she stopped convulsing. The hum that surrounded her dulled. I placed my hands upon her and felt only the hum of my healing. The shield had been removed.

She sat up slowly, her eyes wide with disbelief. "He's dead," she said. A smile replaced her doubt as she scanned her arms and body. "The pain is gone."

Tria came over and gave her mother a hug. "Thank you," she said to me.

I nodded then rushed over to help Maiyun. Her ribs had been broken, and blood trickled from her nose. I allowed the energy to flow through my hands like water from Heaven. Maiyun lifted her head and licked my hand then relaxed and allowed the healing to continue. When the hum stopped, I removed my hands, now warm and shaking. "Okay Maiyun, get up."

Maiyun rose to her feet with a groan and hearty body shake. "Good girl," I said, scratching the thick fur on the back of her neck. She licked my face with her warm, wet tongue.

The door slammed opened and Ian ran in. "Skye, come quick. It's Khalen." I jumped to my feet and followed Ian to Case's yurt. Maiyun and Eve came as well, followed by Sunjia and Tria.

Khalen lay on the ground, surrounded by Aidan, Case, Caleb, and Drew. He was barely breathing. "What happened?" I asked, completely forgetting Sunjia had just announced her mate's death. I didn't put the pieces together until now. "Oh God," I said. "Who killed him?"

Case looked down. Aidan looked away, tears welling in his eyes. Through their thoughts, I knew it was Khalen who had taken his brother's miserable life. With a prayer, I placed my hands on Khalen's chest. It was cold and still. I closed my eyes and asked the Father for all the help he could give me. "Don't take him from me," I pleaded. My hands shook, remembering my same plea when Derrick was slipping away. I couldn't save him. What if I couldn't save Khalen?

Sunjia kneeled down beside me. "You carry a part of his soul," she said. "Offer it back to him."

I took a few deep breaths, and reached in deep to the place where I felt him the strongest. I imagined that part of himself he had offered to me mingling with the blue mist. I then offered the blue mist to him. I didn't know if it would work, but I had no idea how to offer his soul back. Healing energy, I knew, was not particular as it relied on pure intention. The stronger the intent, the more focused the energy became. I felt his soul drain from my body, and felt his body respond with new life. His chest grew warm beneath my hands, and his heartbeat strengthened.

"Khalen, my love. Come back to me." I continued offering myself to him, feeling a dark, cold void in the pit of my stomach.

"Enough," Sunjia, said, pulling my hands away from him. My hands were cold. The vibration was gone. Khalen lay still and silent. His breathing was stronger now, and his body was warm. I lay down beside him, and curled into a ball. A huge hole filled my center, cold, dark and empty. Khalen was gone from me, along with a chunk of my own soul. I was an empty shell, shivering between the cool space that separated life and death.

I heard the voices around me, but could not make out the words. I was drifting away, bodiless, soulless, and without direction. I saw Khalen's face as it drifted by, along with the beautiful green eyes of our daughters; their laughter filling my ears like a dulcet song. Then I was on that familiar cliff surrounded by a waterfall and bright purple flowers, with Derrick standing before me. He smiled.

I wanted to reach out for him, but my vow to Khalen kept me bound. Strangely, I felt as if I had betrayed Derrick. "I'm sorry," I said.

"Don't be." He walked toward me, his smile never faltering. "I always knew you had so much more to offer. I thank God every day for the time I had with you."

I gave him a hug. Our time together felt like an entire lifetime ago. I knew I loved him, but now my heart felt empty of all feelings. I was confused. Before, I wanted nothing more than to be with him—to stay here and never return to my life on Earth. Now I hungered to feel the life I had with Khalen, to feel his warmth and his love.

"I won't see you again," said Derrick. "This is the last time. I have to let you go." He stepped back, his hazel eyes sparkling with love and admiration. "I love you, Skye." His image faded before me. I was alone in the meadow now. Alone, empty, and afraid.

A dark figure came toward me. He looked like Khalen but it wasn't him. He reached his hand out toward me. "Come to me, Skye." I shrank back. Something was wrong. This man was not Khalen.

I shook my head. "No, you're not him."

The man drew closer, the hum surrounding him like mosquitoes hungry and aggressive. "Take my hand, Skye."

Was it possible that I had lost all sense of recognition? Was I so dead inside that even my own mate could not reach my empty heart? "No," I said again. "Go away." I curled up into a ball and hugged my legs to my chest.

The darkness in me felt like heavy tar, making it hard to breathe. The cliff, waterfall, and purple flowers began to fade, along with the scent of lilac and lavender. Darkness surrounded me now, and with it came a blissful sense of peace.

"Skye," a familiar voice broke through the void.

I saw nothing through the darkness. A bright blue light filled my vision as if it came from the inside of my head. As it drew near, I made out a handsome man with silver hair and sea-blue eyes. "Shanuk?" My voice was distant as if I had spoken the name from several feet away.

He smiled down at me then raised his hand. A sharp bolt of energy pierced my chest. I fell into a vortex, spinning and falling with streaks of light flashing by me. I couldn't breathe.

"Breathe, Skye. Please, breathe for me, love." A warm burst of air filled my lungs then another. I felt firm, even pressure over my chest then a sharp pound. My eyes sprang open. My lungs gasped for air. Maiyun's warm, wet tongue lapped over my mouth. Fuzzy figures milled around me, talking and laughing. Another wet lick urged me to sit up. That was a mistake. Everything went black again and my body collapsed against something warm and hard.

"Why can't you stay bloody down?" was the last thing I heard.

When my eyes finally opened again, Khalen's face was inches from my own. His hair hung loose and provided a dark canopy around my head. "Welcome back," he said in a wonderful, velvety voice.

I tried to sit, but his hands firmly held my shoulders down. "Stay put," he said.

I lifted my hand and weaved my fingers through his hair. The soft strands felt like silk. I smiled. "You have your hair down." My throat felt dry and rough.

"If I let you go, will you promise to stay down?" he asked, his golden green eyes boring into mine.

"I don't want you to let me go," I teased. My words came out slow and weak, hardly sounding like my own.

He drew me into him and held me so tight it was difficult to breathe. "Khalen," I rasped. "I need to breathe." He gently laid me back down then rested his forehead against my chest.

"God," he said. "I thought I'd lost you." I felt a warm tear trickle down my chest.

"Me too," I said.

Chapter 27

The battle between right and wrong is infinite. The division between the two fluctuates like the tide and changes with each perspective.

KHALEN AND I PACKED FOR OUR trip to Brazil in the morning to meet with the clan elders. I was prepared to stay behind, but Khalen was not comfortable with leaving me. He assured Case that I would be safe in Arcadie's guest cottage while the meeting took place. As a compromise, however, Case insisted Eve go as well so that I would have company. Maiyun, of course, was to stay at the camp under Aidan's care. When things had settled, he formed a bond with me as my templar. The sting of it nearly dropped me to my knees as we connected. It was supposed to have been done after the ceremony, but Khalen was too impatient.

The council meeting was arranged in short order, and the leaders were prepared to meet at Arcadie's manor. Our plan was to arrive at the manor one day in advance. Not knowing how long the meeting would take, we planned to stay the entire week, maybe longer if necessary.

Khalen convinced me to pack my cane, since he would not always be around to guide me should I venture onto the massive grounds of the manor. I never liked using the cane. The red tip, to me, was an eyesore and drew too much attention.

"It is not for your benefit," he said. "It alerts others around you that you have a visual impairment."

"Why do they need to know?" I asked.

"So they don't think you're drunk or something when you fall over an unseen chair." He handed me my folded cane and watched as I reluctantly place it in my satchel.

I continued to pack my few belongings, wondering what in the world I was thinking. I hadn't traveled out of the United States since I was nine years old. That trip to England was nothing but a distant memory. I was apprehensive about leaving Maiyun, but knew she would be in great care. Aidan and Ian would no doubt take her to work every day and spoil her rotten.

Khalen looked at me as if assessing my mood. The right side of his mouth started to curl. "Why so apprehensive?" he asked, looking at me as he carefully tucked his clothing into the garment bag.

I shrugged. "I guess I'm just not sure what to expect."

He walked over to me and wrapped his arms around my shoulders. "You'll be all right, my love. Relax."

"Are you sure I should come? Case was shocked that you insisted I be there. Perhaps it would be better if I stayed here?"

He crooked his finger under my chin. "I am the clan leader and you are my mate. Where I go, you go."

"But Case said that it might not be safe for me there."

He groaned and rested his chin on my head. "That is true, but you are not much safer being left here with

Case and I gone. Caleb and Drew will stand watch, along with Ian and Aidan, but the Shadows are on high alert now, especially since Traeger is gone and his mate is in our camp. I think it's best to keep you by my side. Besides, things are sure to get dicey during the meeting, and you might be needed to offer some healing. Negotiations can turn aggressive among Spirians."

"So I've heard," I said, silently praying that my mate would have the sense to stay out of the fire line.

"I'll be fine," he assured me.

"I'm not sure if traveling while being so early in pregnancy is such a good idea," I said.

"Skye," he said, his voice stern now and deep. "I want you with me. You will not stay here." It was more of a statement than a request. Knowing I would lose this argument, I simply nodded.

Khalen gathered our bags and placed them next to the door. He took my hand and led me toward the bed. "Come," he said, "let's get some rest. We leave early tomorrow and I doubt you will sleep much on the plane."

He slipped my nightshirt off over my head and draped it across the bench at the foot of our bed. He quickly shed his own clothes, climbed under the covers and snuggled up next to me. His warm, demanding lips claimed mine with such possession, it took my breath away as it did each time he kissed me.

"Tonight," he said, his tone low and gentle, "I make you mine again."

I knew what that meant. Every time we made love, he reaffirmed our union, offering a bond to his soul that several lifetimes couldn't sever. I was complete beneath his skillful command, and assured that I was, indeed, loved.

It was nice not having him disappear in the middle of the night anymore when he could not sleep. Now he simply woke me and loved me until his body was spent. Before our union, he explained, he wanted me but did not want to take me without ceremony. The frustration of lying beside me without having his way was too much for him, so he had to leave. Knowing that provided a relief of sorts. At least I knew he didn't find me unattractive.

He made our loving last that night, long, slow, and deliberate. "Sleep now, love," he whispered, gently brushing the clinging hair from my dampened forehead. He rolled off me then pulled me beside him until my head rested in the crook of his shoulder, his large arms wrapped around me like a protective blanket. I slept listening to the sound of his heartbeat, slow, strong, and steady.

K HALEN GENTLY SHOOK ME FROM the side of the bed, and then placed a hot cup of coffee on the end table. His warm lips trailed a line of fire down my neck until I opened my eyes. "Rise and shine," he said. He was already up and dressed. The smell of spicy Italian sausage and onions permeated the air.

I groaned and sat up, squinting against the bright full-spectrum lights that illuminated the room. He handed me my coffee. "Did you sleep well?" he asked.

I nodded. "Like a stone in a lazy river," I replied. "And you?"

He smiled, obviously amused with my simile. "The same. Are you hungry?"

"Always," I replied, savoring the first sip of my coffee. It had a hint of dark chocolate and cinnamon powder. I smiled. "Mmm, this is good," I said, closing my eyes and breathing in the earthy aroma.

I watched him cook and toss scraps of food to Maiyun. How he could cook in a white long-sleeved shirt without spilling anything down the front of it intrigued me. The shirt hung loose over his massive frame and did not have the usual creases down the arms. This shirt displayed a more casual look as it draped free over his jeans.

I reached over and grabbed my nightshirt. I donned it, and then took my coffee up to the breakfast bar. "Khalen," I said, scooting onto the high stool.

"Hmm?" he replied, adding a bowl of scrambled eggs to the goodies in the frying pan.

"When the Shadows came, I removed my shield, but still no one could touch me. Why is that?"

I could see a hint of a smile on his face when he turned to check on the coffee. "I placed a bond around you for protection."

"A bond? Like the one that kept me from leaving camp?"

"Yes, exactly. If anyone tries to harm you or touch you without your acceptance, a good shock would deter them from trying again."

"How long does the bond last?"

He turned to face me. "Until I remove it."

I frowned. "How does it work? I mean, how does it know who to shock and who to let in?"

"It is activated whenever you are frightened, alarmed or uncomfortable." He slid half of the omelet onto my plate then neatly arranged sliced apples, bananas and pears around it.

My stomach growled loudly. "Then you had best remove it when we fly to Brazil because I will be uncomfortable the entire trip."

He laughed. "I'll be with you, Skye. There is no need

for you to feel discomfort." He warmed my coffee then sat beside me, taking my hands in his. After a gracious prayer, we began eating.

"Can women place a bond around things?"

He shook his head then finished his bite. "Women can shield, but their gifts typically lean toward nurturing, as where male gifts lean toward protection."

"But Kiara could set things on fire. That is hardly nurturing."

"It is when used correctly. Just as your shield can send a man flying or cause an electrical explosion to occur, like what happened in the illusion with Aidan and Ian."

I took another bite of the tangy, spicy omelet. The sweet orange bell peppers played nicely with the hot spice of the sausage. "I feel like my gifts have grown much stronger since we married."

He sipped his coffee; his lips hinted at a smile. "When you join with a mate, you acquire his or her gifts to a degree."

"To a degree?" I asked.

"I cannot heal, for that gift is reserved for females, and you cannot reinforce commands, a gift reserved for lead males. A woman's gifts cannot overpower those of her mate. When the woman's gifts grow stronger, so does her mate's. The man chooses which gifts he shares with his mate and which gifts he acquires from her."

The benefits of a union seemed vastly unbalanced in the male's favor. "That hardly seems fair."

He popped a pear slice into his mouth and chased it down with a sip of coffee. "It is when you view things from the Father's perspective."

"Explain." I enjoyed my apple portion while Khalen gathered his thoughts for what was sure to be an enlightening answer.

"Man was created to labor and protect his land and family. Woman was created to love and nurture her mate and children. Yin and yang, soft and hard, gentle and firm. Together we provide perfect balance." Obviously satisfied with his answer, he continued to eat his fruit.

"Women can also be strong," I affirmed.

"Yes, but never stronger than her mate." He held my hand. "I am not undermining the power of a woman, Love. I'm simply explaining how things are in the Spirian realm. Humans often choose female-dominant relationships, and they work fine in the human world. If a Spirian male joins with a stronger female, the balance will be destructive. Also, if a Spirian male joins with too weak of a female, she may not survive the union."

"Is that why Ian and Aidan do not have wives?" I still had a hard time with the word mate and Khalen was obviously amused by it.

He laughed. "An illusionist is very strong. They require an equally strong mate." He emphasized the last word.

I narrowed my eyes. "Mate sounds so barbaric," I said.

"But it means so much more than mere wife," he explained. "A mate is your equal, the very thing that completes you. When your mate dies, a part of you dies as well."

I reflected on the past weeks. "Yes, I remember," I quietly said.

He frowned. "Sunjia said that you had given not only my spirit back to save me, but a good part of yours as well. Why would you do that?"

I pushed my plate away, having had my fill of food for now. "I wanted nothing more than to bring you back. I wanted to offer you my life in return."

He took my hands and urged me to look into his fiery gaze. He was trying to see through me. "My love, do you not understand that without you, my life is nothing?"

I laughed and looked away. His finger gently brought me back to his piercing stare.

"Khalen," I said, my voice shaky. "You managed to survive eighty-three years without me by your side. I believe you will survive without me again someday."

A soft smile formed on his face and he closed his eyes. "Then you still do not understand how you affect me and how much you are a part of me now."

"I don't understand permanence in a world that constantly changes. Everything I have ever loved has left me, except you. When your life was seeping from this world, I—."

I looked down, unable to continue.

"I won't leave you, Skye. You are a part of me now, in this life and beyond." He pulled me against his chest and cradled my head with his palm.

Chapter 28

A journey begins with momentum and ends with quiet stillness,
only to be reborn and traveled again with renewed light.

THE TWENTY-THREE-HOUR JOURNEY to Manaus Brazil played havoc on my senses. Though we flew first class, the close proximity to so many people was nearly unbearable. Humans, I discovered, share their emotions generously through the way they walk, talk, and spend quiet time. So much pain and sadness quenched and dulled with alcohol, music, novels, and movies. I wanted to reach out and heal their hearts with a peace they may never know stands right before them.

"Your heart seems heavy, my love," said Khalen, squeezing my hand as he led me expertly through the crowded airport. Eve and Case walked in front of us, snuggling and laughing like young teens in love.

I softened the wrinkles on my brow; previously unaware I had been so tense. "I have never noticed how sad humans are. I guess I never really paid much attention. I feel as if I had distanced myself from everyone for a very long time."

"There are advantages to our race," he said. "We are closer to the Father than most humans and, therefore, can feel His peace. Unfortunately, technology and busy lifestyles have taken the place of quiet time for most humans. Not many of them spend time in front of a crackling fire, listening to the sounds of the night, or the wind for that matter. They watch TV, work on computers, or tune into their MP3 players. There is not enough time with the Father to feel His presence."

I looked around at the crowd meandering through the corridors. Many of them seemed lost in their own little worlds. Their energetic vibrations were dull and tired. "Funny, I've never noticed it before."

He wrapped his arm around my shoulders. "You did, it just didn't register. Now that you have spent time with people of your own kind, you notice how different humans are. Before, you noticed how different our race was, picking up on our energy and bright auras. Remember?"

I nodded. "Yeah, I do." I rested my head against his chest, relishing the comfort he offered.

We followed Case and Eve through a restricted wing in the airport. It led to a small terminal where a private plane waited for us. A handsome man with silver hair held back in a braid, slightly longer and thinner than Khalen's, greeted us.

Case greeted the man with a smile and a hug. "Arcadie," he said warmly, "great to see you again, brother."

Arcadie stepped back and admired Eve with sparkling blue eyes that reminded me of Shanuk. "Eve, you look more engaging each time I see you," he said, his brilliant teeth shining like pearls in sunlight. His British accent was slightly thicker than Case's, with a hint of Scottish undertones. He was immaculately dressed in a cobalt blue silk shirt and jet-black pants. His boots were shiny and flawless.

He turned toward Khalen and invited him with open arms. "Khalen, my boy, you've grown since last I saw you. Damn handsome, you are."

"Good to see you, Arcadie," he said then turned and gestured toward me. "Allow me to introduce my mate, Skye."

Arcadie's eyes sparkled. "Oh aye, we've heard about this one. He bowed, took my hand and gently kissed the back of it. "It is an honor to meet you, my lady. Your brilliance precedes you, but it offers meager justice to your beauty. You are more magnificent in person."

I felt myself flush and lowered my head. "Thank you," I stammered like a shy child. His presence was so close to Shanuk that I felt as if I were staring at his twin.

He laughed, obviously reading my thoughts. "His twin, no," he clarified, "just his eldest son." He turned toward Case with sadness. "I understand he has returned to the Father."

Case nodded. "Indeed, he has."

The silence was awkward, but filled with utmost respect for Shanuk who had played such a vital role in many lives.

"Come," said Arcadie. "My mate, Kitta, has prepared an early dinner for us all." He ushered us toward the private plane painted in bright colors of blue, purple, orange and red. There was no apparent format to the design scheme, just a relaxed blend of colors that swirled about the fuselage and wings like wild wind.

Inside, the plane was furnished with comfortable leather chairs, tables, and a small bar. The pilot turned and greeted us all with a smile. "My son, Dirk," said Arcadie.

"Hang on," said Dirk. "It's going to be a bit of a ride. The wind is relentless up there." His accent carried more Scottish overtones than his father's, and pleasantly rolled off his tongue like a song. He had black hair and obsidian eyes that mirrored Case's. In the bright sunlight streaming in through the window, I could see Dirk's long, straight nose ended with a triangular tip that brought attention to the natural curl of his lips. When his eyes rested on me, I felt his intrigue build. I suddenly felt obligated to meet expectations that were far too high for my comfort. I looked away and allowed Khalen to guide me over to a chair.

The cabin was darker than the front of the plane and the details were lost to me. Khalen secured the complicated five-point harness that surrounded me with confining efficiency.

"I'd offer you all drinks, but fear the turbulence will be too much for you to enjoy them properly."

Khalen reached over and squeezed my hand. "Relax, Love."

I hadn't noticed that my fingernails were clenching the soft leather arms of the chair. My eyesight began to shrink as if my pupils were shutting out all traces of light. This had happened once before, when stress overcame me, but it had been months ago. I closed my eyes and willed the pupils to expand.

"Have any others arrived?" Case asked.

The roar of the engines came to life as Arcadie secured the door. "You're the first. The others will arrive sometime on the morrow." He sat next to Case and secured his harness.

The city of Manaus soon became a small speck as the plane banked over the Rio Negro, which Khalen had told me means black river. I could see why. It literally looked like a black ribbon winding through thick patches of green and geometrical shapes that outlined the city. Arcadie, I was told, lived on an island that had no name. He liked anonymity and had enough money to ensure he maintained it. He spent mostly summers here, and had other mansions throughout most of Europe.

The plane banked sharply left, leaving my guts in a state of weightlessness for a brief moment. I held my breath and gripped the arm of the chair. Khalen laughed. "Skye, breathe."

The plane lurched forward then jostled back again. "Hang on," Dirk announced over the speaker. "The landing is going to be a bit rough."

I closed my eyes and imagined us safely on the ground. Given the amount of turbulence bouncing us around, that image was distant at best. I placed my hand over my belly as if trying to assure my young that all would be fine soon. Somehow, calming them calmed my own fears. I smiled as Khalen placed his hand over mine.

We landed safely on an island that looked to be mostly trees. Dirk expertly negotiated the narrow airstrip to a small building that seemed oddly out of place here in the midst of old-growth trees. It looked like it was constructed of metal posts and beams, tinted glass, and metal siding—a sterile structure amid nature. My sight still had not completely recovered and I felt as if I were looking through murky water, even though there was enough sunlight for me to see.

A black Escalade waited for us. The driver stepped out and opened the doors. He was dressed like Jungle Jim, in khaki shorts, a safari vest, and a wide-brimmed hat. His ankle-high hiking boots added to the outfit that screamed adventure. A handgun rested in the holster over his right hip.

Khalen sat me in the back seat with Eve then helped the others load the luggage. After traveling for nearly two straight days, the fatigue was catching up with me.

"Case has a handsome family, does he not?" Eve said, breaking the silence.

I nodded. "Yes, very." I noticed the sadness in her eyes. I knew that she wondered what her own child would look like if it had survived. Case had chosen her life over the child's before swearing to never try having children again. From what I understood, the last time nearly took Eve's life as well. She had given birth to a pre-mature boy that was much too large for her to deliver. There was really nothing I could say to ease her pain, so I remained silent and simply placed my hand over hers.

I understood the pain of not being able to have children. Derrick and I had tried multiple times, not really understanding why I couldn't get pregnant. We were both fertile and healthy. The doctors could not provide an explanation, which further heightened our frustration. Eve knew why having children was not possible, yet still she longed for them. I hoped that her grandchildren would help ease that longing.

The ride to the mansion was quick, perhaps twenty minutes. We were greeted by a horde of women and young children. One woman stood out from the crowd. She was tall, and held herself in a manner that illustrated her stature in life. She wore a pale blue dress and had her long black hair twisted in a braid that fell to her tiny waist. She stood at the top of the stairs and watched as we walked from the car toward the mansion.

The mansion had been built of large stone and was

integrated among the many trees that dominated the island. The dark green vegetation that grew over the stones made it difficult to know where the mansion began and the forest ended. The clever design made it impossible to detect from the air.

"Kitta," Arcadie began, and then spoke to her in what sounded like Portuguese with a twist. I assumed he was introducing us all, but couldn't be certain. I did not speak or understand the language.

"Of course," she answered in English. Her accent was clearly not Scottish. And then her dark eyes rested on me. She reminded me of an ancient Egyptian queen minus the gold and makeup. "And who is this?" She held her hand out to me.

Khalen lifted my hand and placed it into Kitta's. "This is Skye, my mate," he said with far too much pride for my comfort. I felt the blood rush to my face.

Kitta bowed to me then released my hand. "The legend," she said. "I'm honored."

"No legend," I said, "just Skye."

Kitta laughed, followed by her husband and a few other bystanders. I felt as if I was the brunt of an old joke. Khalen offered me a reassuring squeeze.

After offering hugs to everyone, Kitta turned toward the huge wooden doors. They must have been at least twelve feet tall. The black wrought iron hinges and accents lent the feel of an old Scottish castle from the 1700s. It was too dark for me to see any detail.

"Come," Kitta said, "let's get you settled then we eat. I have prepared something special for you."

Our bags were carried inside for us by servants and were no doubt taken to our rooms. "I hope you don't mind," Kitta said over her shoulder. "Instead of having you stay in the guest cottages, I have arranged for you to stay in the main house with us."

She led us up two flights of stairs and down a wide hallway. The floors were hard like tile or stone, but warm under my thin-soled shoes. I couldn't wait to remove them.

"Case, Eve, this is your room," she said. I could hear the two of them veer to the left. Your bags have been unpacked for you. Dinner will be served in an hour."

"Lovely, thank you, Kitta," Case replied.

We continued down the hall. "Khalen, Skye, this is your room. Your bags have been unpacked as well."

Khalen nodded his head, leading me slightly to the right to let me know the direction of our room. "Thank you."

Kitta turned to face him. "You have grown into a fine young man, Khalen, and have chosen a lovely mate."

"Your accommodations are very gracious, Kitta. Thank you."

She smiled. "Of course, only the best for family. I'll see you both in an hour."

It was odd to hear an eighty-three-year-old man being addressed as young, but compared to Case and his older brother, I supposed Khalen was young. Given that I was nearly half his age, I was like a teenager in the grand scheme of things. I rather liked that.

"What are you smiling at?" asked Khalen, as he closed the door behind us.

"The fact that she called you a young man."

"Kitta is over two-hundred years old. To her, I am young."

I walked over to the sliding glass door that opened to a spacious deck overlooking a wild pond. The sounds of the jungle were something akin to a Tarzan movie. The air smelled green and damp like Irish moss. It was humid, but not intolerable.

Khalen came up behind me and wrapped his arms around my waist. "Are you happy you came?" he asked.

"I'm happy to be with you."

"But?" he prompted, knowing already what laid heavy on my mind.

"I don't like being considered 'the legend.' It makes me uncomfortable."

He laughed and turned me around to face him. "I'm afraid it is something you must get used to, my love. News travels fast among Spirians."

"Well," I said, tracing a seductive finger down his chest, "you can help set things straight and deny the rumor."

He took a deep breath and growled, gripping my hand. "I could," he said, his voice raspy, "but I won't lie. You are the legend and denying that fact disgraces Shanuk." He led me back to the room.

"Now, my love," he continued. "We have an hour. I suggest you finish what you just started with that seductive touch of yours." He led me over to the bed and began stripping my clothes.

DINNER STARTED WITH MANDIOCA FRITA, fried yucca. Khalen moved a candle before me so that I could at least locate the food on my plate. It tasted similar to a potato but slightly more fibrous with a heavy flavor of rosemary. A white wine, Loios Branco Alentejo, was served. I reluctantly opted for water, which rose more than a few brows, as I gathered from the sudden quieting of conversation.

"She's with child," Eve explained. That bit of news raised a flurry of excitement. I wanted to crawl under the table and stay there. I was never one to enjoy being the topic of conversation, especially when the word "legend" was used.

Arcadie raised his glass. "To new beginnings and hope," he said. Everyone nodded, clinked their glasses with one another, and took a hearty sip. Khalen offered me his glass to seal the toast. The sweet wine offered the flavor of crisp fruit, similar to a pear with attitude. The rich minerals of the land were evident in the finish. I liked it.

Served next was a green salad with a colorful variety of julienned vegetables, some of which I couldn't identify. What followed was a hearty entrée of Brazilian Stroganoff. It consisted of tender beef sautéed in mushroom sauce with onions, and served over a steaming bed of hearty, vanilla-scented rice. A heavy accent of black pepper dominated the aroma, but was not overpowering. I could only eat a quarter of the portion served to me. Khalen eagerly ate the rest.

Warm bread pudding served with rich coffee ended the meal. By the time I was done, my stomach felt close to bursting. The men retired to the study where they could discuss the details of the upcoming meeting, while we women retired to the sitting room. Not being familiar with the layout of the huge mansion, I stayed close to Eve, who took over for Khalen and protectively led me from one room to another. Even if I had my cane, I could not negotiate the massive maze of rooms and corridors, not without memorizing the layout.

"How far along are you, my dear?" Kitta asked.

"Two months," I replied. The morning sickness had

not yet begun, but I noticed a subtle queasiness now.

Kitta suddenly grew quiet. "You carry twins," she said with apprehension in her voice. "Khalen must—"

"I'm fine," I interrupted.

"But, dear, it is dangerous to—"

Eve patted her hand. "Not now, Kitta."

The older woman sighed. "Very well."

"You have a lovely place," I said, hoping to change the mood and the topic. My father always commented on my ability to skirt around a subject that I didn't want to discuss. It worked well with most people, but not so well with Khalen. He always seemed to circle back to where we left off.

Kitta took the hint and carried it off beautifully. She described the tapestries that covered the walls in great detail. I found the history behind them fascinating. Most of them were brought over from the Scottish Highlands and told stories of past wars and triumphs. The way she described them conjured memories of the movie Braveheart.

"That's when I met Arcadie," she giggled. "There he sat astride a large black beast with steam billowing from its nose. He was a handsome man," she added, sounding almost distant now. "And built like a fortress."

"If I remember right," said Eve, "your father refused to offer you as his mate."

"True, true," she laughed. "My father called him a wild man with no direction. Arcadie had to prove himself for years before my father blessed our union."

"Prove himself?" I asked. "In what way?"

"Arcadie had to provide for me in a manner that my father believed was appropriate. He had to build me a fine house, in a strong clan community, and demonstrate a wide variety of gifts to prove his stature."

"Well," I said. "Being the son of Shanuk, I'm sure Arcadie did not disappoint your father."

Kitta laughed. "No, he frightened the hell out of him," she said.

"What did he do?" I asked.

"Well, he brilliantly demonstrated telekinetic powers by effortlessly rearranging the furniture both upstairs and down. He then read my father's thoughts and revealed an embarrassing story from his youthful past. After that, he started a lovely bonfire in front of the barn, kept it very controlled—even though hay and straw surrounded the area—and then quickly quenched the flames with a simple wave of his hand."

"And that," Eve added, "was a small demonstration of his capabilities. A precursor, he called it."

"Needless to say, my father blessed our union without further proof. Arcadie neglected to tell him he was the son of Shanuk until our union took place."

"It would have saved him some time," I said.

"That it would have," she agreed. "My father's eyes nearly fell from his head when Shanuk was introduced. He apologized profusely for asking Arcadie to prove himself. Shanuk, of course, was amused and proud that Arcadie held up to the challenge."

Eve must have noticed my exhaustion. She stood and offered her hand to me. "Well, it's getting late and we didn't get much sleep on the plane."

"Of course," said Kitta. "You must be exhausted. I'll bid you good night then."

Eve led me back to my room. "Get some sleep, Skye. You look spent."

"I am a bit. Thank you for your help tonight," I said.

"With everything."

I could hear the smile in her voice as she said, "Good night, Skye."

After being led to my room, I closed the door and went straight to the washroom, where I started filling the tub with hot water. I had taken a shower earlier, so getting clean was not my intention. What I wanted now was heat, darkness, and blissful silence.

Khalen returned sometime later. The water had turned cold after the first forty-five minutes of my bath, before I fell asleep, and now I was shivering cold. He lifted my limp body from the tub, and laid me down onto the bed. After drying me off, he covered me with blankets and the warmth of his body.

"Khalen," I whispered. "I'm so cold."

"Lying in cold water tends to have that effect," he said.

"I fell asleep."

"Evidently." He rubbed my body to generate some heat. When that didn't work, he removed his clothes, cast them onto the floor then crawled beneath the covers. "Ahh," he shivered. "You're too damn cold."

"You're not," I said with a smile. "You feel warm." I snuggled up next to him.

"Jeeze," he screamed. "Even your feet are like ice."

"I think I know how to warm them up," I said mischievously. I began exploring his now shivering body with my hands.

"Yes," he said. "I think it's working."

A couple of hours later, I was feeling quite warm and had to stick my feet out from under the covers. Khalen rolled over onto his side and placed his hand on my belly.

"You're two months along," he said. "If I wait any longer the risk is greater."

"Wait any longer for what?" I asked.

"Skye, love. One of the twins must die, or you risk losing them both."

I sat up and stared at him incredulously. "No," I said, removing his hand from my belly. "I won't allow it."

"It is not your choice alone. If I do this now, your body will simply absorb the fetus without complications."

I started to get out of bed, not really believing his words. He pulled me back. "Skye, be reasonable." My instinct was to pull away from him and leave the room, but I knew better than to try such a feeble act. If I wanted to change Khalen's mind, I would have to employ a more effective tactic.

"I saw them," I said, "when I nearly died. They had black hair and vivid green eyes, Khalen. They were alive and well. Please don't take one of them from me."

"You were hallucinating, Skye. You were on the verge of death, for Pete's sake."

My eyes pleaded with him now, knowing that it would take nothing for him to claim the life of one of our babes. "I'm asking you to trust me on this, my love. Please."

He rolled off the bed. "Err," he growled. "You are so stubborn and naive. You ask me to go against the very thread of my instincts. By all rights, I should do what I know must be done and deal with your wrath in the wake." He turned to face me then pressed his hand on my belly. There was no need to form a shield around the twins. Intuitively, I knew he would not take one of them. He closed his eyes and took a long, deep breath. "Damn your will," he said between clenched teeth.

"I know your heart. You would rather die yourself than hurt me. And you know that taking one of our daughters would be far worse for me than anything that may arise from their birth."

He pressed his forehead down upon my belly. "I pray you are right."

"What good is a legend who cannot fulfill her obligations?" I teased, trying to coax a smile onto his weary face.

He lifted his head and looked at me questioningly. "So are you finally accepting your fate?"

"If it means making you smile, I do."

He held my hand and brought it tenderly to his lips. "You do make me smile."

"Sometimes," I added in a clarifying tone. I urged him down next to me and cradled his head in the crook of my shoulder.

Chapter 29

Those who become a part of our lives walk beside us for a time before venturing away, but their spirit remains in our hearts forever.

MORE LEADERS ARRIVED THIS MORNING, along with their respective successors. None of them were introduced or even brought near us women. They were immediately ushered to the meeting room. I was told they represented the Shadow clans. Those who represented the Protected were here in the house waiting for the meeting to begin. The mansion hummed like an old engine in desperate need of a tuning. I felt the hair on my back rise as if I stood in the center of an electrical storm. The meeting was to take place this morning after breakfast. Arcadie arranged to have it in the sub-basement where the energy would have less effect should an argument arise. Given the domineering attitudes of many of the leaders, everyone was sure to feel at least a dozen tremors I was warned.

Arcadie was careful whom he invited into the living space of his mansion. Many of the leaders had agreed to stay at a hotel in Manaus and fly over for the meetings. Dirk was more than willing to accommodate them. He didn't care for their company in the mansion any more than his father did.

Khalen brought me down to the sitting room where Eve and Kitta sipped tea. He sat me down and took both my hands in his. "Skye, promise me you will stay in the mansion. I don't want you wandering around with Shadows lurking about."

"Won't they be in the meeting with the rest of the men?" I asked, slightly disappointed that I would not be able to take my walk through the gardens.

"Some, but not all. I want you to stay inside. Understand?"

I nodded, feeling like a young child appeasing an overprotective adult. "This is going to be a long week," I sighed.

He kissed my hands then tenderly kissed my mouth. "Not long," he assured. "These meetings are typically short; you'll see why. I'll see you at dinner," he said. "We'll go for a walk then, all right?"

"I love you," I said as he stepped away. "Stay safe."

He nodded then left the room.

- K h a l e n -

A S WE APPROACHED THE MEETING room, my insides began to feel the pressure of conflicting energy. This was the first of these meetings that Case had me attend. Before this year, he later explained, I was not ready for the challenge. Other successors who were destined to lead a territory were asked to stay on the grounds, but not attend the meeting. Case explained that these meetings had taken too many young lives and the leaders were cautious about who could attend. I had to admit, my nerves were on edge.

"Shield yourself," said Case. "Make it strong." He squeezed my arm with a firm grip. "Keep your emotions in check, Son. Never weaken your shield." His dark eyes illuminated with deep cobalt hues. "If you feel a breech in your shield of any kind, leave the room. Understand?" He shook my arm with emphasis. "No one will judge you for it."

I nodded. "Yes, I understand."

Case hesitated before entering the room. His grip on my arm tightened, and then released as he closed his eyes and twisted the knob on the door. His own shield was so tight I could not even detect his emotions.

Arcadie sat at the far end of the huge round table. The room was circular and void of decor. The walls were lined with something that resembled a sponge-like material. I assumed it was meant to absorb some of the energy that would soon fill the room. Already the bone-jarring hum was making me nauseas.

I recognized many of the leaders in the room. Victor, the Shadow ruler of North America sat next to his eldest son, Sage. Victor was an energy bender, having the ability to change an object's form to suit his needs—a handy gift to have in the midst of a war. His son, Sage, looked much more confident than the last time I had seen him. His gifts were not as refined as his father's, but useful all the same. His telekinetic abilities rivaled my own and he could manipulate weaker minds with little effort. He would be hard pressed to find such a mind in this room.

Lasset, the Protected leader of New Zealand sat to my

left. He was a tribal elder who maintained the traditional ways. His form of dress was a simple robe woven from wool, slightly lighter than his sun-darkened skin. His gifts were a bit of a mystery, but Case had assured me he was a formidable ally to have on our side. He reminded me of an ancient voodoo sorcerer delivered in true form from Edgar Allen Poe's imagination.

I was unfamiliar with the other gentlemen occupying the room.

"Gentlemen," Arcadie began. "Thank you all for agreeing to meet on such short notice. As you are well aware, we have some situations that require our complete cooperation with one another. You have all been given an opportunity to read the issues at hand and add your own to the list. We will also use this meeting to announce changes in regional leadership.

"To keep damage to a minimum, I suggest we all have a chance to speak our opinions one at a time. At the end of each session, we will agree upon the most likely solution. Debates will not be permitted. Those who cannot conform to these rules may leave now."

He glanced around the table gleaning silent agreement from all in the room. "Very good then. Let us begin with the first issue at hand."

The first few items were minor and easily resolved. When the bone of contention concerning multiple mates was announced, an audible roar filled the room.

Arcadie stood, his cobalt eyes glowing with disapproval and evident threat. With a slight gesture of his hand, he managed to silence the three leaders who refused to acknowledge his request. Each of them held their throats as if some unseen force was squeezing them.

The subtle curl of Case's lips hinted his approval. He

had often spoken about his oldest brother's gifts with admiration. Now his eyes shone with support as they searched the room for possible counter-assaults. The other leaders felt his inclination and immediately stood down. It was clear who held the power in this room.

"Victor," Arcadie said, removing his chokehold on the three recalcitrant leaders. "We will begin with you." His eyes scanned the room as if pledging penance on anyone who interrupted.

Victor thought quietly for a moment before stating his opinion. He was a man of few words but those he spoke had powerful impact.

He rubbed his clean-shaven face, deeply tanned from hours in the sun. His good looks and abundant money flow ensured he had a steady influx of beautiful women to enjoy. Like most Shadows, he was not particular about his women being human or Spirian.

"The humans," he began, "do not seem to mind our affections." A sly smile stretched across his face. "We do not intentionally impregnate them. The women have the ability to—protect themselves, yet they do not. I understand that their offspring have shorter, barren lifespans and they must be around Spirians to survive, but that hardly poses a threat to our kind. I do agree, however, to having only one Spirian mate with whom to breed. There are simply not enough of them around to horde, and we are sorely in need of fresh Spirian blood."

It was Sage's turn to speak next. He did so while staring directly at Case. "The humans are weak. Their demise should not concern us."

I felt Case's energy surge then dampen. Sage's meaning had not gone unnoticed. When it was Case's turn to speak, he did so with harsh intent.

"I would be hard pressed to look our Holy Father in the eyes and tell him that his human creations were weak. If that were the case, young man," his eyes were on Sage, "their kind would be extinct instead of ours. My mate is human, true enough. It is my choice not to impregnate her. Victor's claim that we cannot prevent the female from conceiving is not entirely true. Humans are not always fertile. We are able to sense when they are likely to conceive. As we have stated, our original intent to taking a human female was to increase our numbers after careless Shadow males destroyed many of our Spirian females. Our mistake is well known and it is irresponsible for us to continue to interact with the humans intimately." He closed his hands indicating he was done speaking.

The hum in the room increased. If the table had not been bolted to the cement foundation, it would have levitated. I found it hard to breathe and had to concentrate on keeping myself centered and filled with light. When it was my turn to speak, I felt the piercing blows of the other leaders, testing my shield as Case had promised would happen. My years of training with Case made it easy to deflect the assaults with little effort.

"Humans are not the issue here, nor is their value. It is our Father's law that must be enforced. He wanted us to live in harmony with the humans. That does not involve altering their existence."

"Your adoptive mother is a human, is she not?" Haley voiced then quickly settled under the weight of Arcadie's warning glance.

"She is," I replied. "Our attempts to strengthen our race were futile and we have since learned that humans and Spirians are not meant to join in union. Repeating that mistake is blatant disrespect toward our Father. We are merely asking that we repent and cease all intimacy with humans, lest a union already exists." I closed my hands, indicating that my opinion had been voiced and I was done speaking.

Each leader spoke their opinions. The Shadows were not eager to relinquish their human relations. It was clear that they had made slaves of the females who proved useful for curbing anger bouts, and keeping the young males calmer until suitable mates were offered.

Arcadie stood. "I suggest that we break from this meeting and gather our wits. When we return, we will come to an agreement."

~ S k y e ~

DESPITE OUR PROMISE TO ONE another, Khalen had to keep his thoughts to himself and carefully guarded. Not knowing what was going on was equally frustrating for Eve and Kitta but they both understood having been through them before. Charges sparked throughout the manor as if an intense electrical storm was sifting its way over the island. An occasional rumble rattled the walls, reminiscent of an earthquake.

Eve gripped my hand. "Something tells me they are just getting started."

"Reminds me of the meeting in 1936 when the clans were divided," said Kitta. Massive floods were felt as far as North America."

Eve's brows arched in remembrance as she nodded. "I remember that. Having it so far from the equator was devastating."

"I'm not sure having it on an island is much better,"

said Kitta, looking at the fierce rain pelting the glass.

After a few hours of walking the grounds and talking, things became suddenly quiet. "They must be taking a break," said Eve.

Kitta poured us all a cup of tea. "Thank God for that."

"You both seem very calm about this," I mentioned, my hands raw from rubbing them together. "It seems as if they just got started. Why are they taking a break so soon?"

Eve held my hands. "The energy in the room downstairs is so intense, it takes everyone a bit of time to acclimate to it all. Case once told me that it is synonymous to standing in the midst of an electrical storm and enduring multiple lightening strikes."

Dirk came around the corner and focused in on me. His black eyes reflected the firelight like brilliant opals. "May I have a word with you?"

I stood and walked toward him. "What is it?"

"Come," he said. "Walk with me."

I glanced back over my shoulder at Eve who looked on with concern in her posture. Kitta emitted mild curiosity.

I allowed him to lead me down the hall and toward the gardens. I stopped before the doorway. "Khalen has asked that I remain inside for the duration of the meeting," I said.

"Surely you are safe with me," he countered, urging me forward.

I gently pulled my arm from his grip. "I gave him my word," I said, raising my chin slightly so that I could meet Dirk's gaze.

He sighed. "Very well. We'll talk in the study." He claimed my arm again and led me to a room. The lights were insufficient for me to see any detail. He guided me to a soft leather chair and urged me to sit.

His dark eyes lowered to stare at my belly. My hands instinctively moved there. "You carry twins," he said. He snorted then his hands turned into fists. "Why Khalen?" he asked.

"I'm sorry?"

"Why were you offered to Khalen? He does not carry Shanuk's blood, nor is he of Protected blood. He is a Shadow, and the son of Damon, spawn of the devil, himself. You should not have been offered to him," he seethed.

I stood, having heard about all I wanted to hear. He grabbed my arm and pulled me back down. I tried to jerk away from him but his grip did not ease.

"You should be mine," he growled. "I am the rightful heir in Shanuk's line."

Again I pulled away from him, this time succeeding. "My mate is Khalen, Sir, and he was my choice."

"His blood is tainted," Dirk said. Again, he glanced down at my belly. "You dishonor your stature by carrying his devil seeds."

"My stature?"

"Aye, you are the legend, the mother of our race, and yet you chose to mate with a Shadow."

"Khalen is no Shadow, Dirk, I assure you."

"He has no right to you." He looked off into the distance. "For years, I listened to Shanuk tell my father of your tale, your legend, and I waited. I've seen you in my dreams, I felt you beneath my touch." His hands shook with the memory.

My skin crawled. I felt spiritually violated and fought the urge to vomit. "Perhaps you dreamt of another," I said, "for I have never dreamt of you."

He reached for me and I retracted back against the chair. His hands rested on my thighs, and then he jerked back, screaming a blasphemy. "Agh, the bastard has bound you." He held his hand, shaking with rage.

Khalen entered the room, followed by Case and Arcadie. "What is the meaning of this, Dirk?" his father asked.

"She should be mine, Father, and not the mate of this Shadow demon."

Arcadie's eyes widened. "Khalen is not a Shadow demon, nor will you ever speak of him as such again!" he commanded, shaking the walls with the power of his voice.

Dirk's eyes lowered, showing respect. "He does not carry Shanuk's blood."

"But he carries his respect, and that is good enough for me." Arcadie turned to Case and Khalen. "I apologize for my son," he said with disappointment etched in his frown. His eyes fell back on Dirk. "Perhaps there is a reason that Shanuk chose Khalen over you. It is the same reason why you do not participate in the meeting."

Dirk stiffened and growled then pushed past his father, mumbling, "This is not over" as he left the room.

Arcadie looked over at me. "I'm sorry, my dear. He has waited for you since he was able to talk. He has much to learn but is reluctant to do so, I'm afraid."

A shiver ran down my spine. I felt as if I had a whole other life I knew nothing about; like I was an ordinary woman launched into an extraordinary world born long before I was ever conceived.

"I will speak with him and assure him that this is, indeed, over," Arcadie said then turned to leave.

Khalen pulled me up and wrapped me in his arms. "I

fear that bringing you here was a mistake."

"No, Son," Case said. "You were correct in bringing her here. She is rightfully your mate and deserves to stand by your side."

"Father," Khalen said, a hint of sadness in his voice. "Does my blood shame you?"

"Khalen, when Shanuk assumed you as his grandson, and blessed Eve's and my decision to raise you as our own, he assumed you as if you were from his blood. His blessing, as you well know, extends beyond mere genes."

Khalen's lips curled slightly. "Thank you, Father."

"I don't question my father's decisions. I trust them—completely." He said the last word while looking at me. "I must speak with you before we get back to the meeting, Son."

Khalen nodded. "Give me a moment. I'll meet with you soon."

Case smiled and left, granting us privacy.

I held Khalen's shaking hands. "How are things going?" I asked, my words barely audible.

"It's intense," he said. "Worse than I ever imagined—like being under Case's wrath for hours on end."

I shuttered, remembering the stinging blows that held me down many months ago. "I don't like this."

He kissed the back of my hand. "I know. But this is the life of a leader. It only makes me stronger."

I lowered my eyes. "Dirk knows about the twins."

He lifted my chin. "They are not a secret, my love. They are a blessing. It won't take long for all to take notice."

I rubbed my belly. "They are a blessing."

I sensed sadness in him as he drew in a long breath. He kissed my forehead. "I'll see you in three hours," he said.

I kissed his trembling hands, and then let him go. Enjoying the blissful silence, I remained in the quiet room for a while until Eve came to check on me. I joined her and Kitta in the kitchen to help prepare dinner.

Kitta had many servants, but she enjoyed cooking the meals herself. Eve and I were more than eager to assist. The kitchen was a chef's dream, sporting Wolfe ovens with their commercial gas burners. The counters displayed a useful mix of granite and something that resembled granite but was warm and softer in texture. "What is this?" I asked, rubbing my hands over the warm surface.

Kitta glanced over at me and smiled. "It's Silestone. You can cut directly on it and it doesn't stain."

"Hmm," I said, admiringly, "I like it."

Kitta laughed. "I'll let Khalen know. He'll appreciate the price, I'm sure." An odd silence followed that comment, as if she wanted to ask what her son Dirk had wanted to talk to me about but was not sure how to ask.

Eve noticed that I had picked up on Kitta's intention, and silently persuaded me to evade the subject. "So, what are we preparing for dinner?" I asked.

Kitta's black eyes sparkled. "Shepherd's pie, one of Arcadie's favorites. He likes it best with chunks of lamb and wild boar instead of ground beef as you are accustomed to in the Americas."

A rumble shook the building and caused the heavy cast-iron pans to bang together. A flash of lightning pierced the sky.

"Good thing the meeting is several feet underground," said Kitta. "I can only imagine the destruction if they held it topside."

Eve laughed. "At this rate, though, we might just be swallowed by some unforeseen fault."

"Or tsunami," Kitta added.

Another flash of lightning followed by a thunderous roar shook the windows. Hail pelted the glass.

"Hmm," Eve surmised. "Haley must be taking a stance."

"Haley?" I asked, feeling very naive about this entire event.

"A Shadow from Jamaica," Kitta explained. "He's an elementist—one who can control the elements."

"He leads the largest Shadow clan of any continent," said Eve.

"Perfect," I mumbled, staring out at the pea-sized balls bouncing off the windows. "I can only imagine what the energy feels like in the meeting room."

"If you are not properly shielded," Eve explained, "the vibration will kill you. It is the main reason these meetings are kept short with many breaks. Over the years, the leaders have learned to reconcile their differences more efficiently. Hundreds of years before, many of them lost their lives due to conflicts of opinion."

"Conflicts of opinion," I quietly muttered, staring out at the violent storm.

Eve smiled, obviously picking up on my anxiety. "Case has informed me that the negotiations will end this evening. There are still a few items to discuss but tempers are flaring too high for Arcadie's comfort. He has had to intervene far too many times and the Shadows are rebelling. If it goes too far, nothing will be settled. It is best to end on a neutral note than on one pitched with anger."

"Who represents the Shadows in Washington?" I

asked, mildly curious. I had not recognized the names of the leaders that had arrived.

Eve placed a knife and five onions in front of me to chop for the meat mixture. "I believe his name is Sage, and I would hardly consider him a leader."

"His father, Victor, is a powerful man," said Kitta. "He is the true leader. Sage is merely a product of weak breeding."

"I take it you don't like his mother?" I concluded.

Kitta's eyes narrowed. "She is a witch. I will not speak her name in this house."

"Anyway," Eve continued. "Sage was given charge of the Pacific Northwest, under Victor's confining scrutiny. Sage makes no decision without his father's blessing."

"Are they both here?" I asked.

"Yes," said Eve. "Victor's family oversees the Shadows on the entire North American continent."

I frowned. "Who oversees the Protected?"

Eve chopped the ends from a bunch of carrots. "Shanuk's family oversees three continents: North America, South America, and Europe." Eve looked up at me. "Before Shanuk passed, he was the most powerful Spirian alive."

I had no doubt about that truth. Just being in the man's presence made one feel small and weak. I missed him terribly, but always felt him watching over me like an angel of sorts. "Who's the most powerful now?" I had to ask.

Eve shrugged. "It's hard to say. Shanuk had many sons and daughters, all very strong. Time will reveal the one who takes his place."

After several ground tremors and a treacherous storm, the meeting ended one hour early. The leaders, exhausted

Rowena Portch

from the ordeal, returned to their respective lodgings. Dinner waited until Dirk returned from his transporting duties. His spirit was dark and sunken, like a man who had indulged in too much drink. As he took his seat across from me, his posture revealed his torment. I had to look away.

Talk about the negotiations dominated the conversation. New leaders had been assigned, and rules had been established for all Spirians. Unions with humans were now forbidden, apart from those that had already happened. I was sure that Case had a major vote in that one. Territories were to be respected by all Spirians, and the act of taking another's mate resulted in death.

Then there was the issue of widowed mates. They were to be offered to their assigned templar with no dispute. If the templar did not want the woman, he was to find her another mate within the extended clan.

I immediately thought of Sunjia. She would rather die than return to the Shadows. Khalen must have read my mind. He squeezed my hand under the table. Sunjia had told me how to save Khalen's life. If she hadn't been there, I would not have known what to do.

Case had been granted the entire European continent to lead, which meant Khalen was to lead North America. That bit of news did not go unnoticed by Dirk. His energy suddenly shifted.

I felt his eyes look directly at me. "Khalen," he said, "do you intend to allow your mate to continue carrying twins?"

My stomach sank. I wanted to answer for him, but he silently warned me to say nothing.

The conversation dwindled and fell silent. All eyes were on Khalen and me. My hand began to sweat in his.

He didn't let go. I read Dirk's intention. He aimed to invoke Khalen's anger, something that typically got out of control very quickly. I relayed my thoughts to Khalen. He was already savvy to Dirk's ploy.

"That decision is between my mate and I, Dirk, I don't see how it concerns you."

Arcadie's eyes widened. "She carries twins. Certainly you cannot allow them both to grow inside her?"

"Khalen, you can't," Kitta added.

"I believe I also have a say in what does and does not grow in my belly," I said, my voice surprisingly strong. "Khalen does not make this choice on his own."

Arcadie started to stand. "He is your mate, Skye. He is the only one who can make that choice."

"Enough!" Case roared. "What Khalen and Skye decide is their business and none of our own."

Arcadie sat back down. Dirk started to smile. He had gotten the reaction he had hoped for. "Apparently, Khalen does not fully understand who he has been favored with. Something as important as this should not leave any question."

"It leaves no question," Khalen retorted. "Whatever decision we make, it will be the right one, I assure you."

Dirk scoffed. "What kind of man allows his mate to sway his decisions?"

"A good man," I answered. "I'm curious," I said, changing the subject, "if a law was broken prior to the laws being established today, what are the consequences, if any?"

This earned the attention of everyone at the table, including a few of the elders who had attended the meeting. Until now, they had kept their conversations to themselves.

What are you getting at? Khalen asked in thought.

I didn't answer. I wanted to hear the response prior to revealing my plan.

One of the elders, earlier introduced as Lasset, was a gangly old man with golden eyes and a short white beard. He was shorter than me and had a delightful New Zealand accent. He cleared his throat. "That depends upon the law that is broken and what can or cannot be done about it." He paused. "Some laws," he added, "will be enforced no matter what the circumstances."

"And who has the final say?" I asked.

"The regional leaders," he replied, leaning back in his chair. He was trying to read me, I could feel it. I purposely kept him out. I imagined a smile stretched across his face before his pipe bumped against his teeth. "Why are you wantin' to know?"

I shrugged. "Just curious how it all works," I said, keeping my thoughts to myself.

"Ah," he said. "You keep very quiet until you have something to say, do you not?" He laughed and turned his attention to Khalen. "Your mate is reserved, but she's got some sass to her when a burr clings to her blanket, eh?"

"You have no idea," Khalen said, squeezing my hand. *What are you up to?* he added in thought.

I'll tell you later.

Chapter 30

When a heart bonds with another, the love that is forged knows no enemy.

WE RETURNED HOME A WEEK LATER. Maiyun was the first to greet us, followed by Aidan, Ian, Seth, his mother and sister. They all looked so relaxed, I hardly recognized them. Maiyun had gained some weight back in my absence. Her fur was soft and she carried the faint smell of bleach—remnants from the vet clinic.

I rubbed her fur and buried my face in the scruff of her neck. Beneath all that chemical smell was the Maiyun I recognized and missed. "Oh, it's good to see you," I told her. "I missed you."

After getting settled and having some dinner, we all met outside by the fire. I was exhausted and planned on socializing for just a bit before turning in. Aidan and Sunjia chatted and laughed on the other side of the fire, while Seth and Ian teased young Tria who was far more clever than they gave her credit for. She would give them a ride for their taunting when she finally reached of age, I was sure.

Khalen sat next to me and jostled me out of my trance. "Are you ready for bed, my love?"

I gestured toward Aidan and Sunjia. "He has a different air about him tonight," I said.

Khalen followed my focus. "She does as well."

"If I didn't know any better, I would say that Aidan is smitten with her."

Khalen's eyes narrowed. "He damn well better not be."

"Why not?" I interjected. "He has a right to find a mate like everyone else."

"Not that one," said Khalen. "She is not—available."

"Khalen, I—"

"Do not think for a moment that hiding your thoughts from me keeps me from reading your intentions." A wry smile curled at his lips. "I acquired that unique gift from you, my love. I know what you are thinking and it will not happen. Sunjia must be returned to the Shadows."

I stood from the log on which we were sitting. "No, there must be another way." He reached for me, but I pulled away. "Khalen, tell me there is another way."

He looked over at Aidan, who was all smiles and obviously taken with the widow. "Christ," he groaned. "My life was much easier when I was just a doctor."

This time, instead of reaching for me, he telekinetically pulled me into him, despite my efforts to thwart him. "Listen to me, Skye. Do not get involved with this. I must uphold the law."

Struggling against him was futile. His strength had increased tenfold and I felt as if I fought against a gripping tornado. "Case and Eve have an unlawful union and they are allowed to stay together."

"You cannot break a union," he said, clearly irritated with my logic. "Aidan cannot join with that woman."

"That woman," I said, "has a name. I might also remind you that she is responsible for saving your life."

"By nearly costing your own."

Again I tried to pull away from him. "She told me to stop." I could feel the hum of his anger building. I was dangerously pushing the line.

"She was my brother's mate," he said through clenched teeth. "She will not stay here."

"And what about what Aidan wants?" I asked.

"Wait for me in our yurt," he said. It was not a request, but an order. "I will have a word with Aidan." His golden eyes warned me to listen this time and do as he asked. Since I couldn't see much in the dark anyway, I figured I could hear just as well from inside as I could out here.

From the warmth of our yurt, I tuned into their thoughts while petting Maiyun, who lay beside me on the floor.

"Aidan. May I have a word with you?" Khalen asked.

When they were alone, the conversation started. "What is it, my brother?"

"Are you getting close with the widow?" Khalen asked, lacking all forms of tact.

"I find her—intriguing."

"She cannot stay here, Aidan. She has a templar and must be returned to him."

"He has not come to claim her, and the woman and her children want to stay."

"I cannot allow them to stay." I could feel the anger welling in Khalen like a deep itch that couldn't be scratched. It came from somewhere darker, though, than a mere law that must be upheld.

"She is not one of them," Aidan claimed. "I have spent some time with her. She is different and very gifted. I think—"

"You must keep your distance," Khalen interrupted. "For the sake of the clan."

"Is that an order?" Aidan asked.

Khalen's heart softened. "It is a request."

"Then it is one I cannot honor."

When Khalen entered the yurt, a chill filled the space, despite the fire I had stoked. I remained on the floor with Maiyun, watching as he paced the floor.

"This battle you fight," I said, "runs deeper than any river governed by law." He said nothing, but his heart told me everything I needed to know. "You fear she will turn Aidan, and that she may have joined with multiple Shadows. If she has, Aidan may unknowingly link our clans."

"Yes," he said. "Now you understand."

"Have you thought to ask her?"

"She could lie," he seethed, the anger in his voice making him sound hoarse.

"Then use your gift of intention, Khalen. Read her and know if she tells the truth. She will not be able to lie to you without first intending to do so."

"The Shadows have taken so much from us. Aidan is your templar, Skye. If he is turned and something happens to me, you will be consumed."

"Aidan will not turn."

His golden eyes glowed. "You do not know that. It is a risk I will not take!"

I stayed silent as I watched him prepare for bed. I was not too eager to join him.

"Come to bed," he said.

I didn't reply.

"Skye, please. I need you beside me."

The pain in his voice was unbearable and far more powerful than any other force he could project toward me. It was also something I couldn't neglect. I stood and crawled into bed beside him.

He began removing my clothes. "Tonight," he said, his voice low and gruff. "I want to forget about life and get lost inside of you, my love. The morrow will take care of itself."

KHALEN WAS GONE WHEN I awoke. The bed beside me was cold. Maiyun had left with him. He had gone hunting, perhaps, I thought. My head pounded from the effects of last night. Khalen's lovemaking was becoming more intense, nearly driving me over the edge of tolerance. I felt the rawness of it between my thighs. With a groan, I sat up and reached for the cup of coffee he had left for me. Like the bed, it was cold.

I could not read Khalen, nor could I feel his presence in camp. A shot of panic zapped through me. I hopped out of bed, quickly got dressed, and headed for Case's yurt. Their front door was left open.

"Come in, Skye," Case said from the kitchen. "Hungry?" Maiyun sat beside him, waiting for another tasty morsel. I ticked my tongue to her. She nudged my leg in greeting then returned to her previous location, which was sure to earn a few more treats.

"No, not at all." My hand covered my belly.

He handed me a cup of tea. "Here, drink this. It will help ease your sickness."

"Where's Khalen?" I asked, sipping the tea. It had a calming flavor of mint and ginger.

"Aidan left last night."

"With Sunjia and the kids?" I asked.

He glanced up at me after flipping two eggs. "Yes."

I pressed my forehead into my palm. The headache increased tenfold and it took all that I had just to remain sitting. "Is Ian with Khalen?"

"Yes."

"How does one find an illusionist who wants to remain hidden?" I mumbled as if talking to myself.

"It's nearly impossible."

"I can't read him," I said. "He promised never to block me out."

"These past five days have pressed his limits, Skye. As you well know, his power runs deep and carries violent tendencies. For him to stay in control during all this, it takes more than you and I have combined. You must be strong for him; be his anchor."

"I don't know how," I admitted. "He is so intense and guarded right now."

"Reach out to him. He'll feel you. Just knowing you are there with him will be enough to pull him through," he said, flipping the eggs onto a plate.

I moved over to give him some room beside me. "What's going to happen with Sunjia and the kids?" I asked.

"She will be offered back to her templar and he will decide what to do."

"And what about Aidan?"

Case ate silently as if weighing his answer carefully. "If he claims Sunjia without her templar's blessing, Khalen must kill him, Skye."

This time, I couldn't fight back my stomach's retort. I ran outside and bent over a log. The heave was painful and dry, threatening to purge my organs on every contraction. I heard Eve call my name as she tossed her gardening gloves aside and ran toward me.

"Lord, Skye, are you all right?"

Another heave left me speechless. I tried shaking my head. Case walked up with a cool damp towel. I took it and wiped my perspiring face. "Thank you," I said.

"Aidan has not claimed her," I said. "He would never do so haphazardly."

"Men do things in desperation, Skye."

I looked up at him. "He has not claimed her," I growled, immediately regretting the disrespect in my voice. "Khalen will find them. He will make things right." I grabbed Case's arm for support and hauled myself up.

An image clouded my mind. Aidan and Sunjia stood by the ocean. I could make out a jutting rock through the water. It resembled the shape of a cone. "I see them," I said. "They are by the ocean." I remembered seeing Khalen in that same ocean after we parted in anger several months ago. "Khalen's beach house. Aidan wants to be found," I said. "He's reaching out to me."

"Come with me," Case said, taking my hand. All three of us entered his yurt and sat on the floor. "Take my hands, Skye. Together, we can break through to Khalen and let him know where to go."

I did as he asked and concentrated on contacting Khalen. I sent him images of his beach house with Aidan and Sunjia standing on the deck. The queasiness in my stomach made concentrating difficult. My eyes sprang open when I felt Khalen. "He hears us," I said. "He knows."

Case squeezed my hands. "Well done."

I bolted and headed straight for the woods.

Union

-Khalen-

I WASN'T SURE WHAT TO SAY to my brother when I approached him. True to the images Skye had sent, I found him standing on the deck of my beach house. He was alone for now. Ian stayed by the truck, stricken by the same sickness that gripped my guts.

"Aidan," I said with my hands extended and facing upward, indicating that I came as an equal and not his leader.

He nodded, acknowledging my message. "Where do we stand on this, brother?"

"It is complicated," I replied, leaning against the rail. "Have you claimed her as your own?"

Aidan's eyes narrowed. "Your mate knows me better than you, apparently."

"She believes strongly in your favor and has a powerful way of expressing her feelings."

Aidan smiled, but it was a sad one. "Is there anything Skye doesn't feel strongly about?"

"Yes," I said, "but I never hear of them."

We both chuckled at that. It was true. Skye rarely spoke of things unless they merited the words to express them. Trivial events were left in the shadows.

After a long silence, Aidan finally spoke. "Sunjia cannot go back, Khalen. If forced to do so, she promises to take her own life."

"The choice is not ours, Aidan, you know that."

"What if it were Skye?

"Yes," said Khalen. "What if it were Skye? You are her templar, Aidan. Would you be so willing to let her fall into the hands of the Shadows, or would you want to take her as your own?"

Aidan's jaw clenched, his eyes reflected pain. "I would let her choose." My heart caved at the possibility that Skye would chose a Shadow for a mate should anything happen to me. Still, Aidan's honesty and sense of honor warmed me. Skye would appreciate his respect for her choice as well, I was certain.

"I pray Sunjia's templar has the same heart as you."

Aidan turned his back to me and stared out at the ocean. "Do you know of him?"

I walked beside him and leaned against the rail. "No, but he is sure to make himself known to us soon."

"He has contacted her already," said Aidan. "She and her two children have been ordered to come to him immediately."

I read the name of this man from Aidan's mind, and immediately felt the blood drain from my face. "Bloody hell," I groaned. "Dirk Graham."

"You know him?"

"He is Arcadie's son. We ran into him at the meeting in Brazil. He was very put out when he discovered that Shanuk had offered Skye to me instead of him." I thought for a moment. "Shanuk must have known about him turning."

"So I take it you are not on good terms with this man."

The expression on my face was answer enough. "I must speak with Sunjia."

The corners of Aidan's lips curled. "She fears you."

My expression turned serious. "As well she should, for what she has done. Not only has she placed you at great risk, but her children as well." I knew she was listening and purposely played up my anger. Aidan knew me better and was unaffected.

"Sunjia, come here," I said, trying to sound as

commanding as possible. No self-preserving female would think twice about ignoring a leader's command. She came around the corner, eyes down and hands clasped in front of her.

"My Lord," she said.

"Relax, woman. Honestly, your submissiveness will accomplish nothing but make me angry."

Aidan reached over and took her hand. "Come, sit." He led her over to a couch in the small living space. I took the chair across from them. Seeing Aidan's affections toward the woman was alarming. He sensed my concern, but held fast, his eyes locked on mine. I let it go for now, concentrating on more pressing matters.

"Tell me what you know about your templar," I said. "And please, look me in the eye when doing so."

Her dark brown eyes focused in on mine, her pupils tight with fear. "My union was arranged by Damon. He knew that Dirk would lead the South American territories and he wanted that connection to Shanuk's clan. Dirk was the perfect choice. No one would know that he had chosen sides with the Shadows."

I narrowed my eyes. "Someone knew. Dirk leads no territories." It all made sense now. What didn't make sense was the fact that his parents didn't seem to know he had changed sides. Or, perhaps they did know but were ashamed to admit it. No, I thought, I would have sensed that in Arcadie. The man knew something was amiss with his son, but like all fathers, he was blind to it.

"What if something happened to his father?" asked Sunjia.

I straightened my shoulders. "Dirk would acquire his territories, without question."

"I believe that is what Damon counted on. He was

a patient man, but a ruthless one. By placing me in that circle, it offered the Shadows a very strategic edge. I am the daughter of Carlos Montoya, Shanuk's oldest ally. How fitting it was to join the daughter of one great power with the grandson of another."

"Your children, sired by Traeger, links the clans in a very persuasive way," Aidan concluded. "Brilliant."

"So long as I am left alive," she added. "I am your worst nightmare." Aidan's hand gripped her harder.

"If something happens to you," I said. "Dirk will claim your daughter."

Sunjia's eyes grew wide. "He wouldn't dare."

My attention focused on Aidan. "I need to know where you stand on this, brother."

Aidan looked thoughtful too long for my comfort. His lips pursed as if weighing his answer. "I trust you will make the right choice."

"That is not an answer," I said. "I know you have feelings for this woman, but you and I both know what the consequences will be should you—"

"My loyalty is and always has been to you, Khalen. You of all people should know that without question." His words were hard and had an edge that sliced through my soul. "You have honored me as Skye's templar. Do you honestly believe I would deliver her to the hands of our adversary?"

I met his gaze. My lips firm and tense. "Thank you," was all I could say. I felt the pain in his heart and it nearly doubled me over. I stood and placed a hand on his shoulder. "Stay here for as long as you like. I will contact you if anything changes."

"It already has," said Sunjia. "We will return tonight."

The mood that evening back at the camp was as dark

as the moonless sky. Groups of people warmed themselves by the fires and conversed quietly among themselves. Sunjia and Aidan sat across from us, holding hands but not speaking. Case and Eve had retired early and were making plans to return to England soon. It would be difficult staying here without them. Skye remained dutifully by my side, but her thoughts were distant.

She and I were the last ones to retire. Her color was pale and she looked emotionally worn. Even Maiyun lay lifeless on her bed with barely a glance in our direction as we crawled into bed. Skye snuggled down, pulled her soft blanket up to her chin, and rested her head on my shoulder.

"Skye," I said, breaking the silence.

"Hmm?" she replied, sleepily.

"I promise, I will do everything in my power to ensure Sunjia stays."

She sat up and stared at me with her sea-gray eyes. A small smile softened her features. The firelight played upon her loose hair, forming a golden halo around her head and shoulders. "Well, Khalen Dunning, knowing you will do your best, I am confident that you'll succeed."

"I pray you're right," I said, not sharing her level of confidence.

"I have never known you to fail in getting what you want. It is one of your many gifts."

I pulled her down then quickly rolled on top of her, making her giggle. "Right now, I want to claim my most powerful gift."

"Fabulous love play?" she teased, her eyes sparkling in the firelight.

"No, my love—you."

Rowena Portch

-The End-

A Note From the Author

I hope you have enjoyed reading Union. The relationship between Khalen and Skye reflect my own relationship with my mate, Gregg. Sometimes we battle what is ultimately best for us, even if it comes disguised as what we never wanted.

Many of us have a story to tell but are afraid tell it for one reason or another. My goal is to encourage and inspire you all to tell your story, be it as a memoir or as a fictional tale such as this one.

About the Author

Rowena started writing at a young age, feeling an inherent need to tell stories that inspire and reflect aspects of life that are rarely considered.

Being a descendant of James Hudson Taylor, author and founder of the China Inland Mission, Rowena comes from a long line of story tellers, including her mother and father. The tradition of writing continues through her daughter, Erika.

Rowena's goal is to inspire others to tell their stories and share the wonderful gift and adventure of life. She often speaks before groups, sharing her experiences of writing and telling stories. It is a passion of hers that she shares with her mate, Gregg.

Together, they are writing a book entitled, *Finding Peace Among Chaos*, due to be released in Spring 2013.

Though she is over seventy-five percent blind, she doesn't allow that to derail her ambitions. Her husband is deaf, so they make the perfect pair. They live on the Olympic Peninsula in Washington with her guide dog Skye-Bear.

Other Books by Rowena

Protected
Legend
Aeon Pneuma
Illusions
Fealty

www.Rowena-Portch.com

Book a Speaking Engagement with Rowena and Gregg

Rowena and Gregg love to inspire people to tell their story and to follow their passion no matter how unobtainable it may seem.

Both of them have been on their own since age fourteen and have some incredible stories to share. Though both of them are disabled—she's blind and he's deaf—neither of them allow their impairments to deter them from their dreams.

If you want Rowena and Gregg to speak at your next event, please email them at:

Rowena@Rowena-Portch.com